EXPOSING
SECRET SINS

Curses & Secrets Book Two

A novel by Elisabeth Zguta

Other Books
by Elisabeth Zguta

Breaking Cursed Bonds

Seeking Redemption

IN THE WOODS:

Murder In The North East Kingdom

DREAMER:

A Ukrainian World War II story

Copyright

Prologue

1972 Vision Quest

T he man knew he wasn't alone. *Was his animal familiar out there?* Something was out there even if he refused to believe in the Chief's ancient tales about power animals and familiars, who dwelled at the edge of the threshold. For the first time in his life, the man was afraid. Fear speared through his being.

It appeared as if by magic and stared straight at him. The creature, a monster of the night, loomed in front of the man. It was larger than any animal he had ever imagined. A growl from the creature's throat, low and guttural, filled the air with an echoing menace. It was a gigantic wolf and stood not ten feet away from him.

Drool dripped from its teeth. It growled and twitched its head from side to side. The monster measured the man with its keen dark eyes, positioning himself as the predator. A monstrous dark shadow in the charcoal night. The beast's ivory fangs, sharp and ragged, stood out stark against its midnight black coat. It absorbed his emotions; the man weakened. As the wolf consumed the man's fear, its eyes smoldered from the emotive hostility. The monster thrived on the man's terror and appeared to grow along with the man's mounting horror.

The man heard the creature's breathing, the huffing sound as it exhaled air, and saw the steam leave its nostrils and mix into the cold night mist. He heard the rumble that vibrated from deep within its throat. The beast's wet fur smelled wild, a feral reek.

This creature was worse than anything the man had ever

imagined. He understood that his own natural tendency leaned toward a psychopath; he had never been afraid of anything in his life. Now, he was petrified, frozen with fear. The man wanted to flee, but he couldn't move his muscles, the message was lost in the delivery somewhere between his brain and limbs. Without additional warning, the beast lunged forward and attacked.

Teeth gripped the man's entire shoulder blade, digging in deep as it gorged his flesh. It wrestled him to the ground, and the two bodies rolled about, kicking up stones and dry dirt. The man grabbed a rock, yanked it up to the wolf's head, and pounded it, over and over again, against the monster's skull. There was a brief yelp of surprise, but the beast never loosened its grip for a moment.

Searing pain shot through the man, every nerve ending jumping out against his skin. The fangs pierced through to his limbs. Warm liquid oozed out from his wound and dripped down his arm. The rust smell of blood filled the night air and melded with the rank of the beast's wet fur. In a final attempt to survive, the man grabbed the monster's coat with great force, but nothing registered with the animal; it just kept chomping away at his shoulder and arm, devouring his meaty muscle. The more panic the man generated, the more blazon the beast's attack grew. It was futile to battle; any attempt to protect himself from the deadly beast failed.

The terrorized man gave up. His aggressor penetrated one last deadly bite into his neck. The man lost consciousness as his blood rushed out like a river. His spirit floated away from his body. Peacefully, his soul rose into the sky between the world he lived in and the other world on the other side of the veil.

A flash of lightning filled the sky, and his being dispersed, becoming part of the burst, and the world became visible to him in a blinding illumination. The ghostly white animal that had once been the dark wolf was now holding his limp human body in its arms. The massive wolf had somehow become a walking creature, and it carried the man's corpse to a place up high, into the sky, toward the bright light. Another streak zapped through the ether, booming a thunderous explosion. The strike burned through him, scorching his insides and cauterizing his skin closed. His internal organs were singed, blackened.

It was his turning point—that night of the bite. The man transformed, and his new life had begun. He turned into his new supernatural being, filled with animal instincts that surged within each cell of his body.

He awoke back on the ground and realized he changed and was no longer merely human. He was a skinwalker, a shapeshifter, a wolfman.

The black creature no longer gnarled at him. Instead of fearing the beast, the man felt a bond with it. This creature was his animal power, his supernatural link, and he intended to keep it near, always.

Transformed into a transcendental creature of the night, the man was a supernatural beast from the other side of the dweller's threshold. His primal instincts were strong. He could smell everything with a new sharpness, the rocks, the dirt, everything. When he lifted his head, he smelled human fear in the breeze. This would be his secret weapon to use for his own gain. That night the man embraced his renewed evil nature, his true destiny all along.

Chapter 1

Autumn Present Day

Michelle de Gourgues sped up the driveway in her silver Porsche 918 Spyder, clipping ahead as she passed under the trees edging the road and leading to the house. The Memphis mansion presided there, prominent and indifferent. She rounded the driveway and parked. Streaks of sunshine bounced off the car's shiny coat; she squinted despite wearing sunglasses.

Curiosity gnawed at her nerves. Her brother made an urgent call requesting her to come home right away. *Something wasn't right.* Robert hadn't spoken to her for the past few months. Tension hovered between them since the reading of Father's will. That was the day Robert discovered he hadn't inherited the business and had no access to company funds. Now his sole revenue was generated from a joint trust held with his new wife, Rachael.

Robert had fumed with anger and blamed her for the last-minute changes to the will. Michelle wanted to explain so many things to her brother, but Robert rebuffed her, not even giving her a glance. *It wasn't fair; it was his own fault after all.*

Unconsciously twisting the cuff of her sleeve, wringing it with her fingers as if it were wet, Michelle recalled the last conversation she had with her father before he died. He had warned her to be careful and had said Robert would try his best to take back control of the family money. *Robert put the entire family in jeopardy once, but it won't happen again.* Michelle got out of her car and hurried to the front door.

Apprehensive to enter, she waited a moment, drew in a

deep breath, and exhaled. To herself, she counted to three while shaking her arms along her sides trying to loosen up. Running her fingers through her dark, short hair, she tried to appear calm and at ease. Most days, she fought off the feeling that she was an impostor, a little girl playing businesswoman. She grasped enough to keep her insecurities hidden, especially from her brother. She opened the heavy front door, walked through the foyer, and entered the parlor.

It was a grand room enclosed by a high tray ceiling and stuffed with eclectic furnishings and antiques. A large gold velvet sofa dominated the center of the space.

Robert stood peering out the window in deep reflection. She stopped, her breath caught in her throat. He looked so much like Father, tall with dark wavy hair and deep brown eyes; most women saw him as handsome. He swirled the drink in his glass, his usual Highland Park scotch, as he gazed out dreaming. He seemed so innocent, but appearances can't be trusted. He was, after all, a master of life's stage.

Her pulse quickened with the idea. Even though intimidated by her brother, she couldn't afford to let her guard down. She choked back her angst, swallowing her fears.

"Hi, Robert." She put on a confident smile, walked over to him, and stood by his side. "I'm happy you called me. I hate this rift between us," she said.

Robert flashed that wise-ass grin of his but remained standing to the side of her, and he avoided a direct glance at her face.

She felt small with that same sick feeling she experienced as a kid on the first day of school. Her stomach ached with a familiar unease. *Why had he summoned her only to ignore her?* There was an awkward silence, then he spoke.

"I called you here to discuss the business, as you might have guessed. I think your time running things will be over soon." Robert stared off into space, his face expressionless.

She let his words sink into her head. There was no way for him to immerse himself back into the business; they both knew that, *didn't they*? What was he trying to pull? Pretending his words didn't bother her, she cleared her voice, fabricating a confident tone.

"Rob, what the hell are you talking about? Father was quite clear in his will about how the business is off-limits to you. Believe it or not, it's to protect you, to keep you out of jail, and to protect the rest of us, too. I know you don't want to believe me, but Tom Bennett lied to you, Robert. He used you. He only wanted the money you provided, not your friendship," she said. "Besides, why do you need anything from the likes of that old man?"

Robert wheeled around, red-faced with anger, and glared down at her. She stepped back.

"You know nothing about the situation." He scowled with stormy eyes.

She saw evil. It wasn't even Robert in there; her big brother was gone. Maybe it was his tone, or maybe she was just tired of feeling helpless like a frightened little girl, but something inside of her snapped. Blinded by the temper instigated from her burning rage, she exploded.

"I know plenty! You embezzled company and family money and flushed the funds into Tom Bennett's bank account. He only had you do it because of his vendetta against Father. I still don't understand it all, but Bennett used you, Robert. Now he's richer and you're banned from the company. Nice—real nice."

There were other questionable things her brother did, horrible things. But Michelle preferred not to waste time with rumors. *Don't trust Robert, period.* She held back tears that burned the corners of her eyes, her heart torn between the brother she loved and grew up with, and the bitter man who stood there now. She was tired of Robert's abuse of privilege and wasn't prepared to cover matters up as Father had in the past. Stewing in her mixed feelings, she gazed up and noticed a change in his expression. A shiver skated down her back.

"There's a rumor going around that once upon a time, you were under suspicion for murder? Tsk tsk. Not exactly good PR for the CEO. After news of this gets out, nobody will do business with you. And of course any of my past indiscretions—" He flung his hands into the air and smiled. "Forgotten next to a charge like murder. Swept under the rug, and they'll forgive me."

Shocked, his words buried her. Panic ensued, her breathing quickened, and her pulse vibrated in her head. She wiped the sweat off her brow with the back of her hand. *Calm down, take control.* From somewhere deep inside herself, she mustered up a brave voice.

"Robert, you know it's not true. Besides, I was only questioned, never a real suspect. Lord knows I could never kill anyone, not even you. Who told you such a thing?"

Ignoring her, he walked to the bar cart and topped off his drink. The liquid dribbled into his glass over the ice. She turned and saw the light reflect off the golden bourbon. A sudden urge for a swig of his drink consumed her. She wanted anything to forget those days, anything to make her feel better. Her mouth watered at the consideration of the warm, smooth whiskey. *Snap out of it, girl! Those days are gone. Remember, you left it behind years ago. So why is it still so raw?* She hated Robert's meddling into things he could never understand and chastised herself for her defensive banter, falling into his trap.

"It doesn't matter how I found out; it sounds bad no matter the source." He swigged his scotch.

Michelle stared as he swallowed, his Adam's apple bobbing up and down as he gulped the entire drink, then he slammed his glass down onto the marble tabletop. It cracked, smashing into tiny pieces. He shook his hand free from loose shards, wiped himself with a napkin, and left the mess there. He spun around with a look that pierced her blue eyes, now blurred with the threat of tears.

"It doesn't matter if it's true or not, either. Your innocence or guilt is of no consequence to me. All that matters is the image portrayed to the public, especially the customers and stock-holders. After the press gets a hold of this, companies we do business with will request your resignation from every board seat. You'll become viral on social media, a parasite. I can see the headlines now—" Robert raised his arms in the air, display-ing an imaginary banner. "'Heiress involved in old murder case' and 'Young businesswoman had checkered past in col-lege'."

Furious, her fists tightened into balls.

He kept grandstanding. "That's when I'll step up to the bat-ter's plate."

Robert improvised a batter's stance, swinging into empty air.

"They'll beg me to fill the empty slots reserved for our com-pany, realizing what a fool Father had been to take me out of the picture in the first place. You're not the only one with friends. I have people who love me. You used to be one of them."

He held his hands to his chest and looked up toward the high ceiling, waiting for showers of light. *Robert's delusional.*

"I might just find myself a way to override Father's wishes concerning who controls the family money. Once they convict you in the press, you might even end up in jail. Let's face it, even innocent people get convicted. After all, once the mem-bers of the board have faith in me again, they'll listen to me. And who will believe you?"

He pointed his finger at her, wearing that evil grin again. Hard to believe this was her brother, the same Rob she gallivanted with her in Boston while going to school. Now, he stood there and taunted her, treating her like a nobody.

Michelle wanted to smack him across the mouth. Robert acted the slithering snake and skulking traitor, waiting to consume the leftovers of the family fortune. The board members would be crazy to ever trust him again, *but they didn't all know the truth, did they. Did father's will leave a loophole? Could he serve on a board?*

Confused, she froze, lost for words. She never anticipated this move, twisting her past for his advantage. Her hands were tied, and she could never expose her brother for the scoundrel he was because Michelle had promised her father, moments before he died, that she would protect Robert's secret. *Yet he's so willing to threaten me.*

"Nothing to say, Chelle?"

He turned and left the room. The heavy front door slammed.

He's such an arrogant ass.

Chapter 2

Michelle hated living in this big old house with her brother and his wife Rachael; it was more than an intense situation. They had eloped just before Father died, and now they tried to justify their rash behavior, clinging to their marriage. Day after day, Father Eddie, their friend, and local priest, came to the house to counsel them. He always checked in with Michelle, too, whenever she was home. He was the only one speaking to her, other than an occasional comment from Rachael about trivial things as they passed each other in the house.

Luckily, Michelle was busy enough with her new responsibilities for it not to bother her. She had a flair for leading the business, and she wanted to do well to prove that her father's decision to empower her was sound. So far, she had gained the trust from most department heads and was held in good esteem, or so it seemed. She kept her eyes on the few who remained faithful to her brother. If they only knew all the facts about Robert and why he was removed. Still, no one could argue that she made good decisions, despite her young age of twenty-seven. *What will they think of me when they learn about my past in Boston?* Images from the past flooded her mind.

Tears brimmed her eyes, and she allowed a couple of them to fall before she rubbed her face dry with the back of her hand. She stormed out of the parlor, rushed through the foyer, and opened the doors to their father's library. No one had entered this room since the day the lawyer had read the will. Everything remained the same. The lawyer had taken all the files. There had never been any photographs nor mementos displayed in this room. It was sterile.

The room stayed vacant, just like Father had been for most

of her childhood. He'd managed to stress the importance of the public persona, which was crystal clear. They were expected to be responsible and keep a scrupulous record, the philosophy ingrained in all three siblings. Her brother understood how to manipulate and keep his image unscathed, no matter what he did. He understood how to twist reality to look pristine; it was second nature for him. Robert loved being in front of the camera, the center of attention. Michelle actually admired that side of him. *He's so clever.*

Michelle pretended to be confident, but inside she was still a vulnerable child. Naive when it came to keeping secrets — obviously, she hadn't hidden her secrets well enough, but she wouldn't allow Robert to use her past to inject himself back into the company, not in any capacity. She had to take action.

The only option she saw to keep her name free from any negative press was to identify the real killer and close that chapter for the last time. To accomplish this Michelle needed help. She picked up the phone on her father's desk and bit her lip. Hating the idea of bothering her big sister Emilie, she hesitated but realized options were limited. Her sister was literally the only person for the job. She needed her to step in and run the company so that Michelle could go to Boston and find out the name of the real killer.

She dialed the number and waited, tapping her foot against the hardwood floor in a jittery beat, her eyes raised, looking at the ceiling. The seconds passed like hours. Emilie finally picked up.

"Good morning, Michelle. What's up, Sis?"

"Good morning? It's afternoon, girl. I know that tone of voice. You're not alone, are you? Is Jeremy there, too? Hello, Jeremy."

Jeremy was the love of Emilie's life. She had been going through a tough time since Father's death, and Michelle was glad he was with her sister.

"Hello, Michelle," he said, laughing. "Yes, I'm here. You're on speakerphone. What's up, Michelle?"

"Seriously, I need you and Em. Emilie, remember our last conversation? I told you how Robert is still giving me the cold shoulder, right? Well, ten minutes ago he exploded a bombshell in front of me!"

There was a noise on the other end, like something dropping, then her sister's voice came back on the line.

"What do you mean? You said he's not talking to you. Michelle, you're not making sense."

"Robert dug up some dirt on me, something that happened when I lived in Boston, and he's using it as leverage against me. Don't you understand? He's trying to get me overthrown by the board of directors. I need you here, Em, to fill in as CEO while I work things out. Maybe you can talk sense into him. I need you—are you coming?"

The line was silent a moment. Michelle watched from the corner of her eye, hoping no one stood in the hall within earshot, eavesdropping. She wouldn't put it past Robert to have Evans, or some other servant, spying on her. Often that creepy feeling sent a shiver down her back.

"Yes, of course, we'll be there if you need us. Can you give us some details?" Emilie asked.

"It's hard to discuss over the line. Someone might be listening."

Another worry—telling Emilie the entire truth and chancing the possibility of disappointing her.

"Hi Michelle, Jeremy again. We'll get there as soon as possible as long as you think it will help. We've got your back kid."

"You want the truth? Come soon. I need you both now."

Michelle hung up the phone, a burden lifted. Emilie was the

only person she trusted. They had been through so much together. When Michelle was eight, they lost their mother, and just a few months ago they lost their father, too. They grieved together, sharing a bond, and both needed a lot of healing. The loss of Father had been heartrending.

Emilie left Memphis, taking time off to sort things out in her head. It's not that she couldn't process the grief; quite the contrary. She had experienced the ordeal as a clairvoyant. All the emotional baggage they each carried ended up in Emilie's head. Her gift was empathy, being able to feel other people's emotions. That gift had led Emilie down a dark and lonely place at times.

Michelle had been useless helping her sister. She couldn't understand and actually hated to acknowledge the paranormal nature of things. Supernatural things had always scared Michelle. The memory of their father's death frightened her the most and still haunted her dreams. The day he died they had witnessed the surreal, as his soul leaped into another realm.

She pressed her fingers against her head and massaged in circles, trying to get rid of her mental vision and block the memory. Even after six months, she couldn't wrap her head around what happened that day. Only Emilie understood because she had empathized with what Father experienced during his journey. She hadn't spoken of it since.

Emilie had fled to Florida and got her head squared away. Things seemed to be working out for her. She was fine when they talked on the phone. Of course, long-distance isn't the same thing as being at the house. Michelle hoped her sister's old pain wouldn't stir up by coming back.

Life choices Michelle had made while in college were exposed and raw again. Her past naivety made her skin crawl with self-loathing. The past seven years, since her sophomore year at Harvard, she worked through her demons. When Father showed his faith in her, Michelle believed everything was going to be fine.

Soaring on new wings, things were gliding smoothly for her. Her self-confidence was a sturdy rock, but now everything crumbled beneath her. She was right back where she began, the old insecurities returning. She hated public scrutiny over her life, and the judgments were soon to surface. It was too much; she wanted to run away and hide from the world.

Michelle gasped, struggling to breathe, her heart pounded in an anxiety attack. She was overwhelmed by the smell of the old books, the dried ink, the drapes, the dust, all of it in this closed-up space. Everything reeked like stale perfume as the room crept in closer. Claustrophobic, her chest burned.

Making a quick exit, she ran out of the room, through the front hall, and tugged at the massive door's handle, pulling it open. Frantic, she ran away from the house, toward her car, gulping in deep breaths. *Get a grip*.

She slid into the driver's seat and raced off, away from the house and her brother's spying eyes, heading for her favorite thinking spot, a place she used to hide away when she was a teenage kid. *You won't win this one, Rob. I'll squash the story before it's let out*. Emilie couldn't get back to Memphis soon enough.

Chapter 3

Michelle drove down the road looking for her special place, watching the street signs, but everything looked different. A new sprawling development stuffed with McMansions of the new Mid-south replaced the empty fields of her childhood memories. Finally, she found the road and parked. There was a footpath down a steep hill, its cliff overlooking the Wolf River's currents. In the spring, the water was rampant, but on this autumn day, the water appeared calm. That's exactly what Michelle yearned for now.

She scampered down the embankment, sliding a bit and stirring up dust that peppered across her black designer boots like red chili powder. A familiar rock formation awaited; she sat on the boulder's edge, took in a deep breath, and filled her lungs with the humid air. She smelled the catfish that lingered in the swirling muddy water below.

Calmer now, she replayed in her head the conversation with Robert, processing every word. He hadn't been very nice, but she refused to argue with him. Instead, she would go around him. According to the will, both sisters were responsible for the business, and Emilie could step into the role of CEO with no problem. *But will Emilie understand if I tell her the truth?* More than anything else in the world, she needed her sister's approval.

Michelle stared at the water, allowing deeper reflection to flow to the surface. Tied in knots of stress, she conjured up a story to tell her sister, but nothing sounded legitimate. *Hell, even the truth didn't seem real! But I have to tell Emilie the truth. It's not that bad, is it? My only sin was being young, rebellious, and naive.* She rubbed the back of her neck and closed her eyes, and drifted into memories of her college days . . . It was only seven years ago, but an eternity to Michelle.

Until the day she left for school, Michelle had lived a sheltered life in Memphis. True, the family had traveled around the world, but always under tight supervision. Nina, their cook, and homemaker had monitored them with her strict Christian ways. Pierre, their father, let Nina have her way because it had made his life easier, but Michelle's life had been a prison. She applied only to schools in the north, far from Memphis. Her time served was up when she left the house for college.

Finally, she had exposure to the real world. She had embraced her newfound freedom with open arms, more than a little wild at first chance, and curious about everything that had been off bounds. The only ramification that concerned her then was her father finding out about her escapades. Some days a twinge of guilt plagued her, but not enough to stop her from living the new lifestyle.

The affair had happened in her sophomore year of college. Crazy days spent with Professor Silas Kain, a teacher in the Literature Department at Harvard. He had the reputation on campus of being a ladies' man, and Michelle had taken him on as a personal challenge—one of the most exciting times in her life, fooling around with her professor. Michelle enjoyed the rush of being a bad girl.

Silas wasn't only a young teacher but a promising new author with a newly published book. He exhibited the same work ethic as her father, which Michelle secretly admired. His career as a brooding author turned professor to support his art was in its infancy then, barely introduced to the literary world, but Silas had plans to climb to the top, young and ambitious with energy to burn. She recognized he would be famous someday and trusted that he had as much reason as she to keep the affair secret. Disclosure would damage his career. Sleeping with a student was against all rules and had to be kept secret.

She closed her eyes and envisioned his body . . .

The attraction had started the first day of class, infatuated with his charm, his ash brown hair, misshaped, wavy and free, his face and nose long and prominent, like a statue she had seen once, stationed at a street in Florence. His long, lanky body glided as he skated back and forth in the front of the class, expelling his views on Shakespeare in the LIT97 course. Michelle had seated herself in a front-row desk, crossed her long legs with skirt up, and gazed at him shamelessly with her bright blue eyes. At the opportune moment, she fluttered her lashes. Flirtatious foreplay had come naturally to her, and she loved testing her wild ways for fiery reactions.

Silas had noticed her, of course. Their relationship had been brutally honest, and their bond grew intense quickly. If she could do it all over again, she would stay away from Professor Silas Kain.

The affair exploded the first night together. The two of them drank wine, smoked pot, and got silly. She was liberated, and the drinking led her to behave feverishly. They had sex, sizzling sex. The affair turned into a sensual frenzy whenever they were together. Day after day, they rendezvoused at his house on Trowbridge Street and indulged in their fantasies. They had sex in the loft area while looking through the skylight at the stars and in the solarium among the plants intoxicated by fragrant orchids. They loved each other in all positions and places imaginable, up and down the stairs in his townhouse. Not a spot on the floor or a piece of furniture was unused.

Recalling a special long weekend they had spent together when she had actually imagined they were in love, she remembered being naked on his big bed upstairs. The music played softly, *You Found Me* by the Fray. The cotton sheets had touched smooth against her skin. He rolled on top of her, and she embraced his warm body against hers and deeply inhaled his after-shave cologne. It was spicy, manly, and erotic. Tingling, she had shamelessly wanted his lovemaking.

He watched her face and traced her cheekbone with his finger, gently sending shivers through her body, then a dreamy expression slid across his long face. His gray eyes smoldered, edged with tears of passion, then he pushed his hardened organ into her with a smooth thrust. Her hands grabbed the brass pipe of the headboard; she burrowed her butt into the mattress and allowed him to slip into her repeatedly, releasing all inhibitions. She savored the intensity of every move he made, every vibration he provided her. It had been glorious.

Her reverie sent a twinge of excitement and awakened her body. Her nipples hardened while fantasizing about the things Silas had done to her years ago. She closed her eyes and touched her lips, remembering his touch and envisioned his smoldering eyes again, as a heat built up inside her from the embers remaining of her love. Oddly, the flurry she experienced inside of her body helped calm her down. She kept her eyes closed and breathed deep, remembering more of those days . . .

The affair had ended just as abruptly as it started, after Silas's father, Frank Kain, was murdered. That horrible night had ruined everything. The police dragged her into the station the day after the dead body had been discovered. They questioned her about her relationship with Silas.

She shivered again as she remembered that dreadful night.

Frightened, she had walked down the long hallway in the precinct, the overhead lights buzzed. She was led to the back room and seated at a table. It had been sleeting outside, and she was wet and cold. She waited, twisting her sweater sleeve, and ended up stretching it to the point beyond repair. It never looked the same again. They made her wait for a long time, shivering in the cold room.

The lead officer had finally graced her with his presence, his interrogation was etched into her brain. She remembered his face, his olive-toned skin, covered with open pores. He had sweat dripping down from his forehead, which seemed odd because the room was so frigid. His dark eyes probed hers. She had felt violated, transparent, as if he was peeking at her through clear wrap, seeing her naked and vulnerable.

"What's your relationship with Silas Kain?" he said.

"He's my teacher."

"Oh, come on, Miss de Gourgues, you can do better than that. What do you two teach each other?" The detective tapped his pen against the table. "I know you go to his house, and I'm pretty sure it's not to study. I bet you let him touch you." A roguish smile crossed his face. "Word is, you're pretty tight with the Professor. Maybe infatuated even. You might even be willing to kill for his sake."

"I would never do something like that," she cried aloud.

"I know who you are, Michelle. Just another spoiled brat who thinks she can get away with murder. I know you're a killer." He gawked at her with contempt. "You're a heartless rich girl with no reverence for other people's lives. You come up here to Cambridge thinking you can run the place with your allowance from daddy."

Tears had brimmed her eyes, from fear and anger. She had wanted to scream at the arrogant man, police or not, but was afraid of her father finding out.

"I have no motive to kill a man I never even met," she had snapped back.

The detective banged his fist on the table right in front of her face and made her jump. "Don't lie to me."

She had tried hard to block his intimidation. It had all seemed so odd and pointless. Scared, desperate, and unwilling to call the family lawyer because then her father would have definitely found out about her affair. He would have flipped out. Then she remembered that her mother's sister lived nearby. Michelle took a chance that her aunt would keep her secret.

"I want to make a phone call, now."

She phoned Aunt Victoria. It had been the first time she reached out to her, and Michelle didn't know what to expect. She never anticipated that her aunt would end up being such a blessing in her life. Aunt Victoria had demanded Michelle to be released, and they finally had to let her go.

Of course, Michelle never had anything to do with the man's murder. Unfortunately, she never heard if it had been solved, still no closure. *No one can even imagine for a moment that I got away with murder. The insinuation alone is dynamite to my public life.* The clock ticked. She needed to act now before any messy business leaked out. She climbed the hill and walked back to her car, pulling out her cell phone. She leaned against the warm hood of the car and called Silas, dialing the number listed for his university office.

"Hello, Professor Kain speaking."

His voice sounded different from how she remembered.

"Hello, Professor."

A frozen moment lingered in the connection.

More feelings whirled in her mind, anxiety about what to say, and curiosity about latent feelings apparently released from a dark corner of her mind.

"Michelle?"

"How are you, Silas?"

"Michelle, it's you. I'm doing great now that you called."

Michelle didn't like being patronized.

"My goodness, you're laying it on a bit thick, Silas, don't you think? It's been seven years."

Quiet filled the air, except for scratchy crackles in the line. Michelle didn't know what to expect from him, but needed answers, so she blathered on.

"Silas, I'll be in Boston the day after tomorrow, and I'd love to see you. Would you be up to meeting with me, let's say for a cup of coffee at our favorite shop?"

"Michelle, just send me a text with the time, and I'll be at Darwin's like your loyal servant."

"I see that the literary world has devoured your work. Your books are doing well; best-sellers."

"Don't poke fun."

Now the old self-conscious and persecuted soul she remembered appeared, and it touched a soft spot in her heart.

"I'm not joking, Silas. I read your work and they're great stories. Congratulations."

"Tell me more. What's your favorite story?" he asked.

"We'll discuss it over coffee in two days. Send me your cell number to this phone, and I'll text you with the time."

"Fine. It'll be great to see you again. Thanks for calling, Michelle."

She ended the call, relieved that that part was over. Michelle drove back to the house and got ready for Emilie's return home.

Chapter 4

Silas

Silas hung up the phone. Memories of Michelle flooded his meditation. He leaned back in his desk chair, closed his eyes, and let his imagination fly. Vivid images of her body rushed through his mind. He remembered the way she had looked back then, her tanned supple body sprawled across his Greek handmade flokati rug, his most precious piece of decor, made more so after her sweet fragrance enhanced its beauty. Her dark strands of hair feathered out around her face contrasting against the ivory-colored shag, her big blue eyes closed so slowly when she succumbed to rapture. Their intimate moments had been wonderous. No lover had been as intense as she.

He missed Michelle. Excited by his memories of her, Silas closed his eyes and daydreamed. His groin hardened from his fantasy. A noise disrupted the silence; he wasn't alone in the office. A student stood near the door. Flustered, Silas appreciated the heavy desk he sat behind, blocking the view of his body. The student cleared his throat.

"Excuse me, Sir, is this the History Department?"

Frustrated, Silas said, "No. Can't you read? The sign on the door clearly states Professor Kain, Department Head of Literature. That's me."

"Sorry to trouble you."

"Close the door p-l-e-a-s-e."

The door slammed. Silas leaned back and tried to get back into his fantasy. Elated that he was going to see Michelle again after all these years, he smiled. It seemed a lifetime ago, and so much had changed. His mind drifted once more, but this time he remembered other things. . . . Silas remembered the night his mother died and how that set everything in the wrong direction.

There had been a blizzard that night; the snow piled high by the time he and his brother Milo had reached their mother's house in Maine. He remembered how she had looked while dying, lying there on her bed so thin and pale, losing her battle with cancer that night. A tear ran down his cheek as he envisioned his mother's frail body. She had meant the world to him, a strong woman who had raised her two sons on her own after their father walked out on them.

Silas had always agonized over the stigma following him, enduring years of teasing dished out by mean-spirited boys, all because his father had been a loser and left them stranded to fetch life on their own. Silas hated the man he never knew.

On the night his mother died, his estranged father, Frank Kain, emerged out of nowhere.

"Hello, boys. I figured the two of you would be here by your mother's side," Frank Kain said.

Silas couldn't believe his eyes. The nerve of the man, to come to his mother's house after all the years, and on the night of her death without any show of remorse. Silas opened the door wider, stepped out to the porch, and pushed the man away, back toward the steps.

"Get the hell out of here," Silas screamed.

Milo, his younger brother, came running to the door.

"What's going on?" he said.

"Your brother is beating me, that's what. I'll go away quietly if you just give me a few bucks. You are, after all, my sons, like it or not. I know you're coming into money, Silas, what with your mom dying, and now you have a book published and all. Just a few thousand, that's all I ask."

Silas moved closer to Frank Kain, raising his fist.

"You've got to be deranged to think you're getting a cent. We owe you nothing."

Silas had reacted on impulse and punched Frank Kain in the face. They struggled in a scuffle until Milo had pulled them apart. Frank Kain slipped on his ass, landing hard, he cursed. Silas laughed at him.

Frank Kain got up and yelled with a vengeance, "That's how you want to play? Okay, you asked for it. I'm going public with your brutality. Punching your dad, who only wants to amend the bridges burned. Just wait until the press hears about this."

Frank Kain wiped his face with his shirtsleeve.

"Good, I'm bleeding. It'll make a great picture for show and tell."

He turned away, laughing as he went down the street.

Enraged, Silas had screamed at the old man, "You'll get yours, old man."

A neighbor was walking his dog, turned, and glared at Silas. Boyhood insecurities rooted in his humbled past surfaced. Silas felt ashamed and small. He loathed his contentious father and, combined with grief over his mother's death, Silas's desperation drifted to a point of no return.

In his distress, Silas had reached out to the wrong person. He made a deal with the devil that night and had been paying for it since. In his panic, Silas confided his situation to a new friend of his, knowing full well that this friend had influence in all kinds of circles, including connections with the underworld.

Silas called his new friend asking for a favor. He received help that night in return for his pledge to return the favor in the future. Unfortunately, his request for help was twisted in the interpretation. Silas wanted Frank Kain gone, but not dead, but that didn't matter now. The deed had been done because of his appeal. Silas, an unwitting accomplice, was now entrapped with the group. He had become a full-fledged member that night and owed a favor to one of the most influential secret societies in the world.

There's no way out. He shivered from the memory of that horrible winter night, his worst nightmare. Frank Kain had been murdered and would never bother Silas or his brother again. Silas was never told who actually performed the deed, still, the Society clearly had been implicit in the murder of his father. This made him an accomplice, now that Silas was a member of the same secret society.

The deal deepened later on when Silas was promoted as a world-renowned author, using the society's financial backing. His success spiked because of their influence, power, and long reaches into social circles. The deal was sealed, and now Silas owed his allegiance to his fellow members. Somehow his affair with Michelle had been known to the grandmaster of the group. Silas was given strict instructions to inform the Society if any de Gourgues family member ever reached out to him.

Now backed into a corner with horrible choices, he was conflicted. Part of him still loved Michelle, never stopped loving her, but he owed his loyalty to the Society. They kept his secret all these years. He wished he could forget about the call from Michelle, but crossing the grandmaster of the Society was like signing his own death warrant. *The choice was stripped from me years ago, that awful night cursed my sad life. I lost my mother and my muse, Michelle.*

His mood darkened, and his stomach burned. Fearful of what they might do to Michelle if he called in the alert, Silas lost his edge. It didn't matter anymore; his soul was already lost.

"Well, there's no way to get back that fantasy about Michelle," he said aloud. He rubbed the edge of the desk with his fingers, deliberating. He picked up the phone, hesitating, his nerves raw and unable to decide.

Chapter 5

Emilie

The next day Emilie and Jeremy arrived at the house in Memphis. It was a warm autumn day. The leaves on the trees looked thirsty for water, a few tinged with gold edges and brown tips. Breezes intermittently crossed the yard and brushed against the skin on Emilie's arm, warming her with harmonious sensations. Happy to be home again, Emilie gazed up at the grand front columns. Fond memories filled her head.

She was reluctant, at first, to come home, afraid of reliving those last days when at the house. The pain that she had experienced back then was thankfully gone now, and she refused to relive the drama of when her father died. Shielding herself from those memories was an easier task with Jeremy near, her lifesaver. His positive attitude about life anchored her with good vibes. Emilie gazed up at his face, happy to see his deep dimples and warm hazel eyes, smiling back at her. Their love was strong and saved her soul from plummeting into madness; she accepted that now.

There was a loud ruckus. Emilie turned her attention to Nina, who scampered out of the house and down the stairs to greet them. She beamed with joy.

"Oh my Lord! Thank goodness you're home, Miss Emilie."

Nina wrapped her warm brown arms around her in a hug. She smelled like clean cotton sheets and sugar cookies at the same time.

"You look so wonderful!" Nina smiled, giving her a look, up and down. "Miss Emilie, you haven't looked this good in a long while. Last time I laid eyes on you, you looked like death itself."

"Oh, thanks for that," Emilie said.

"It's true. Your hair is a bit longer, but so soft with those brown waves. You're glowing like a woman in love." Nina smiled and gave Jeremy an approving nod. "I see that dark mood of yours is gone."

"I feel much more like myself these days," Emilie said.

"Let's just hope it stays that way," Nina said. "Don't pay any attention to your brother's infernal opinions. I know you can feel them sprouting out of him. Just remember, like I told you when you wuz a child, keep pushing the bad away. No need to harbor evil intentions in that head of yours. Thank goodness your young man here knew enough to bring you back to me."

She hugged Emilie again, so hard she almost toppled over.

"Okay, enough already, Nina."

Jeremy smiled, showing off his deep dimples.

"Do you think this is funny? Wait until she gets a hold of you," Emilie said.

Jeremy quickly grabbed the luggage, filling his arms, and headed into the house.

"I called your sister. Miss Michelle is at the office, but I told her you're here. She's so happy and said she'll be here shortly. I'm planning a special dinner tonight, the whole family together again. My Lord, your Mama, God rest her soul, would be so happy. I feel Miss Bethany smiling down on us right now. Do you feel it, too, child?"

Emilie and Jeremy gave each other side glances.

"Yes, as a matter of fact, I do feel like Mother is smiling on me, and it feels good."

Nina laughed aloud, snatched their bags away from Jeremy, then almost ran up the stairs. Evans, the house manager, stopped her, took the bags, and brought the luggage upstairs to Emilie's room and Jeremy's bag to a guest room. The perception of discretion was everything in the Mid-south.

Nina turned toward Emilie, leaned up, and whispered into her ear. "I'm so glad you're here. Your brother and sister haven't spoken a word since you left. And the poor child Rachael is stuck in the middle. That priest of yours comes here to counsel them, but I don't think it helps much."

Emilie took her hands in hers.

"Don't worry, Nina. Things will work themselves out. I'm here to help Michelle, and hopefully, Robert will have a change of heart."

"Humph. We'll see about that one. I'll keep praying for his soul," Nina said, then walked away.

Jeremy came over to Emilie, and they strolled into the parlor hand in hand. They stood there for a few minutes, looking around the room. Emilie sensed his concerns flowing from him, her empath gift kicking into gear.

"Don't worry, Jeremy, I have it under control. I feel pretty good and proud of myself for being able to rein in the vibes so well. During my time alone in Florida, I exercised the boundaries of my gift and practiced controlling them. I know how to turn them off. In a way, it sounds cold, turning off empathy to others, but it helps me stay me. If you ever notice me seemingly indifferent, you'll know why."

"Thanks for the warning," he said.

She smiled and pulled some stray hair that fell into her face back behind her ears.

"Is there still negativity around this place?" he asked.

Smiling, she nodded.

"I believe we're about to find out."

Emilie turned her gaze toward the doorway.

"Hello, Emilie, Jeremy." Robert walked into the parlor with Rachael at his side. "Glad you could pull yourself away from the beach to visit your family."

"You sound like you care, Robert," Emilie said.

"Em, of course, I care."

"Then why don't you answer my calls? Why not return them?"

"You know I hate phones. All water under the bridge now. I'm glad to see you again, honest." Robert walked over and gave her a kiss on her forehead.

"Now that you're here, you can help Rachael and me plan our wedding reception. We've waited long enough. It's going to be a huge affair with anybody who's somebody attending."

Emilie walked over to Rachael and hugged her friend. "I'm so happy for you and glad you're family now."

"Thank you, Emilie. Now instead of friends, we're sisters. And it's about time we all behaved like a family." Rachael shot a glare at Robert, who rolled his eyes.

"I promise to be a good boy," he said.

"Robert, will you please talk with Michelle? It's not her fault or mine. The changes concerning the business that were made in a new will were done to protect everyone—you included."

"I don't want to discuss it, Em," he replied.

"Then what's all this about holding things over Michelle's head? And about trying to get on the board again?"

Robert smiled while assessing everyone's faces.

"Would that be so bad for me to be on a board? The reason I haven't been speaking to my little sister is that she keeps going off. About how bad an influence Tom Bennett is, but he's been there for me, and I wish you all would be more understanding and forgiving. Besides, if there are secrets hidden by Michelle, maybe she's the one who should be explaining things," Robert said.

"Explaining what?" Michelle walked into the room. "What

have I missed?"

Emilie greeted her sister with a hug.

"We all decided to make peace and speak to each other again. And promise not to mention the name Tom Bennett," Emilie said.

"I second that if it means we can be civilized to each other," Robert said.

Michelle pulled her lips together tight and drew in a deep breath, then nodded.

The grandfather clock in the entry hall chimed eight; it was time for dinner.

Chapter 6

They all drifted into the dining room. The smell of home cooking blanketed the table, warming Michelle's senses and conjuring feelings of safety, tenderness, and the sentiment that came from familiar people and places. Nina bustled into the dining room behind them and uncovered dinner, pulling the stainless tops off the silver chaffered dishes, unveiling works of art.

"I made your favorite, Miss Emilie."

Smells from the steamed salmon sprinkled with dill and lemon wedges filled the room.

"I could use some home cooking," Emilie said. "Thank you for making me fish without the whiskers. You remembered — no catfish for me."

"Did you catch this one, too, Nina?" Robert joked.

She slapped the back of his head and laughed at his jibe, like usual, then mumbled prayers to herself. They sat down and began serving themselves.

"I'm starved," Michelle said. "Nina, what else do we have for dinner? Something smells good."

"You know I cooked your favorite, too; fried chicken and sides." Nina uncovered a Wedgwood dish, raising the lid carefully, revealing a grand prize.

"Nina, I think that's your favorite." She laughed. "But I like it, too. Got any of your famous coleslaw?"

"Of course. Nothing but the best for you princesses around here. Oh, I'm sorry, prince, too." Nina laughed at her joke. "Just holler if you need anything." She left the room.

"Maybe you can have salmon as a meal choice for the reception?" Emilie said.

"That's a great idea, Emilie." Rachael looked over at Robert.

He nodded, adding nothing to the conversation.

"Michelle, we need to shop for dresses soon. Tell me, what's your favorite flower?" Rachael said.

"Oh, anything is fine with me. I like them all." Michelle was being polite. The conversation about the wedding reception plans seemed a safe topic.

"How have things been going, Robert? What have you been filling your days with?" Emilie asked.

Quick to answer, he seemed happy to be asked. "I have a few non-profits that I've been sponsoring. Rachael and I are doing the work together, part of our marriage counseling with the Church. Father Eddie said we could build a stronger relationship and keep our marriage on track if we learn to work together. I guess counseling is required to get the Church's blessing during the reception. As far as I'm concerned, we don't need any of it. Rachael knows how much I love her. Don't you?" He leaned over and kissed her cheek.

"Yes, of course. I love you, too." Rachael blushed.

Michelle noticed that Rachael seemed uncomfortable with public affection, or maybe having the whole family around the table together was intimidating. Understandable, the three of them were all obstinate.

"Robert, are you free tomorrow?" Jeremy jumped into the conversation. "How about you and I ride the horses? Maybe you can show me the rest of the property. I've only seen the area around the river outlet at the back of the property line. That was months ago when I worked on the Wolf River project. I'd love to see the rest of the estate."

Michelle dropped her fork. It clanged against a china plate, and everyone looked at her. Michelle looked at her sister. Hell, Emilie seemed surprised, too. The tension between Jeremy and Robert was well known, more so after father's will was read.

Michelle remembered the look on Rob's face that day when Jeremy had grabbed him by the shirt, lifting him off the floor, choking him after Jeremy had learned of Robert's involvement in his uncle's death. Robert had hired someone to steal a precious book from Jeremy's old uncle, and the event caused him to have a heart attack. Jeremy had lost his better judgment that day, and Rob's face had burned beet red.

"That's right, you worked back there. Of course, Jeremy, if you're genuinely interested in the property from an environmental engineer viewpoint, I think it would be good. You can fill me in on the work you completed with that group, documenting the Eco-system of the Wolf River, and explain to me all the effects of flooding in the area."

Robert wiped his mouth with his napkin and smiled back at Jeremy.

"I noticed my sister is wearing a ring. It seems we're going to be relatives, no matter how uncomfortable we are with each other, so we might as well make the best of it. Besides, you'll be on your own most of the time since Emilie will be tied up working, helping Michelle out. Say, don't you have a job anymore, old chap? No work back in England?"

Robert leaned back, head raised, waiting for a response. He could be sarcastic without any effort. Jeremy shook his head, smiling, pretending the snarky remark rolled off his back, but there was some frustration behind his grin, and Michelle didn't blame him.

"I work free-lance, which means I pick and choose my work projects, as you well know. I'm on vacation right now, but since you mentioned it, maybe I will stop by and see if the watershed project needs a helping hand," Jeremy replied.

"For free, of course," Robert said.

"Of course. Just like you, I help non-profits." Jeremy smiled.

Robert couldn't help from grinning, too.

"Robert, how did you know I asked Emilie to help me at work?" Michelle asked. "I never mentioned it to anyone, except Emilie, of course."

He shrugged. "Just a hunch."

Nina entered the room and started to take away empty dishes while the family prattled as they ate dinner. She nodded, smiling.

"A little nosy tonight, Nina?" Michelle said. Nina ignored her, like usual.

"Miss Emilie, you need to be home more often," Nina said. "Thank goodness you came. The last few months were dreadful. Robert and Miss Michelle, not speaking a word to each other, and poor Miss Rachael, stuck in the middle. All I want is for things to stay good between you children."

"Oh, stop your fussing. Nina. We're all big boys and girls now. Time for you to get on with your own life and family," Robert said.

"Humph," Nina returned back, indignant, as she left the room.

Rachael shot Robert a sideways glance of disapproval.

He just rolled his eyes. "What?"

"Well, that was a nice dinner." Emilie stood.

"Em, you and Jeremy up for after-dinner drinks?" Robert asked.

"Sorry, but I'm a bit tired." Her glance turned to Jeremy.

"No, thanks. I think I'll call it a day also," Jeremy added. "I missed a night's sleep flying the red-eye." After making their excuses, they went upstairs.

Michelle followed them up a few minutes later and barreled into Emilie's bedroom.

"So, Emilie, are you ready to take over?"

She plumped herself down on the bed beside Emilie and looked her straight in the eyes.

"Sure, no problem. Calm down, Michelle. Someone will think you're high."

"I wish." She giggled. "Did you hear Rob downstairs? Gawd, he's so arrogant. He tries to make me sound helpless as if I need my big sister to help me do my job. And poor Nina." Michelle reached over and hugged her sister. "You don't buy Robert's act downstairs, do you?"

Emilie whispered into her ear, "Don't worry."

"Michelle, we know him well enough. Don't worry your pretty head." Jeremy nudged her shoulder playfully.

"Okay then. Tomorrow morning I'm going up to Boston first thing. I'll try to get things cleared up quickly. I'll return before you know it."

She jumped off the bed and turned around, ready to flee.

"Hold on," Emilie said. "Before you take off, are you planning on telling us what this is all about? What was your little indiscretion that's so bad Rob can hold it over your head?"

Michelle dropped her eyes to the floor. Red-faced, she was so embarrassed and knew she couldn't lie to her sister. Emilie would only see through it with her clairvoyant power. Sweat formed on her brow, and she wiped it off with the back of her hand. Michelle gulped back her pride and started her story.

"Well . . . if I tell you everything, do you promise not to judge me?"

"Of course," Emilie said. She and Jeremy were both sitting on the bed, looking up at Michelle with anticipation. *This has got to be good.* Michelle stood center stage, getting her nerve to tell her story.

"First off, I need you to know I'm not too proud of myself."

"Okay, we get that."

"Well, I had an affair with one of my professors."

They didn't flinch.

"Okay. Good. Well then, something happened, unexpected. I was pretty tight with the professor when his mother died all of a sudden. Then, his long-lost father showed up. The professor was so upset, I mean really pissed, and he threatened the guy. His estranged father, I mean."

They nodded and Michelle continued.

"The next day the guy turned up dead. Murdered. Somehow, the police had found out that I was seeing the professor—and they pulled me into the police station, asking me all kinds of questions. They kind of assumed that I murdered the professor's father—to prove my love for him." She burst out laughing. "It sounds ludicrous, and of course, I didn't do it. Hell, I never even met the guy."

"Okay, Chelle, finish up the Cliff note version. How could any of this help Robert?" Emilie said.

"After the interrogation at the police station, I was shaken up and stopped seeing the professor. I wanted to disown him completely, and so I never knew exactly what happened to the dead guy or how it all ended. Aunt Victoria had rescued me from the cops and brought me to her house. I stayed with her awhile until I came to my senses. That's all of it, honest."

She took in a deep breath, relieved.

"Stupid, I know, but that's the entire story. I kept it hidden from Father, for obvious reasons, and I figured it was filed away somewhere, purged by now. But somehow, Robert found out. He threatened to make it public and run a PR campaign against me. He claims even though I didn't do anything wrong, just the rumor of trouble would be reason enough to be ostracized by the board."

Michelle felt guilty.

Emilie got up from the bed and hugged her sister, patting her back gently.

"Don't worry, Michelle. People make mistakes. You used poor judgment, but you were young, and besides, you didn't do anything wrong or unlawful. If anyone did, it was the professor."

Michelle leaned away from Emilie, stepped back, and grabbed her hands.

"Yes, I know, but here's the thing. I plan to meet with him tomorrow."

"The professor?" Jeremy stood, alarmed. "Why?"

Emilie shook her head. "That doesn't sound like a good idea, Chelle."

"I know what you think, but I have to find out if he knows anything else about his father's death. Maybe they caught the guy who murdered him already? I hope so because that definitely would put me in the clear."

"Do you think that wise? To see him, I mean. Maybe you can just call the police."

Michelle looked up. "No way. That detective still haunts my dreams, thank you very much. Maybe the professor knows something about what happened that night. Besides, I want to see his reactions when I ask him, you know. And Rob's right about one thing. I was questioned about a murder, and that knowledge could be bad PR. Especially worse if there's still room for doubt."

She paced the floor. "I avoided Silas for the next two years. I changed my major, I changed my habits and the places where I hung out. I never had closure, and I certainly have no idea how it all played out. Maybe the case is solved, but if not, then the only way to keep my name in good standing is to catch the real killer, once and for all."

"Michelle, that sounds dangerous." Jeremy stepped closer. "We'll go with you."

"I need Emilie to watch things here because I don't trust

Robert to be alone. You heard him—he already knew I asked Em to come here. Somehow he spied. If I need you guys, I'll call. Promise."

"All right, but what's the professor's name?" Emilie asked. "Just in case we need to locate you. Who knows, he might hold you responsible and clobber you on the head."

Michelle smiled. "I was so worried about telling you what a fool I was that I forgot to say his name." She laughed. "He's Silas—Silas Kain."

"Silas Kain, the author of horror stories?" Emilie said.

"Yes, he's the guy, and his murdered father's name was Frank Kain. Let's just hope I can find some closure so I can get rid of every doubt. That way Rob has no secret hanging over me. Being in the spotlight is nerve-racking. I guess I've been lucky that all this time it remained hushed, which only makes me wonder how Robert even knew about it at all. Oh well, it'll get resolved soon enough. I'll be off tomorrow morning, first thing."

Michelle kissed them both goodnight and left.

Chapter 7

The next day Emilie was up early to say goodbye to Michelle. She stood on the porch waving as the car drove away. Evans, the house manager, was there, too. He never said much about the family's goings-on, but Michelle wondered if he considered them all crazy.

Relieved knowing Emilie and Jeremy had her back, Michelle was on her way to Boston early in the morning. She never doubted her sister's loyalties or capabilities. Robert was the problem. She had hired a specialized surveillance company to monitor her brother's activities, just in case. He had already tried influencing some of the company's executives against her. It took only one person to be fired, the Director of Accounting who had smuggled numbers to Robert in an email before everyone realized that their loyalties should lie with Michelle. No one discussed anything with Robert anymore. She hated resorting to such extremes but enjoyed the power of being in charge, and she wasn't willing to let it be ripped away from her.

She presumed Robert was miffed about Emilie stepping in while Michelle was away. He hadn't anticipated that Emilie would willingly come back, *yet he was all nice and polite as soon as Emilie walked through the door.* Michelle smelled a rat and knew he would try to use Emilie, but she could handle things just fine. Besides, Michelle would only be a phone call away.

Michelle used the family's private jet, and while en route, texted Silas with the time to meet at Darwin's. She hoped he had an update on the murder case of Frank Kain. Silas's enthusiastic reaction somehow troubled her. The idea of seeing him again made her a bit nervous.

Her stomach ached the entire plane trip. Her plans riddled with anxiety, she tried putting her mind at ease by reading.

However, she kept going over the same sentence, so finally, she closed the book and tossed it onto the adjoining seat.

She turned on some music and put the Bose headset over her ears, blocking out everything except Coldplay, then the Killers, but still she felt no reassurance. Michelle told herself, *you can handle this, he's only a man.* She kept repeating the mantra until in control of her emotions.

The small jet landed and parked on the tarmac at Logan Airport.

Michelle stepped onto the wet pavement.

The air was foggy and damp, and a cold breeze swept across the airfield. She pulled her jacket tighter around herself and reached into her bag, grabbing a scarf. She wrapped it around her slender neck. *I forgot how cold it can be in Massachusetts.* Only a year ago, she had lived and worked here, in this busy old city, but it seemed like ages had passed. She had many fond memories of Boston. It had been seven years since she had seen Silas.

Michelle wondered about her stray feelings for him and his toward her. There had been no closure; their relationship just abruptly ended. She just couldn't be with him anymore. Deep inside, she always wondered about his involvement in his father's death. He had hated the man for all the years of neglect, and Silas had blamed his perfidious father for everything that went wrong in his life. Not that he turned out too badly. Silas Kain was one of the most celebrated authors of the day, after all.

The pilot escorted Michelle to the limousine that waited at the curb. She told the driver the first designated stop, Harvard Square. She slid into the back seat of the car, and as soon as the door closed, she noticed the quiet. She disengaged as she gazed out the window watching the bustle of the airport, without any of the sound seeping into the car interior. It was like a silent movie without the music, and everyone looked so mechanical and unreal. Michelle sat back in the leather seat and closed her eyes for a moment. The car tugged as they mingled into the congested morning traffic.

The sun evaporated the early morning haze. Michelle appreciated the radiating rays through the car window, warming her hands that rested on her lap. Sunbeams danced on the diamonds embedded in her rings and bracelet, casting shimmering rainbows across the back seat. It was unfolding into a beautiful autumn day. By the time they neared Harvard, the sun was bright, reflecting on the leaves' yearly turncoat foliage.

Looking through the back seat window, Michelle witnessed life as they passed the old neighborhoods, admiring the old houses and fall scenery. This was the best time of year in New England. She loved the warm, color-filled days and the crisp, cold nights, which invited everyone to snuggle near cozy fires in a hearth. It suggested excuses to drink mulled wine, or any warm spirits to warm the soul. Michelle missed those cozy nights.

The driver honked his horn and swerved to miss another car. Michelle was rattled back to reality. The roads, all merging together, creating one messy snarl of snakes from the hectic migration of vehicles making their morning commute. Traffic wasn't something Michelle missed about Boston. The ride to Harvard Square took longer than expected. She would be a little late. The plan was to meet at a cafe they used to frequent, Darwin's Limited, on Cambridge Street, not far from Silas's townhouse. They often went there for a quick bite. The Skywalker sandwich was Michelle's favorite.

Today just a scone and coffee would do. Her stomach growled. Maybe a bite to eat was a good way to cover up her nervous tension.

Michelle's anxiety sabotaged her theories. *Had he changed much? Would he still desire her?* Her face flushed. She wasn't supposed to care about those kinds of feelings anymore. The last thing she wanted was for Silas to think that she was still infatuated with him. All of that was a lifetime ago and in her past. She wanted to forget him and asked herself, *why am I doing this?* Too late, they arrived.

Chapter 8

The car stopped in front of the shop. Michelle stepped out and waited as the driver left. The tires slushed through a puddle and just missed spraying her with muddy water. She turned and walked into Darwin's alone. When she opened the door, the heat stung against her cold face. The bright colors of the food displayed in the deli case, combined with the smell of freshly roasted coffee, woke her senses. The old brick walls and familiar decor welcomed her back to her old stomping grounds.

Her nerves eased a bit after being reminded of a happier time. Michelle scanned the large open room and saw Silas sitting at a table against the back wall. He stood and motioned for her to join him. She stared for a moment. He wasn't as tall as she remembered but more handsome than she dared dream. Silas appeared different. Confidence radiated from him, noticeable even from across a room. His eyes were still smoldering gray and sexy. Michelle made her way to the table.

"Michelle, my beautiful flower," he said. He wrapped his arm around her skinny body, and to her surprise, he kissed her on the lips, a gentle kiss that lingered a moment. Michelle's face burned, blood rushing to her cheeks. It took her a moment to recover from the unexpected sensation, just from a small peck of a kiss.

"Hello, Silas," she mumbled, annoyed with herself for still having a reaction to his touch. *Those feelings evaporated a long time ago,* she fooled herself. She reminded herself of the reason for this lunacy, determined to smother the surfacing memories. They belonged buried in the past. She slipped into a chair, pulled her arms out of her coat, and without a second thought, waved her hand in the air requesting service. She noticed Silas watching her from across the table, grinning. "Is something funny?" she said.

"Yes, as a matter of fact, there is. No one is going to be coming at your beck and call here. You have to go to the counter for service. Don't you remember?" He grinned. "Don't worry, Michelle, I remember how you like your coffee. I'll be right back."

"Get me a cranberry scone, too." After a second, "Please." She batted her eyes.

Silas nodded and hurried to the counter, lucky there was no line. *Perfect timing on his part, just like always.* Still good-looking, he managed to keep himself lean. Silas seemed happier than she recalled. The shadow that used to follow him around wasn't dragging him down any longer. Obviously, when his father died, so did the insecurity that had haunted him throughout the years. Michelle was glad for him, he deserved to be happy. Random notions buzzed in her head. Did he have someone special in his life? Maybe he got married? How could she ask him without sounding like she cared? *She didn't care, of course; was she fooling herself?*

Silas was back balancing the coffee. "Nice and hot, and one scone for me lady."

"Thank you."

He sat back down, handed her a cup, and watched her from across the table. She could feel his steel-gray eyes on her and suffered the heat from his stare. Michelle wrapped her hands around the steaming cup and warmed her fingers, looking down, away from his gaze. She meticulously stirred her coffee. She stalled while thinking about how to ask her question. Michelle chanced a few glances up and noticed his different hairstyle, cut and neat, refined now — mature. He had a tan leftover from summer. He was as charming as ever, flashing white teeth behind his smile. Michelle found it hard not to look at him. Her glance steered to his face, still drawn to him and those eyes.

"You look terrific, Michelle. All dolled up in business attire, I see. I never dreamed I'd see you so sophisticated. I hear you're running your father's enterprise now. Bravo."

"Yes, I've been pretty busy, actually. How did you hear about it? Until a few months ago, I was right here in Boston."

"Well, it did make headlines in all the papers after your father died. Besides, a friend of mine knows your brother," he said.

Michelle's interest piqued. *Maybe that was how Robert knew about the murder investigation, through their common friend?* Robert knew almost everybody who was somebody, with his gallivanting around the world over the years. She swallowed, trying to hold back her angst. *Keep your cool,* she told herself. *Don't react with your emotions.* She needed details without raising red flags in case Silas was somehow in contact with Robert. She responded with a playful retort.

"Well, tell your friend not to believe a word my brother says. He lies. Anyway, I'm not here to talk about my family."

Silas lost his smile. He held onto his coffee cup tightly as if preventing it from flying off the table. He stared into her eyes.

"Tell me, Michelle, what are you here for? You walked out. After all these years, why now?"

She hadn't expected things to feel so confusing meeting with Silas again. Too late now, she was here and needed to know. *Ask, you dummy!*

"I need to ask you something important, Silas. I hope you don't think badly of me, but I need to know the status of the investigation of your father's murder. Is it still open?"

Michelle looked down at her scone, not wanting to see the reaction to her question on his face. It would upset him, and she wanted to give him a moment to regain his composure, so she waited a few seconds, then looked up. To her surprise, he sported a big smile.

"Is that why you're here? To check on the case? Wow. And here I was thinking you missed me."

Michelle couldn't tell if he was playing with her or just trying to be warm-hearted, like the young professor she once knew. She took a deep breath and hoped it was the latter, willing to give him a benefit of the doubt.

"Sorry. I didn't mean to blurt it out like that. It's just that it's been on my mind a lot, and I needed to know where it stands. As you recall they considered I was involved, and I took that personally."

Silas looked down. His hands fumbled with the napkin on the table.

"I remember. I remember other things, too."

He lifted his face, focused his gaze on Michelle, and flaunted a sexy smile. She recognized exactly what he craved. He felt the pull of attraction between them, too.

"You must be married by now, Silas. I figured a man with your physical appetites had hitched up with someone for regular meals by now. Chasing young girls around campus isn't as socially accepted these days."

She smiled, teasing him.

He shook his head no and lowered his eyes. Michelle had hit a sore spot and immediately regretted her kidding. After all, he had been good to her and important in her life.

"Michelle, after you, there was no one who could quench my thirst."

Surprised, she gulped to suppress her reaction, but the next moment she couldn't stop herself. "You mean you're celibate? I don't believe it."

He choked and wiped spittle from his mouth.

"No," he said, shaking his head. "Of course, I'm not celibate. However, I mean my words completely. You were special to me. The only one I truly shared my soul with, and after you left—well, there was never anyone capable of filling the emptiness."

They looked into each other's eyes; the intensity of years ago returned. Somehow, it seemed right back on track, as if nothing else had mattered in between. Drawn to each other, steaming in an intense mutual attraction, they swam in a sea of pheromones.

Michelle's heart pumped, ready to boil over. Sensations long forgotten surfaced, and she worried her panties were going to melt. The more her body reacted to him, the more her anxiety built up inside. *Stop yourself, fool!* A few years back, she would have jumped at this chance, but not today. She forced her self-control, not trusting anyone ever again, without proof of the sincerity behind words. The only one she trusted in the whole world was her sister.

"I'm so sorry. Silas, I never wanted you to be lonely. You know as well as I do that we were never meant to be together. It was only a wild affair for you to write about someday in erotic fiction," she said.

"I'm sorry you feel that way. It was much more to me."

Michelle dropped her face into her hands, embarrassed to meet his stare. She didn't intend to have this kind of conversation. *What was I thinking coming back here to talk with Silas?* She grabbed the coffee and sipped, pulling an invisible veil over her turbulent emotions.

"Sorry, Silas. Maybe this was a mistake. I can check with the police station on my own and get the update. I'm so sorry that I bothered you. I hope things are going well for you. I read your newest book, and I think it's great." She smiled.

"Yes, things are going well for me. Don't worry, Michelle, I won't bother you about our relationship anymore. But I will help you for old times' sake. Save yourself a call. The case is cold as ever. No clues surfaced that I'm aware of. It's one of those cold cases no one investigates anymore. No one cared about Frank Kain. He lived and died a nobody. I'm glad he's dead. It was crazy of him to come back, and I have no idea what he was thinking, approaching my brother and me like that, but 'thanks for nothing is all I said to him. You know he was a loser and probably killed because of an old grudge or some gambling debt or underworld thing going on in his life. I wash my hands of it all."

Silas sat back, relaxed now, his hands folded behind his head. A smile swiped across his face. Michelle wondered what his game was and what really happened to his father that ended his life. Maybe Silas was right—he was murdered by an old acquaintance with a grudge.

"So are you staying long?" he asked.

Michelle decided to keep him interested just in case she needed something from him later. She was playing with fire, but for her, this was a game, not real. That thought became her mantra as she batted her eyes slowly and teased with a sideways glance, trying to see if she could still get him excited.

It worked. Silas's face twitched a bit, and his eyes faded into a dazed faraway stare. His pants bulged from his piqued interest. She was shameless but wanted to leave with the upper hand.

"I'll be here only for a short visit. Maybe we can squeeze in more time together, but I doubt it. Don't get your hopes up."

Silas flaunted a naughty smile. "Well, it would be nice if we could spend time together."

He sent his smoldering lover's gaze her way. His eyes caused her to melt in a memory of her own, flustered again.

Even after commanding herself to stay in charge of her emotions, Michelle's cheeks burned hot.

She loosened her scarf from around her neck, internally berating herself. Standing abruptly, she knocked over a salt shaker on the table. She grabbed her purse, pulled out her phone, and called her driver. "I'm ready."

She avoided his face, in a hurry to leave Silas before anything else popped into her head.

"Sorry, Silas, I have to go. Other appointments, you understand."

She hurried out of the cafe and left Silas standing near the table. The car rolled up to the curb in front of Darwin's. She hustled into the back seat, slammed the car door, and said, "Get me out of here fast."

Chapter 9

"Where to, Miss de Gourgues?" the driver asked.

"Washington Avenue," she said.

Michelle gazed out the window as they passed crowded neighborhood streets lined with garbage bags stuffed with autumn leaves, dragged to the curb. They drove toward the edge of town, closer to the limits. She noticed how the setting changed, now showing off affluent suburbs with larger homes. Lost in her thoughts, she happened to notice her own reflection on the glass window—a lost girl in a crazy world. A person she desperately tried to understand—herself.

Aunt Victoria's house was on the north side of Cambridge. Victoria was her mother's sister, and she still lived in the old family house they had grown up in. Everything was kept the same, like a time capsule of her mother's past, captured and sealed. Her aunt had given Michelle a safe haven when she had needed it most. It had been months since her last visit, and Michelle needed some family love right now.

Victoria was tall and youthful-looking for a woman in her fifties. She was a pleasant person, with soft blond hair and pale blue eyes, just like her mother. Victoria spoke clearly with distinct command. She was Michelle's hero.

On the night Michelle had been interrogated by the police, she had called her aunt for help, not knowing what to expect. She had been there within an hour. When Victoria entered the station that night, no one had dared harass her. It was made clear that no one was going to keep her niece for another minute. All of the policemen had apologized as Victoria and Michelle exited the station with heads held high. Once they had gotten into her car, Victoria leaned over to the passenger side and hugged Michelle.

"Don't worry, Dear, everything will be all right." Her voice was like an angel's. Aunt Victoria drove Michelle to Washington Avenue and the house where her mother had grown up. From the moment she stepped her foot onto the gray porch floor, she felt at home. Victoria showed Michelle to her room without a third degree. She gave her loving care instead. They had enjoyed each other's company that evening and had remained in touch since.

After Michelle graduated from college, she remained living in Boston and visited her aunt at least once a month, often staying the entire weekend. Aunt Victoria shared memories about Michelle's mother Bethany and told stories about when they were young girls. It gave Michelle some needed connection, something she had missed in her childhood since she had been only eight when her mother died.

Aunt Victoria told childhood stories about her mother. Michelle remembered that her father once had asked her if Victoria ever talked about Tom Bennett. Her parents had some problems with the man in the past. Tom Bennett was the same man who had turned her brother against Father, and now the rest of the family, as well.

Victoria had never mentioned Tom Bennett, but Michelle knew she had knowledge of what had happened between her mother, her father, and Bennett. She planned to ask her Aunt Victoria some hard questions and prepared herself to hear even harder truths.

The car pulled up to the house.

The large Victorian home sat on top of a slight hill, with a large front porch. Fancy woodwork embellished the rounded turrets and the corners of the roofline. It was painted yellow with crisp white trim, capped with gray roof shingles. The porch railing scrollwork enhanced the old style. The bushes were all neatly groomed, creating a welcoming path toward the gigantic oak front door.

The house was a real home, a place where people cared for each other, unlike the big house in Memphis where she grew up. She wished her sister Emilie was there with her to share this feeling. Michelle returned home every time she saw this big old house on the hill. She eagerly left the car and walked to the front door. Aunt Victoria opened the door and hugged her niece as soon as she stepped foot on the porch.

"Oh, I've missed you," Victoria said. She held Michelle tight as if she'd never let her go. Michelle smelled her rose perfume and felt her soft cashmere sweater against her face while cuddled in her embrace. Her aunt dropped her arms, opened the door wide, and welcomed Michelle to enter. She walked into the large hall with dark oak floors and wood-trimmed walls.

"How is Memphis?" Victoria asked.

"It's great. At first, I wasn't sure if I wanted to be back in Memphis, and I miss Boston sometimes, but it's been so busy. Time flies, and I love the work. My father did a great job putting together some wonderful talent." A sly grin slid across her face. "I'm a great boss, and I plan on staying there, even though I do miss you."

Michelle pouted, and Victoria laughed.

"You'll just have to promise to visit more often, and I won't take no for an answer."

"I promise," Michelle said.

She sauntered into the living room. Michelle was content to be there, with everything the same as she remembered. She plopped herself onto the sofa. Victoria slapped her hands together and drew them to her face like in prayer, her smile beaming across the room. Michelle tapped the sofa cushion near her, inviting her aunt to sit.

"Okay, enough small talk. I need some answers. I've been having problems with my brother. Seems Robert just wants to destroy me."

Victoria shook her head, not believing her words.

"You're worrying for nothing. Your brother loves you and would never hurt you," she said.

"He does want to hurt me. He wants to take control of the company. That means getting rid of me. Robert has been so angry since our father's will was read, and he keeps listening to that Tom Bennett. What an ass."

Victoria gasped, her face paled as if she had just seen a ghost.

"Are you all right, Auntie?"

"What does Tom Bennett have to do with things? How does he know Robert?"

Michelle watched her aunt's face as it wilted. The smile on her face vanished. Her hands visibly shook.

"Are you okay?" Michelle repeated. A sick creepy feeling hung in her gut. Victoria's face showed fear as if something horrible was about to happen.

"I'll be all right, just tell me. What is your brother doing with Tom Bennett?"

Remembering the promise she had made to her father, she was reluctant to reveal the secret. She had pledged to keep it hidden.

"Well . . ." she stammered. "It seems that Tom Bennett and Robert are friendly. His son Jackson was Rob's roommate in college, and somehow Rob became best pals with Tom. Well, without getting into details, I need to know everything about him. What happened between Father and Tom Bennett? Why is he out to ruin my father's good name? And why do you think he's still hanging around Robert? Emilie says the man's a menace . . . she sensed it. His son Jackson warned me about him, too."

Victoria sat on the sofa and patted the cushion for Michelle to scoot closer, then took Michelle's hands in hers. Victoria's stare was intense. She swallowed hard, and her eyes started to tear up.

"Tom Bennett hated your father. It's a long story. I wish to God that man was out of our lives for good. I had hoped you would never know about this, but well, now I think you need to hear. We need to keep that man away from your entire family." Victoria shivered.

Michelle sympathized with her aunt, who obviously didn't want to relive the story, but Michelle had to know the truth. "No more secrets."

Victoria nodded. "Some people just refuse to go away. He should have died, not your father."

Suddenly Michelle was afraid to hear the truth. Her dry mouth parched, that safe feeling gone, replaced with dread. It had to be really bad if her aunt wished someone harm. She stared at the floor and waited for Victoria to tell the story of what had happened years ago.

Chapter 10

Victoria stood and paced the floor, wringing her hands, then stopped in her tracks and sat back down beside Michelle. Taking her hands in her own, Victoria stared at Michelle, demanding her full attention.

"When your mother was young, she was a spitfire. You know, you look a lot like she did at your age. You've seen her pictures of when she was younger, right? Of course, your hair color is different."

Michelle nodded.

"You remind me of her, the same spunk and all. Back in the seventies, lots of young men wanted your mother's attention, Bethany was so beautiful. Things were a little wild back then, but we were raised to be careful about things. Your grandmother put the fear of God in us." She chuckled. "We went to church every week and on holy days, too." Victoria looked up into the air at nothing in particular. "Your mom loved to dance and to have fun, and she loved to be with people. College back then was filled with fun parties, and Bethany was such a trusting soul. Some people suggested that she trusted too easily, but . . ."

The silence while Victoria collected her poise left Michelle wondering if she was up to telling the story. Her aunt looked woeful.

"Bethany wasn't promiscuous or anything like that. It was all just fun for her. She loved dancing. We had so much fun back in those days."

Victoria was smiling as she recollected.

"Then Tom Bennett came along. He went to Harvard, too, just like your father. Bethany was introduced to him at a mixer. He was handsome, tall, and dark-haired, and had a mustache.

Back then, that look was hip. All the men had mustaches and wore their collars open, showing off their chest hair." She shook her head and snickered. "They danced and had fun together with the other kids. Everyone liked Tom. He was charming and joked around a lot. Such a handsome devil, though no one knew how much of a devil he was at first."

Victoria let go of Michelle's hands and began twisting hers, kneading one hand into the other in angst.

"It's okay, Auntie. Finish the story," Michelle coaxed.

Victoria looked up into her eyes, and after a few seconds, went on with the story.

"One night after a dance, Tom drove Bethany home. He went the back way on an old barren street and pulled the car over. Before my sister knew what was happening, Tom groped her. Bethany said she pushed him back as best she could and struggled to get out of the car, but she was a small girl. Bennett easily overpowered her and took advantage of her . . ."

Victoria spoke the last words with disgust.

"Tom Bennett raped her in the car. It was a nightmare for your mother."

"Oh my God!" Michelle covered her mouth. The horror set in, and the dark truth disgusted her. Gagging, she almost vomited on the Persian rug. She swallowed back, burning the back of her throat. She closed her eyes, but images emerged and refused to go away. Victoria grabbed Michelle's hands again, and this time gently stroked them for a moment.

"It's okay. It all happened so long ago. Let me finish so you know the whole truth."

Michelle opened her eyes and saw that Aunt Victoria needed to say more. Michelle nodded.

"After, he dropped her off, acting as nothing had happened." Victoria shriveled up her face, making her look suddenly haggard. "He told Bethany he loved her; imagine that!

And that he wanted her. She was some kind of thing he could put in his closet of cruelty. Your mother, of course, wanted nothing to do with the creep. My poor sister was traumatized."

Tears filled Victoria's eyes, and she brushed them away with her curled finger. She took a deep breath and continued.

"Bethany was changed when she came home that night. She cried for a week, refusing to talk about it. She wouldn't leave the house. Finally, she confided in me and told me the truth about the rape. I was appalled, of course, and wanted to run to the police."

She stopped talking and looked again at Michelle, studying her face.

"You must understand, Michelle, those were different times back then. Date rape was never discussed. No one ever spoke about it in fear of being accused. Many people in authority back then thought it was usually made up, and would say things like it was the girl's fault for being too loose as if she asked for it. No one wanted to bring things like that up, especially in a public court. It was too embarrassing."

Victoria shook her head dramatically, trying to fling the memory from her mind.

"Thank God things have changed. Even then, I wasn't meek and mild-tempered like my sister. I was so angry. When Bethany refused to make a complaint, I took matters into my own hands. I walked up to Tom Bennett and confronted him, right there on the steps of his fraternity house. In front of all his friends. I told him to stay away from my sister, or else Bethany would have the police arrest him. You should have seen the looks people gave him. I felt justified, but then . . .

"Well, he was such an arrogant young man. He persisted in his advances anyway. He sent Bethany flowers and letters in the mail, expressing his love. Of course, it made her sick."

Victoria's face turned red. Michelle could see that hate resided with her aunt; hell, she was revolted by Tom Bennett, still.

"Oh God, he made all of us in the house sick! He kept calling and leaving messages even with our parents. Then one day, I had had enough. I couldn't stand by any longer while he tortured my sister.

I took the letters to the police and told them about the rape. The police didn't take the situation seriously. It was weeks later and with no evidence of the rape. They claimed they didn't want to hurt a promising young man's career, etc., etc. Infuriated, I went to see a lawyer. They had a complaint drawn, and we went to court to get a restraining order against Tom Bennett. That was the only way to stop his letters from coming." Aunt Victoria's nostrils flared.

Michelle tried to sit quietly and listen to the entire story, even though she had a million questions inside her head that she wanted to ask. She couldn't hold out and settled by asking the easiest question.

"Did that work? Did he stay away after that?"

"That's when Pierre de Gourgues came along. Your mother's great love." Victoria smiled. "Your father had heard my rants at the fraternity house that day. Out of concern, Pierre made a point of being nice to Bethany, making sure she was all right. He later claimed he had noticed your mother before and liked her, but was too shy to come forward. After he heard what happened to her, well, he was caring when she needed someone the most. It didn't take long for them to fall madly in love. Your father helped her overcome her fears and heal from the rape ordeal."

"The happy ending," Michelle said.

"Yes," Victoria said, nodding. "But their happiness only enraged Tom Bennett. He started stalking them and made threats against both of them. He had no idea of the power behind the de Gourgues family. Your father had never flaunted his wealth, and most of the young men on campus had come from rich families. But no one heard of your family dynasty. Different social circles back then in the South. After a few days of harassment, the de Gourgues family stepped in. Your grandfather contacted some of his friends from Harvard, who had deep influence, and the next thing we knew, Tom Bennett was kicked out of school. They barred Tom Bennett from any other Ivy college as well. The de Gourgues family ensured he would never be around Pierre or Bethany again."

Victoria squinted at Michelle.

"Are you okay, sweetheart?" she asked.

"Sure. I guess as well as can be expected. My poor mother. At least they had a happy ending, right? Except of course that my parents are both dead, and that creep is still trying to ruin what's left of the family."

Michelle looked down and noticed her hands visibly shook, and goosebumps ran up her arm. Victoria grabbed her hands again and tugged them to get Michelle's attention.

"It's not over, Aunt Victoria. Unfortunately, Tom Bennett seems bent on destroying the entire de Gourgues legacy."

"Well, your family's power and influence ridiculed Tom Bennett and scarred him for life. He was already a monster, a psychopath, and already had enough rage in him to rape my innocent sister just because she dared to reject him. Seems that his fury just grew over the years. He threatened your parents whenever he could, but I had hoped it would all end after they died."

Michelle nodded and tightened her hold on her aunt's hands.

"Yes, and now he's dedicated to destroying the de Gourgues estate. He's using Robert for his gain. He already tricked my brother."

She bit her lip, holding back specific information. She had promised her father that Robert's deeds would remain secret. She peered up, hoping her aunt had missed the reference. Aunt Victoria was far away, and Michelle's words were never heard.

"Tom Bennett is a sick, evil man. We need to keep him away from my brother."

Michelle's skin crawled after hearing the ugly story. Robert needed to be told about this sordid incident and about the horrible things he had done to Mother, and hear what sort of monster Tom Bennett really was. His influence over her brother was dangerous. Robert must be blind if he didn't already feel something was off with this guy. Michelle was afraid of who her brother had already become. *Did his bitterness blind him with rage? Was he as bad as Tom Bennett?*

Weary from the gruesome conversation, she had more information than she could bear. Michelle sat in silence for a while, blankly staring at the wall. She almost forgot about her immediate dilemma that needed a resolution and quick—the Kain murder. She thought about that night at the police station. She hoped her aunt would remember something, any clue that would help the search. Someone had wanted to blame her, and someone out there got away with murder.

Aunt Victoria stood, rousing Michelle from her musings.

"Come. Let's have dinner," Victoria said.

Michelle followed her down a long hallway and into the kitchen. There was a large window, displaying the last streaks of the day's light. The sun went down behind the hills, shining an orange glow that quickly dimmed. The days were short in the fall, and darkness came early.

Lethargic, all her energy was drained with the sun. Her body was slow at responding to her will as she took the plates out of the cupboard. Aunt Victoria pulled some covered pans from the oven and removed the lids. Steam escaped and filled the room with the aroma of herbs and butter. The lids clanged as Victoria placed them into the sink. They each took portions of food, then carried their plates into the dining room, where they sat enjoying dinner together in silence.

Michelle realized she hadn't eaten all day except for the scone in the morning. She was famished and the food satisfied her. It was her favorite fish, haddock, served with some sort of a baked potato dish.

"This food is delicious," she said.

Aunt Victoria smiled. Michelle felt safe in this big old house, filled with her mother's memories, good and bad.

"Auntie, I need to know what happened that night you picked me up at the police station. It's important. Can you re- member who was there, or did anyone at the desk tell you why I was being held, or what really happened that night? Remem- ber, it was a blizzard. That was an awful night."

"It was the day after the blizzard. Everything turned to sleet by then. Remember?"

Michelle nodded and played with her food while waiting for more of an answer. Using the fork as a weapon, she stabbed the fish. After a moment with no response, Michelle looked up at her aunt's gaze and realized she was staring at her.

"Sorry. I didn't mean to kill it again. I guess I'm nervous."

She'd been fidgeting too much. Michelle took another bite and put her fork down again, as she chewed.

"You know as much as I, Michelle," Victoria said. "I got your call and came straight away. The officer at the desk said you were being questioned in the back room. I said, 'Without a lawyer, no way!' then they led me back to get you. That was it, honey. You know the rest; we came home."

Michelle was looking for something that might stand out, something that she missed before.

"Yes, but do you remember why they were questioning me? Who told them I was involved in the first place?"

"I've been wondering that myself since that night," Victoria said.

"I remember Detective Ramsey." Michelle closed her eyes and shook her head, trying to shake out the negative image. "He gave me the evil eye. I kept thinking there was something up his sleeve because it all seemed so odd. Either he truly believed I did it or had an ulterior motive that he wasn't letting on. He questioned me; hell, he drilled me like I was some hardened criminal and scared the daylight out of me. He kept asking me the same questions again and again, where was I. He didn't believe a word I said. Just a big bully, I guess."

Michelle wiggled in her seat.

"God, that night was horrible. I still get bad dreams about it."

Aunt Victoria slapped her cloth napkin down on the table.

"That settles it. Tomorrow we're paying Detective Ramsey a visit. If anyone knows the reason you were pulled in, he will. Maybe we can get to the bottom of this whole affair. No more bad dreams. Life is too short."

Michelle smiled, remembering why she loved Aunt Victoria so much, always looking for the shortest way to get answers. She was Michelle's hero, a woman of passion.

"That's a great idea."

We could go down and demand the truth from Detective Ramsey, but would he help? Something strange had happened back then. There was more to his involvement. Michelle still had that same sick feeling in her gut as she did back then. How did that feeling survive all these years, still shadowing her? She hoped the truth would set her free from this haunting memory.

Chapter 11

Michelle was exhausted and excused herself. She climbed the stairs and went to her bedroom. It was just as she had left it. The walls were covered with a blueprinted paper, the bed was covered with a white Chenille bedspread; white knots created the center medallion design in the shape of pine boughs, a traditional spread made by the Maine Heritage Weavers. The decor was old-fashioned, just like the house, but cozy.

She undressed and dragged herself to the bathroom. She lit a Yankee jar candle and filled the quaint clawfoot tub with warm water, adding Jade Matcha bath oil. The ginseng and shiso leaf extracts soothed her skin while she took a long soak. She was at home, surrounded by the familiar wainscoting walls painted pale blue. The warm water made her sleepy. The candlelight permeated the room with a relaxing herbal scent and cast a soft glow reflecting off the water and walls. When the water cooled, she finished and went straight to bed, tucking herself under the fresh sheets. The book she'd been reading during her last visit was still by the bedside, dog-eared where she had left off.

"There you are. I thought I lost you somewhere," she said aloud to the book. She grabbed the paperback *The Alchemist* and flipped through it until she stopped at a random page and read the first line she noticed. *"Tell your heart that the fear of suffering is worse than the suffering itself. And that no heart has ever suffered when it goes in search of its dreams."* She understood the words of Paulo Coelho written on the page as they mingled with the day's conversations that still rattled in her mind.

Her mother found peace once she went after her dream. Even though she had died young, at least she had found true love and there was joy in her life after being subjected to such brutal treatment. Michelle was searching, but not for her dream. Instead, she sought answers. *How can I have a future if the past keeps pulling me down?* Her secret got out somehow. She turned out the light and tucked herself under the sheets. Michelle fell into a deep sleep and dreamed about that night seven years ago.

In the dream Detective Ramsey loomed over her with a dark ruthless stare, wearing a haughty grin, and his deep voice sounded harsh.

"Tell us. Where were you last night?" The detective howled.

Michelle was frightened and angry at the same time because he wouldn't listen to her. "For the last time, I was at Silas's house sleeping." She cried back at him, but he kept taunting her, asking the same question over and over.

His face grew distorted as he bent his head closer to hers. She was afraid and wanted to run.

"I don't like the way you're treating me. Can someone please tell me what's going on?" she cried out.

She rose from the chair and ran around a table. Someone chased her until she was pushed down into the chair again, forced to sit. She wept.

"Answer our questions now, little girl." The detective bellowed as his dark coal eyes burned through her.

She was afraid of catching on fire. She wanted to call someone, anyone, who would take her out of this place. The dream repeated itself like a skipped record. It kept going around in a cycle until a large phone on the table rang aloud. Everything in her nightmare started to bend, turning topsy-turvy into a freakish place. She grabbed the phone. It was an old-fashioned model, black and heavy, and it took her a long time to move the dials. The cord wasn't connected. Her perspective changed, and she was looking from above while she dialed the numbers, calling Aunt Victoria. The line rang, then an annoying buzz echoed from the walls. The intense noise reverberated in the small interrogation room.

Aunt Victoria answered the call and promised to be there. The door burst open, and she stood on the other side, waiting. Dressed in purple feathers, she fanned herself like a Geisha girl. The silk vane moved in rapid small clips. The wind outside blew against the window, a sea of white waves. The snow surfed against the glass and piled high.

"Michelle, let's go. Let's play in the blizzard," Victoria said.

She handed the detective some balloons, and he floated away. Victoria wrapped her arm around Michelle's shoulders and pulled her toward the door.

"You poor dear," she said. "Let's go home and get you some warm soup. We can talk things over."

Michelle didn't say anything except, "thank you, Aunt Victoria."

They flew to the house, and Emilie greeted them in the front hallway. When Michelle landed on her feet, she and Emilie turned toward the staircase and began to climb the massive treads together. They reached the top and slid down the big oak handrail. The staircase grew longer as they kept slipping down, and they couldn't reach the end. Emilie laughed, her voice filled the enormous house. Suddenly Michelle was stuck with her head between the balusters. She struggled and was frightened until her father appeared and gently liberated her from the stair post by carefully wiggling her head free. He smiled at her, and she wondered why she had been so afraid of him all those years when she was growing up because he was so gentle.

Michelle tried to remember her mother. Only a vague image of Bethany remained. Then a ghost appeared before Michelle; it was her mother. She cried, and Michelle called out, "don't cry, Mommy, I'll help you."

Michelle wanted to save her mother but was afraid and wanted to run away at the same time. She ran fast and faster, until she woke up suddenly, screaming. Flinging her arms in the air, she called out, "don't cry, Mommy. Don't cry."

Aunt Victoria was there by her bedside. She held Michelle's arms down.

"It's okay. Michelle, it's only a dream. Just a bad dream." Victoria hugged Michelle and patted her back.

Michelle cried on her aunt's shoulder like a baby.

Chapter 12

The next morning was bright and promising. Michelle had finally fallen back asleep. She woke up refreshed and optimistic that they would find the answers needed. The nightmare expelled all the dread built up after learning the ugly truth about what had happened to her mother. She couldn't change the past, but she could ensure her future wasn't haunted by secrets or damaged by the likes of Tom Bennett.

Determined to start her day right, she did a few minutes of yoga stretches. *Question one—why was she considered a suspect in the first place, and why resurface now?* She walked over to the window and looked out into the backyard. The ground was covered in luminous multi-colored leaves from the abundant tree line that surrounded the yard. The leaves were colored in shades of orange, red, and yellow. Shining in the morning light, they revealed their burned edges. The bushes were already barren, exposing the rough twig branches that hung with small red berries laid between the thorns. Although the fall was beautiful, soon winter would appear, freezing everyone to the bone. For a moment, she missed Memphis. She pressed her phone and called her sister.

"Is everyone all right at home, Emilie?" she asked.

"Good morning, and don't worry, Michelle, things are fine so far. I promise if anything crops up, I'll call to let you know."

"Okay then. I'm staying at Aunt Victoria's, just in case you need me. Keep a close eye on Robert, and please, try to keep him away from Tom Bennett. That man is even worse than we proposed. I discovered some alarming stuff about him, and I promise to fill you in when I return home. Just believe me when I say we need to keep him away from Robert."

Michelle paced the floor as she spoke. Her throat tightened, thinking of the revolting tale about Mother's attack. She wouldn't tell Emilie the story, not yet anyway. She swallowed hard.

"Em, I know I owe you and Jeremy big time. Thank you."

"It's no problem, Michelle, I'll do my best to keep Robert busy and away from Mr. Bennett. That man has always given me the creeps. Jeremy has been good about keeping Rob busy."

"Just do what you need to do and keep me updated," Michelle said. "Bye for now."

She hung up the phone, and her designs wandered, thinking about Silas and their meeting. The conversation they had yesterday was of no help. Michelle wondered how he felt about her and was a bit mortified that she had such a reaction to him. *I wish there were no feelings left. Still, his eyes undressed me and made me feel —* "

"Michelle, are you all right?"

Her reverie was interrupted by a knock on the door.

"Yes, I'm fine, Aunt Victoria."

She lied and was far from fine. The realization that she still had residual feelings for Silas troubled her, plus she needed to catch a murderer. Michelle washed and dressed, then went downstairs for breakfast.

Aunt Victoria's brainstorm to go directly to the source and visit Detective Ramsey was promising. Michelle decided to visit him first thing. She grabbed a piece of toast and headed for the back door.

"Can I borrow your car, Auntie?" she said.

"Where are you going?"

"I'm following your suggestion and heading for the police department to talk with Detective Ramsey."

"Fine, but wait for me. You're not going without me. Let me grab my coat. If he's still the arrogant man he was back then, you'll need some support. In my experience, people don't change much through the years."

They drove to the station, both quiet with their judgments.

It was a brisk fall morning in the center of town, and frost still covered some of the leaves remaining on the trees and bushes that lined the street. The sun shined streaks of light between the buildings and shed beams upon the silvery leaves; the foliage twinkled like a frosty wonderland. The air was fresh, filling Michelle's lungs with an invigorating clean whiff. They walked to the Cambridge Police Department on Sixth Street and climbed the granite steps. Entering the main lobby, they inquired at the front desk with the clerk on duty.

"Excuse me. Could you tell us where we can find Detective Ramsey?" Michelle said.

"Ramsey? My goodness, he was promoted years ago. Now he's Deputy Superintendent in charge of the Criminal Investigations Unit Division. Check the directory over there on the wall."

"Thank you."

They walked to the directory. What a coincidence, Michelle thought, a jump from detective all the way up to one of the top slots in a matter of a few years; impressive.

"Ramsey sure knows people in important places," Victoria said.

Michelle smirked and nodded in agreement.

"Sarcasm aside, this doesn't leave a good feeling. Something seems fishy here. No one gets to that level so quick, do they?" Michelle asked.

They took the elevator to the floor of his office. The doors closed and the elevator bell tinged. Her stomach flipped as the elevator rose. Something wasn't right, Michelle felt it in her gut, and she had the inclination to vomit. Feeling intimidated, the same fear of years ago, images from the past sucked all her courage. She remembered the look in Ramsey's eyes, dragged under by an undertow. *Pull yourself together, girl.*

"Are you alright? You look pale," Victoria said.

"I'll be fine."

The doors opened and they walked to the end of a short hallway.

"Can I help you?" A pleasant clerk sitting at a desk behind the low counter asked for their names. She jotted them down on a pad, then dialed an extension announcing them. A moment later, she came back with an excuse. "So sorry, but Deputy Superintendent Ramsey is out for the day. Care to make an appointment? I can book you for next week?" she said, smiling.

"That'll be too late," Victoria said.

"Is there anything later today or maybe tomorrow?" Michelle pushed.

"Sorry," the woman said.

"Thank you anyway," Victoria said.

Victoria pulled Michelle's coat sleeve and led her away, shaking her head with disappointment. They went back down to the main floor.

"I wonder how I can get in touch with the man?" Michelle said aloud, but talking more to herself. She snapped her fingers.

"I have an idea. I know he's in the office. Why else would that woman have called the extension? I'm going to sit here and wait for him to leave his office, then I'll follow him. As soon as I get a chance, I'll approach him and ask my questions."

Victoria shook her head while pulling her hat on.

"I'm not sure about this, Michelle. I have things I need to do and can't wait around all day. And I don't want you to face the man alone. We could be here all day for nothing."

Michelle wrapped her arms around her aunt.

"I can do this alone, Auntie. You go home and do your own thing. I promise I'll only speak to him in public. Maybe I'll just see what he's up to." She raised her fingers. "Girl Scout's honor, I won't get into any trouble. Listen, you take the car back home, and I'll call you later. I'll be fine, I promise."

Michelle gave her Aunt Victoria a 'you can trust me' look. No one ever argued with Michelle when she dug her heels into the sand. Victoria reluctantly left Michelle there to spy on her own after she promised to call with updates.

Grabbing a chair, Michelle tucked herself away in a corner, pulled out her iPhone, and started reading an eBook while she waited.

It was just past noon when Michelle spotted Ramsey leaving the elevator.

A surge of excitement rushed through her body. She put her phone in her handbag and followed him. Michelle shadowed Ramsey for fifteen minutes, tracing every step. First, he walked down to the corner, got a coffee, and talked with people in the shop. She pretended to look at a display of greeting cards. Next, he met a man on the street and together they chatted a bit. She stood nearby and listened while pretending to look at the newsprint in the street stand, keeping her back to them. It was all regular stuff that any politician would say. Finally, he walked down Cambridge Street and entered a restaurant. Michelle ducked into the same restaurant a few minutes behind him and discretely asked for a table near his, padding the hostess's palm with a wad of bills. With a wink, she said, "I want to stay close but invisible."

Michelle turned her face in the other direction as they passed Ramsey's table. He didn't seem to notice her. His back was to the booth she was occupying. She sat down and picked up a menu to hide her face as she scanned his back.

He was a handsome man, with silver-gray tints strewed in his thick dark hair. A big man, he toted broad shoulders. *No wonder he intimidated me.* He reached his arm out as someone approached his table. He shook a hand, that's when she spotted Silas.

Michelle froze. The shock paralyzed her. Within seconds, she came to her senses and quickly flung the menu up to hide her now red-hot face. She peeked around the menu to get a good look. *Maybe I'm mistaken? No, it's Silas!* She gasped in surprise and quickly raised the menu again to make sure they wouldn't spot her. She was clueless as to why Silas would dine with Ramsey.

She slid herself around in the booth so that she sat with her back to them. In this way she could stay close and listen to their conversation without either of them recognizing her, she hoped. Ideas bubbled in her head. *Maybe they were discussing his father's murder? Maybe a new lead?* Michelle was beginning to get excited by the possibility that the murderer may have been caught. That certainly would make her life a lot easier.

"Ramsey, thanks for meeting me. I know how busy you are these days, but I wanted to run something past you," Silas said.

"It sounds important. What's up?"

"I had a surprise visit yesterday. Do you remember my friend Michelle de Gourgues?"

Michelle instinctively turned her head at the mention of her name. Silas was smiling. She quickly turned away again. *What was so humorous, and why did he need to share the knowledge of her visit with Ramsey?* Michelle pretended to read the menu but listened intently.

"Of course I remember her. How could I forget? She came to my office this morning, with her aunt, asking to meet with me," Ramsey said.

"And did you?"

"Of course not. The last thing either of us needs right now is to be seen with her. Keep away from her, do you understand?

No smart ideas about brewing up your relations with her again. I know what a lady's man you are, Silas, but that's one dish you shouldn't eat. Just remember our orders. We're supposed to have her take the blame for the murder, not fuck her! Well, I guess we're doing that to her, in a way."

Michelle heard Ramsey, as he wiggled in his chair, obviously uncomfortable. She certainly was and she hoped that he anguished in guilt over what he just said. Their conversation didn't make sense to Michelle. *Who was giving them orders? Why blame her if they both knew the truth, or did Silas really believe she killed his father?*

"Did you speak with him about her yet?" Silas asked.

"No, and I'm not going to either. For Pete's sake, let's pretend we didn't see or hear from her. The last thing we need is to get him angry, or worst yet, to end up owing him another favor."

Ramsey harrumphed with agitation.

"I don't understand," Silas said. "Why, after all this time, is this happening again? They got rid of that man who claimed to be my father and let it become a cold case. So why bring it up again? And why blame Michelle?"

"Who cares why? You know the game."

"I just don't get it, and the thing is, I care for her. I don't want her to get dragged back into all this mess," Silas said.

Michelle dared a peek over her shoulder and saw his face, all red and flustered. She pitied him, which was weird because he just confirmed that they were dumping the blame of the murder on her.

The waitress came up and took her order. Michelle quickly asked for a grilled Portobello sandwich to keep anyone from being suspicious. Besides, she was hungry. As the waitress moved away, she noticed that the two men were still talking, but in lower tones, their heads leaning together. She couldn't discern a word between them, so she replayed in her mind the conversation she had just heard. *Silas said they took care of his father? Did he hire someone to kill him? And Ramsey knew all along!*

She was in deep trouble. Silas not only did something bad, but he was also willing to let her take the blame. *Nice guy!* She had misjudged him and needed to find out more, but nothing was audible more than a mumble as she strained to hear their conversation. A new plan was needed.

Michelle dreamed up another idea—she would play double agent. She would meet up with Silas again and somehow get him to spill more information. Better armed now, she was ready to start the charade. She ate her lunch, hoping to hear more tidbits of information, but nothing else of importance was heard. Michelle left the restaurant following the men out after they finished their meal.

This time she followed Silas, hoping to discover who they were taking orders from and why. It was a gamble, but she didn't know what else to do. Armed with the knowledge that he was implicated in his father's murder, she was happy she had listened to her instinct and broken things off with him. What was her instinct trying to tell her now? Why did these feelings still stir in her when they were close? She should hate him, but she didn't. Pushing her feelings aside, the only important thing now was to invent a ruse to flesh out what Silas knew.

Chapter 13

Silas walked back to campus, and Michelle shadowed him into a lecture hall. She slipped into a seat in the back of the room and hid behind a big football player type. Silas was teaching a class on American Writers in the twentieth century, and they were reviewing Saul Bellow's work *Henderson The Rain King*. She remembered how ambitious Silas was and how he wanted to be famous more than anything else. She wasn't surprised that he kept his teaching gig. He'd do anything to keep building his fan base and book sales. No, he hadn't changed a bit, still teaching and making bedroom eyes at the prettiest girls sitting in the front row. It made Michelle sick to watch him and to think she was once so gullible.

Michelle pulled a camera from her large handbag, zoomed the lens, and focused on the professor. She snapped a few pictures of him while he flirted with the undergraduate. She burned with anger, not out of jealousy, but feeling betrayed.

Nothing could explain why he was bent on her destruction. An image of her brother suddenly popped into her mind. *Did they know Robert? No, that wasn't likely*, she reasoned. She had never introduced Silas to anyone in her family. Besides, Robert was younger than both Ramsey and Silas. A sick thought came to mind. Robert knew Tom Bennett, who was older. *Did Silas and Deputy Ramsey know Bennett, too?* The cogs turned, her brain raced into overdrive. Figuring various scenarios, for some reason Tom Bennett rang right to her ears, though she didn't know why.

A call to Jackson Bennett was in order. He was her friend, her brother's old roommate, and unfortunately for him, he was Tom Bennett's son. A year ago she had met up with Jackson

Bennett. They pieced together the embezzlement scam insti-gated by his father Tom Bennett and her brother Robert. Jack-son had discovered some documents and gave Michelle copies. It was with his help that she had learned so much about her brother's crime against the family's finances. They found out in time, and her father was able to right the wrongs, but he had also insisted on protecting Robert from prison.

Maybe Jackson can help me again. Michelle slipped out of the lecture hall, Silas's voice faded. She pulled out her phone from her pocket and called her friend.

"Hello, Michelle."

His voice soothed her frazzled nerves.

"Hello, you. Guess what? I'm in Boston. Want to meet up?"

"Of course I do. Are you free tonight?"

"Yes. Where?"

"I can get to Finnegan's in thirty."

"I'll see you there. It's so nice to hear a friendly voice."

"Okay, you can explain that in a few," he said.

She hung up and remembered to call her aunt with an up-date before she left for the bar, then Michelle ducked into the ladies' room.

The room was empty, so she occupied the largest stall, hanging her bag on the door's hook. While she was busily re-lieving herself, she heard the door to the lady's room open, then the shuffling steps towards her stall. She looked up, just in time, to see a man's hand reaching over the stall door. He snatched her bag off the door's hook and fled.

"Hey, wait a minute," she yelled.

She pulled her pants up in a rush, opened the door, and found the room empty. Her bag was left on the floor. Michelle bent down and checked the contents; her camera was gone.

The late afternoon sky darkened and a brisk cold wind

swept across the sidewalk. Michelle walked down the small-town street, peering up from behind her scarf as she squinted to read the signs on the storefronts. Finally, she found the place where they agreed to meet, Finnegan's Pub. She opened the door and immediately choked with her first whiff of the smoke-filled room. Giving herself a few moments to acclimate to the cigar haze lingering in the air, she stood and scanned the place. The bar's management clearly rebelled against the new non-smoking laws, refusing to make patrons snuff out their stogies. The aroma brought back a fleeting memory of her grandfather from years ago when she was just a baby. It was a happy place for a split second, a feeling of being loved.

The lights in the room were dim, only amber colors reflected from the Tiffany glass shades dangling above the tables and bar. Music played from the multi-colored jukebox that glowed in the corner against the far wall. A path between the tables led her to a back area partitioned off with a half wall. The smell of stale beer became more notable as she walked deeper into the room. Flashes of party days gone by surfaced, not forgotten, but they soon faded back into her not needed to know compartment of her mind. She spotted him in the farthest booth, Jackson Bennett, a sight for sore eyes.

Michelle forgot how handsome he was, with his sandy blond hair and bright blue eyes. He had freckles sprinkled across the bridge of his nose, leftover from his summer tan. He smiled rim to rim, like a banner for a parade spread across his face, broadcasting enthusiasm. She slipped into the booth across from him and smiled.

"Hello, Jackson."

"Hi. It's so nice to see you. It's been too long."

"Only a few months." She smiled. "I've been busy running things since my father died."

"I'm sorry for your loss."

"Thanks." She smiled.

"So things turned out all right," he said. "The information we gathered helped your father in the end. I hope you got the funds back."

"Yes, your help was instrumental. Your father and my brother stole a lot of money. Unfortunately, they'll never truly be punished for what they did."

"Why's that?"

"Because that's how my father wanted it. He refused to let Robert go to jail, so your father got off, too."

"Man, I'm so pissed about that." He shook his head. "You have no idea. He deserves to be hung. I wish he hadn't gotten away with it. I was hoping that something would come out of it all."

"Jackson, why did you help me? You never said when you gave me the proof, and he is your father after all."

"Don't remind me," he said.

Jackson dropped his head, his face reddened. He looked like a different person, ashamed or maybe angry. Michelle was quiet, not wanting to upset him more.

"I hate him, that's why I helped you. I know exactly who he is, and it's not pretty. Pierre wasn't his only victim. My father ripped off so many people, even his own father, but that's not the worst of it. The worst part is that he hurts my mother time and time again. She's afraid to leave him, so she lives her life trying to avoid him." He shook his head again. "That's not a life. My father is bad to the core and I don't know how to stop him. I was hoping your father would, I guess."

Michelle reached over and took his hands in hers.

"I'm so sorry, Jackson. I never considered what his behavior meant to you and your mother. I guess bad is bad. I found out why he went after my father, by the way."

"Tell me. I'm sure it's some kind of twisted revenge. My

father's M.O. is all about getting back at others," he said.

"Well, it seems he had a longtime grudge with my father going all the way back to college days. They went to school together."

"But your father was from Harvard," he said.

"And so was yours, until he was expelled because of my parents' grievance against him with the college. Do you still want to help me now, Jackson?"

"Of course I do. I'm sure the monster deserved it, knowing my father. He's an animal and he hurts people all the time. No scruples; he's a psychopath."

Jackson's smile was long gone. Michelle hated to see him so wounded.

"Yes, just for the record, he did deserve it and more," she replied.

How fortunate she was, having had a chance to resolve her daddy issues before he died, but Jackson would never have that opportunity with his father, who was beyond redemption. Jackson would always know his father as an evil man.

"I'm so sorry, Jackson. We can talk about something else if you want to. I don't want to make you sad."

She yanked on his hand and smiled. He immediately pulled her hand to his lips and kissed her hand gently. She smiled at him again, and he grinned back.

"No worries, Michelle. You're sunshine to me. You can never make me sad. It's my father who does that, and unfortunately, there's nothing I can do about it."

She bit her lip and noticed she was twisting her sleeve again and stopped herself. Hating to drag Jackson into yet another hunt after his father, she hesitated to ask but finally found the nerve.

"Jackson, I need your help again."

Michelle told him about the night she was pulled into the

police station and questioned about the murder seven years ago, and how Robert threatened to spill the incident to the news.

"So you see, my brother plans to use that information as grounds to question my ability as CEO. In our world, image is everything," she said.

"I can't believe Robert would stoop so low and do that to you, his little sister. Maybe you misunderstood?"

She shook her head. "No, afraid not."

"Of course I'll help you. Let me have a talk with your brother. I'm sure he was only blowing hot air."

"Wait, there's more." She winced. "Today I overheard a conversation between Silas, my old professor, and Deputy Detective Ramsey in the restaurant."

"So you just happened to be there to hear this conversation?"

Michelle hung her head.

"Okay, I followed them there." She patted his hand. "But only to get to the truth. I figured if I could resolve the whole mess by finding out who killed Frank Kain, that would clear things up once and for all."

"So you're asking me to help solve a murder?"

"No, not exactly. You see, I heard something. I found out that Silas and Ramsey are trying to frame me. I don't understand why. After all, it's a cold case from years ago, no one could be pushing this. My brother is the only one who wants me out of the way."

"So what are you going to do?"

"I need to find out why. I have a sick feeling that my brother is involved; I just don't know. The pieces of the puzzle are all mixed up. Robert doesn't know them, to my knowledge, but he does know your father. Whenever something bad happens around Rob, I think of your dad. Sorry, that came out wrong."

"No, that came out exactly right," he quipped.

She peeled the label on her bottle of imported beer and avoided looking at him. She didn't want to see the reaction on his face.

"I need to find out if your father knows Silas Kain and Deputy Detective Ramsey, too. Do you think you can help me? Tell me where I should begin to look."

Jackson leaned back against the red leather-covered booth, extending his arms out in a stretch, then slipped them behind his head, looking relaxed. Michelle gazed up at him and saw the huge smile slide across his face.

"Piece of cake, Michelle. I don't think Robert knows them. You're probably right about that. I'm privy to his hangouts and pretty much run in the same circles as your brother ever since we were roommates, and I never heard of them."

He smiled, but his eyes looked far away. The noise in the bar was getting louder as more patrons arrived, but Michelle blurred them all and concentrated on Jackson's words.

"Here's the odd thing that you should know," his expression intent. "Whenever Robert needed something, anything at all, my father was always there. He had some kind of fetish with Rob. I remember the first time Robert came home with me for a holiday vacation, I think it was winter break. My God, my father was falling all over him. Talking to him, making him feel like the sun rose and fell on his command. It was sick."

"So you think your father is in love with Robert?"

"No. It's not that. I think my father is using your brother and has been for a long time."

She laughed, picturing her brother. "I bet Robert was in his glory. He loves to be the center of attention."

"Yes, that he does." Jackson chuckled for a moment, too.

His expression changed and turned stern. "And my father loves to use people. I'm sure he has ulterior motives for all his praises sung to Robert. Now that your father is dead, I can't imagine what his motives are. But for sure there's a plan he's working. And with these clowns trying to pin you with murder, well, it sounds like my father is trying to take control away from you. Maybe get Rob back in place; he's still after your family's money or something. If these two guys are working for him, we need to find out, and quick."

"I'm afraid to think too much, 'cause you're probably right. This all came up after my father died and Rob didn't inherit the company. Your father's out to ruin the de Gourgues family. He hated my father to the core."

The two of them spent the rest of the evening discussing the situation and came up with a plan. Jackson agreed to rummage through his father's papers to find out if there were any traces of the names Deputy Ramsey or Silas Kain. Michelle would research on the web and social media to expose any links between the men, criminal cases, or anything of that nature. Between the two of them, they hoped they would figure this situation out.

Chapter 14

Jackson

Jackson was delighted to see Michelle again but now was concerned for her safety. His father was a dangerous man, and his entanglement in this mess unfortunately seemed probable. He worried that Michelle might get hurt, and from what she disclosed at the pub, he figured she was already a target and ensnared in his father's web. He reluctantly said goodbye to Michelle and headed for home.

The family estate was about thirty minutes from the city, nestled in a small quiet town. Anyone who lived in New England understood how these places worked. People mind their own business, but at the same time, they don't. People pretended they didn't know someone else's story, yet they were quick to speak up when someone asked, *who is so and so?* Jackson's family lived in such a place.

Their home, preserved for generations, was a big old Victorian at the edge of town with gardens and years of hedge growth that surrounded the estate. A forest stood nearby with places to hunt and ponds stocked with fish supplied by the nearby brook that flowed through the backwoods.

He parked his car and wearily walked up the driveway in deep contemplation. Years ago, his grandfather had promised the property would be his someday, but no one heard from the old man in years. Rumors of a dispute between his grandfather and father led to farfetched tales, *or were they real?* Jackson recognized that his father was a monster in disguise, and there were rumors of things—atrocities that his father had supposedly enacted. Most people in town only dared to mumble in the shadows about the things better left unspoken. Everyone in town knew that Jackson's mother was victimized, yet even she was reluctant to speak ill of the man in public. Instead, she hid in her room with a bottle handy to self-medicate. Often on nights when his father had returned from one of his trips, loud voices filled the rooms with screams, then smashing and breaking of things for what seemed like hours, then complete silence. Jackson would lie in his bed wondering if his mother was still alive.

He felt like a coward on those nights, wanting to be the hero and help his mother, but paralyzed by the memory of the one night he had ventured to help. His own mother had told him to stay away. She yelled and screamed for him to leave and to never interfere again. Betrayed by her, she blamed him instead of dear old dad. After that night he let them torture each other with their fighting and scuffles. He pretended not to hear, turned up his music, and applied the headphones, anything to get through the nights.

It was quiet tonight with both his parents out of town. His father was visiting New York for a few days, supposedly meeting with financial people. His mother was recuperating at a spa, Palmer Ranch, where she was drying out while getting a manicure and massage. Her best friend had always been the bottle, taking refuge there and succumbing to its elusive grandeur. It was her way to forget the memories of her clouded judgments and mistakes, but none of that for Jackson. He vowed to be his best and to never live the wrongs of his parents.

He approached the front doors and gazed up at the three-story home that had been in his family for generations, groomed and well-kept by a fleet of servants hired to maintain it with constant care. Jackson once saw old photographs of this place from years ago when it was first built, when the trees were small and the yard an open canvas. Now the growth around the estate flourished. Proud of his ancestral home, Jackson hoped to keep it pristine.

His father was the only visible cancer that begged to be cut out of the picture. The sickness was spreading to his mother and needed to be severed to save her. The disease named Tom Bennett threatened to disgrace this great and noble heritage. He was determined not to become his father's feverish disease but instead to lance the infection.

Jackson tried hard to pave a wholesome life for himself and rose above all the garbage inflicted on him since boyhood. It wasn't easy.

If he were to help Michelle, a road would unfold, not only the truth for her but his truth as well. This was his big chance to bring his father into the light and expose his secret nature to the world. Jackson needed the veil that covered his father's deeds to be lifted. Then maybe the curse he lived under would be released. Years of listening to his father's ramblings taught Jackson one thing—his father pledged revenge against the entire de Gourgues family. Tom Bennett was responsible for Michelle's troubles, and it had to stop now.

He opened the large door and carried himself through the threshold like a prince returning to a castle. He stood tall and gallant, ready to take action against the giant of greed and an unmentionable horror, his father. Jackson went to the first room off the entry hall, his father's office. He turned the knob and switched on the lights. He headed to the desk, riffled through papers, and pulled open drawers. Jackson shuffled through the files for hours but found nothing in the least bit incriminating. In a fit of frustration, he slammed the last drawer shut.

"Dammit!" he screamed aloud. He gave the room one last glance, then turned off the light and closed the door.

Sprinting up the steps two at a time, he was determined to

find something to help Michelle. Jackson stomped into his father's bedroom, switched on the light, and went straight to the wardrobe, opening drawers and searching the contents, only to find nothing. Then he stopped and took a deep breath, carefully folded and returned the contents into the drawers and shelves, so everything looked undisturbed.

Discouraged, Jackson sat on the bed. Think, think. Where would he hide something? He surveyed the room. Where would his father keep something precious and incriminating? Think like the scoundrel he is, think evil, he mused.

His eyes darted around the room. The furniture was made of mahogany, all heirloom pieces. The drapery was made with Waverly cloth of traditional New England colors and design, swirling ginghams. He shifted his eyes from left to right, pretending to be his father. *Who does Tom Bennett love most?* he asked himself, then his eyes stopped at the dresser. On top of the bureau of drawers was a mirror, a large oval antique glass, with a dark wood frame, decorated with carved bouquets of roses and ribbons.

Jackson leaped off the bed and rushed to the mirror. He examined his reflection. He didn't look anything like his father, thank God. Jackson was blond and had a happy face, while his father was dark all around, with even darker eyes that seemed soulless. Jackson thanked God that he took after his mother.

He carefully lifted the mirror from the hangers that held it to the wall. He placed it, glass down, carefully against the bed covers. He wasn't surprised when he found a safe hidden in the wall. It was an antique safe with the old-fashioned type of combination turn lock that didn't appear to be too complicated. The door was manufactured in cast iron and branded with Meilink, a Retro 1940's model In the center of the door, an Eagle lock displayed a dial that went up to fifty. It was a standard lock used on many old wall safes, which he recognized right off.

Jackson was familiar with locks, having opened many in the past for his friends when they were in private prep school and college. The locks in the private dorms were ancient yet still usable, and he became the resident safecracker. It turned into a hobby of sorts, but only for fun.

Rubbing his fingers together, he was excited for the chance to use his skill again. Jackson scrutinized the lock carefully, making sure he was up to the challenge. Some of the numbers were smoothed from years of use and indicated possible combinations. This type of lock was known to use a certain sequence of rotations, three times left to the first number, two times right to the second number, one time left to the third number, and right to stop. The combination usually started with thirty-two, the factory's favorite start-up number. Slowly he turned the lock's dial left three times, going slow on the last rotation, and stopped when he felt a click, then he turned it right, again slowly. He heard another click. Last, he went left again, turning it slow and steady, biting his tongue and holding his breath. The third click freed the door at the number ten.

Relieved, Jackson opened the safe door wide. He found no mounds of cash, no stock certificates, nor any paperwork of double-cooked journal entries, nothing that he expected. Instead, one large book lay flat inside. Jackson removed it from its hiding place. It looked like an antique with its dark leather cover honed to a sheen.

The book was embellished with a center design of an inlaid mother of pearl, cut thin and intricately layered. The centerpiece was surrounded by a stamped design that was hand-painted with red and gold leafing, adorned like a holy book, but there wasn't a religious bone in his father's body. He opened the first few pages, holding his breath as the pages crinkled. Fancy calligraphy filled the pages with colorful letters, then with a few more pages turned, he began to find handwritten text. The only problem, it was written in a foreign language. *Maybe Latin?* He wasn't sure.

"Ugh!" he screamed aloud. "Why didn't I pay attention in Latin class!"

He needed it translated, but he only had a day, two at most. His father was due back the day after tomorrow. He couldn't waste any time. First, he needed to find a translator and second get it back before his father found out he took it. *Easy!* Jackson needed help and had no clue where to begin. He closed the safe and put the room back in order, then took the old book to his room and called Michelle.

"Hi, Michelle, I hate calling you so late, but time is of the essence," he said.

"Jackson, that's all right. I wasn't in bed yet anyway. What's up? Did you find something already?"

"I was looking through my father's things and stumbled across an old book hidden in a secret safe in his room. I think it might give us a lead, or at least some information we might be able to use. We only have a day to look it over because my father will be back."

"So read it to me," she said.

"Not so simple. I think it's in Latin. Maybe some other language, I don't know. That was never my forte." He laughed at himself aloud.

"Latin! My goodness, I never liked dead languages much. Sorry, I can't help translate it. But I know someone who can."

"Who?"

"My sister Emilie. She's fluent in many languages, I think."

"She's in Memphis and we don't have enough time to wait for her. I need to get it back into the safe by tomorrow," he said.

"I'm going to call her right now and ask her to fly up tonight so we can get it translated tomorrow. She has lots of experience translating old books, believe me," she said, laughing.

"What's so funny?"

"I'm just remembering another old book. They seem to keep popping up everywhere. Emilie translated Jeremy's antique journal that was written in old French a few months ago. They used the translations to help them understand a curse that supposedly plagued my family."

"What are you talking about?" he asked, curious.

"Never mind that, it's ancient history. We need to get this one translated."

"Can we trust her? Will she do it?"

"I trust my sister with my life, don't worry. We'll call you first thing tomorrow morning and can meet up here at my aunt's house."

Michelle hung up before he could inquire further. Jackson stood there looking down at the book. *What mysteries do you hold? Do I really want to know about my sick father?* The quick answer was yes. He wanted to know everything possible so he could use it to end his father's evil reach; however, before slaying the monster, he needed to understand it!

Chapter 15

Michelle hated the idea of dragging her sister into this mess, but she had no choice. She needed Emilie because she was the only person around who could translate Latin on such short notice. Michelle immediately called her after hanging up with Jackson and was surprised that Emilie and Jeremy agreed without much prodding. They set out straight away for Boston.

She used Aunt Victoria's car and picked them up at the airport in the early morning hours, and they drove straight back to Victoria's house anticipating the much-needed coffee and caffeine. The weather was nippy and silvery morning frost covered the lawn and steps. They carefully navigated the walkway as Victoria opened the front door to welcome them in, hugging each of them as they entered the house.

"Aunt Victoria, this is Jeremy," Emilie said.

Victoria took hold of his shoulders and looked him over with a quick up and down. Her eyes sparkled as she smiled, then she shook his hand. Michelle was happy they finally met. It seemed like he was officially part of the family now, and she was happy for her sister.

"Sorry, it took so long to meet you, Jeremy. I should have been at the funeral, but I was out of the country and didn't make it back in time. I'm glad you were there for the girls. It meant a lot to them. And it's a pleasure to meet you now."

"Pleasure to meet you, too, Aunt Victoria," he said.

"Please, come in and take your coats off. We'll sit down for a bite of breakfast while Michelle gets us all up to speed. I'm curious myself about this mysterious turn of events. Whatever happened, I'm glad it brought you two here. I'm so glad to see you both."

Michelle took their coats and hung them in the closet. They piled into the dining room and sat around the family-sized table. Victoria carried a tray of dishes that rattled as she walked, placed it on the table, then filled the cups with coffee. The coffee aroma filled the room; it was homey. Their spoons clinked against the china as they stirred in cream and sugar. Michelle grabbed a muffin from a plate and buttered it, then took a bite.

"So what book needs translating? And why call me for the job?"

Emilie sipped her coffee.

"Well," Michelle said, "my friend Jackson found a book hidden in his father's secret safe, and we only have today to get it translated. He has to put it back before his father returns to the house tonight."

Michelle spoke fast and laughed a little to cover up her nervousness.

"Okay, Michelle. Just tell us what's happening. We need to know everything, no more blind trust. We want to be included in your plans."

Emilie's face was like a smooth, calm lake, her voice soft and even. Michelle blew out a breath in relief, more than happy to share all the details with her sister. She would understand.

"You already know why I'm here, to find the person who murdered Frank Kain," she blurted. They nodded, and she continued.

"Well, yesterday Aunt Victoria and I went to his office to try to question the detective who interrogated me all those years ago, to see who put him up to it. But he brushed us off, so I waited and followed him."

"What are you doing, Michelle? You shouldn't spy on cops," Jeremy said.

He appeared worried, his smile gone, and a tense line above his brow showed.

"Please don't be upset with me. Like I told you before, I need to clear my name. I can't be associated with that case. I just wanted to talk with him and find out who suggested that I had anything to do with it in the first place. You understand why I want to know."

Emilie reached over and patted Michelle's hand, showing comfort.

"Michelle, we know you didn't murder anyone. We're here to support you."

"Hold on. I haven't told you the worst part yet. Please don't think badly of me, but when I first came to college, well, I was a little wild."

Emilie and Jeremy looked at each other and laughed aloud.

"What's so funny?" Michele was defensive.

"A little wild back then? Isn't that the joke? You're still a little wild," Emilie teased.

"Really, you're making this very hard."

Michelle faked a pout, then took a sip of her coffee and waited, making sure there were no more pokes at her expense. Emilie forced herself to put on a serious expression, then Michelle continued.

"Well, anyway, Ramsey put us off, so I stuck around and waited. I followed him when he left his office; that's the detective's name, Ramsey. I followed him to a restaurant where he met up with Silas. You know, my old professor. I admit I was shocked, but even more, I was curious."

Everyone sat still a moment, letting the information settle in. A second later, Victoria placed a plate of pancakes down with a thump.

"Sweetheart, you didn't tell me that."

Michelle looked up at her aunt.

"Sorry, I didn't have a chance to yet, but I'm telling you all now. So anyway, Ramsey, I mean Deputy Superintendent

Ramsey and Silas met at a restaurant, and the conversation between them was weird. Get this—they're both answering to someone else. They were supposed to report back *if they talked with me.*" She made curled finger movements forming air quotation marks. "I have to say it. I was stupefied when I heard them say that. However, even worse, they were instructed to pin the murder on me. So I started thinking and realized since they both had someone pushing this entire charade, I needed to know who. That's when I called my friend Jackson and he found the book."

Emilie looked confused. Michelle watched her sister as she pulled her long hair behind her ears, tugging at the brown strands the way she always did when she got nervous.

"Michelle, explain it again. How is this connected? I feel like I'm missing a link here," Emilie said.

"Don't you remember Jackson, Rob's roommate in college?"

"Oh yes, of course. Sorry, I didn't connect it right away."

"Don't you see? Tom Bennett is pulling the strings. And for some reason, Ramsey and Silas seem to feel they have to follow his orders and do as he says."

"You don't know it's Bennett they're answering to. You're just assuming things," Jeremy said.

"I know that's the connection. I feel it."

"I thought I was the psychic," Emilie said with a smile.

The room was quiet for a few minutes as they let this information register. Any news concerning Tom Bennett was rotten news.

"I need your brain, Em, not your gift, to translate the book Jackson found last night in his father's safe," Michelle finally said. "I think this will help us understand what's going on. It must be important, otherwise, why would Bennett hide it in his secret safe? Right?" She bobbed her head up and down. "But we need to do it quickly before Tom returns. If he discovers it missing . . . Jackson will be in a heap of sorrow."

Michelle reached over and filled her plate with pancakes, giving them more time to let the situation sink in, along with the ramifications of it all.

"Michelle, can we trust Jackson? Tom Bennett is his father after all," Jeremy asked.

Michelle nodded and smiled, thinking of Jackson.

"He hates his father, probably more than we do. Yes, he's on our side for sure. I have another plan, too."

Michelle poured some syrup, then looked up. Everyone stared, waiting for her to finish.

"I was thinking of going undercover and meet up with Silas again for old time's sakes. At least that will be my ruse. He was told not to see me, but I know Silas, and there's not a skirt he can resist."

Michelle smiled, proud of her devious plan. She still liked the idea of playing double agent, and the danger excited her.

"I don't think that's wise. You said yourself he was part of the scheme to blame you for a crime you never committed. If he's against you, it could be dangerous," Emilie said.

Aunt Victoria nodded her agreement.

"Yes, but he doesn't know that I know. You know?" she said, laughing.

"It's not funny Michelle," her sister snapped.

"Silas is implicated in his father's death somehow. Maybe I can get him to slip up, maybe he'll say something incriminating. It's worth a shot. He can't hurt me if he wants to blame me, right? He might like the idea of getting into my pants one more time before he screws me for real!"

Michelle looked up when everyone was still quiet.

"You know what I mean. He's a twisted son of a bitch. I followed him yesterday after his lunch meet-up with Ramsey.

I watched him teach a class. He's still a dirty old man chasing naive girls, too young to know better."

Another moment of silence passed. They all took a few bites and sips. The only sound in the room was the silverware tapping against the china. Jeremy put his fork down.

"I hate to say it, but you might be right about this, Michelle. I agree, as long as you meet him in public. He never met me or Emilie, so we can be in the same place and cover your back," Jeremy said.

Emilie shot him a look and shook her head at the two of them.

"What?" Jeremy asked.

He shrugged.

"You're both incorrigible," Emilie said in surrender. "First let's take care of the book."

Michelle pulled out her phone.

"Not a problem."

She called Jackson and gave him directions to Aunt Victoria's home. He promised to be there soon. Time was precious.

Michelle sat back down at the table and watched her sister, looking for a reaction. Emilie appeared to be happy. Her exodus to Florida after their father's funeral must have worked. Her sitting there next to Jeremy, she glowed. Michelle noticed the engagement ring on her finger.

"Emilie, you're engaged." Without waiting for a response, she got up, went to her sister, and hugged her, happy about the good news.

"Congratulations, Dear," Victoria said.

The room filled with excited chatter, all of them speaking simultaneously, about dates and ceremonies, with tears edging their eyes. Jeremy whistled, startling Michelle mid-sentence. The three women looked up at him like startled deer.

"I'm glad you're all so happy and supportive of Emilie and

myself, but let's not forget the mission. You did say this project is urgent and we've only a day."

They nodded and got busy, wasting no more time. Michelle cleared the table of the breakfast dishes and Emilie set up a work area in the dining room with a couple of laptops and iPads on standby for help word checking while she worked on the translations.

A few minutes later the doorbell rang. Jackson arrived carrying a heavy book. Michelle opened the door and led him straight to the dining room.

"I hope this goes fast," she said.

"It has to. I need to get it back before he gets home. He's due back tomorrow morning, but I want it locked away by tonight, just to be safe," he said.

"What would happen if he discovered you took it?"

"I don't even want to speculate, but I do want to stay alive."

Michelle didn't push with further questions. Clearly, even his son feared him.

Chapter 16

Michelle and Jackson walked into the dining room. "Everyone, this is Jackson. Jackson, everyone," Michelle said.

Aunt Victoria shot Michelle a look, her eyes pinched and forehead wrinkled.

"I mean this is Aunt Victoria." She waved her arm and Victoria nodded. "This is Jeremy and my sister Emilie."

Jeremy extended his hand and they shook.

"Nice to meet you all," Jackson said.

Michelle watched Emilie's face and knew her sister was reading Jackson's emotions using her clairvoyant gift. At first, she smiled, and Michelle was relieved that Jackson passed her test, then, after Emilie shook hands with Jackson, her expression changed. Worry washed over her face, overshadowed by deep concern. *I need to ask her about that,* Michelle thought.

"Okay, let's get started," Emilie said. She rubbed her hands together. Her brown eyes sparkled with excitement.

Jackson placed the old, heavy leather-bound book on the table with a thump.

Emilie reached out and gently touched the dark leather cover with her fingers, passing over the raised design, like reading braille. She was sensing its contents and reading the intentions of those who had touched it. Michelle had watched her do this once before. Emilie opened it and read the first few pages.

"Look at this beautiful calligraphy." She bit her lower lip and smiled. "This is definitely a ritual book, but more. It sounds like our Mr. Tom Bennett heads a secret society of men. They joined this group to help each other succeed in their business ventures. They call themselves NIGRUM LUPUS SODAL-ICIUM," she said.

Michelle laughed aloud.

"So you mean it's like the Elks or Rotary Club? There has to be more to it. A reputable club wouldn't have to keep their rule book hidden in a secret safe and written in a dead language," Michelle said.

"What does that mean in English?" Jackson asked.

"Dark evil or black, wolf, secret group, no. Scratch that, it's probably called The Black Wolf Society," Emilie clarified.

Jeremy stood by Emilie, turned more pages, and paged all the way to the center of the book.

"Hold on." Emilie traced her finger along the lines written on the page. "It's not all in Latin. The beginning pages were hand-scripted in Latin, but there's another language here. It looks familiar, but I can't remember from where."

"And look here." Jeremy pointed. "There's a list of names underneath that strange writing. Let me write the names down so I can check them out on a computer."

Emilie tilted the book toward him.

"What's this shorthand?" she said aloud to herself. She grabbed an iPad and took a picture of the page, then quickly went to work researching the strange letters on a laptop.

"Jackson and Michelle, can you help me with the names on this list? We'll just Google them for now and see what we can find out about them," Jeremy said.

Michelle sat on his side, glanced down at the list, then screamed out.

"Holy crap, look who's on the list; Silas Kain and Deputy Superintendent Ramsey, too. They're both members of this group." She smiled. "They're connected. I was right, knew it. The conversation I overheard yesterday was them taking his orders. What did I ever do to him? Especially back then? I didn't even know who Tom Bennett was seven years ago."

Jackson moved closer to her and put his hand on her shoulder. He let her know he was on her side.

"Michelle, he knows you're a de Gourgues. His vindictive nature is out to hurt anyone with that last name. Besides, he's stirring it all up again just to get your brother back into the business, so he can take the rest of your money."

"Tom Bennett is a royal ass. Oh, sorry, Jackson."

He laughed. "I'm the one who's sorry."

The mood grew more somber with his words. Jackson wiped his hand across his face, trying to clean off something invisible.

"How are you doing over there, Em?" Michelle said.

"I think I might have something, just give me a few."

Emilie stared at the book with her head down.

Jeremy was slumped in the chair next to her, scrolling the web for information on the names.

"You two work well together," Jackson said.

"Yup, that's why they're getting married," Jeremy said.

Michelle smiled. "The only thing I don't understand is why anyone would go along with him. I mean, who wants to be told what to do all the time?"

Aunt Victoria chimed in from across the room.

"He must have some dirt on them."

"Or they were coaxed into doing bad things, just like Robert," Michelle said.

Michelle's heart sank. *How could Robert go along with this evil plan against me, his own sister?* Her throat tightened as the sad reality brought her to the brink of tears. Michelle had believed that she and Robert were friends. They often partied together when they both lived in Boston, and Robert had always played the big brother. She counted on him but was duped just like Father, who assumed Robert wanted to help with the business but really tried to destroy it all. *It was all a lie.*

"We need to look at the list of members closely," Jackson said.

"I'm jotting things down on most of these men. It seems that everyone on the list so far is a who's who, famous for something or sitting in a prominent position."

"Jeremy, sorry to interrupt, but I think I've got something. It seems the group's philosophy was written in Latin. But the information above that list, as well as other parts in the book, are coded using Siksika."

"What's that?" Michelle asked.

"It's an Algonquian language used by the Blackfoot. You see, their language was oral, just like other Native American languages. But it came in handy to use as code during the World Wars."

"I've heard of the code talkers." Jackson looked handsome when he smiled. "But I thought that was the Navajo."

"Yes, the Navajo and Sioux in World War II, and the Choctaw were the original code talkers in the first war." Emilie lifted her head, squinting. "Sorry, but that's not the point here. It's just that these aboriginal languages have been used as hidden codes before. Siksika had been given a chart back in the late 1880s or '90s. A missionary named John William Tims created a chart based on another chart designed earlier by another missionary. They were so determined to translate the Bible." She laughed to herself. "Anyway, this chart is based on nine symbols, each that can be manipulated in various directions, giving it a meaning. I think all I have to do is use the chart to translate."

Michelle laughed aloud.

"What's so funny?" Jeremy asked.

"I never knew the extent of my sister's geekiness."

"I studied languages, remember? Didn't you learn anything at college, or is Harvard all parties and mischief?" Emilie smirked. She wasn't usually a jouster, and Michelle wanted to stop her.

"I learned a few things, too. But my major wasn't ancient religions and languages of the world so long ago that we don't give a crap."

"Michelle." Victoria was outraged. "We're lucky Emilie knows these things otherwise we'd be lost translating this book."

"Sorry, Em, just joking." Michelle wondered why she had opened her mouth. Guilt-ridden, her face burned and she turned to look at her sister. Emilie gave her a smile. Michelle was thankful her sister was such an easygoing person.

"So I'll start translating using the Ojibwe syllabary," Emilie said.

"You mean the chart?" Michelle asked. Emilie nodded and smiled.

"Okay then . . . let's see where we stand." Jeremy clapped his hands to get everyone's attention. "So now we have a few more challenges here. First, we need to use the chart and translate. Hopefully, then we can see if it lists who murdered Frank Kain and learn how or why they intend to pin it on Michelle, and last but probably most important, we need to figure out what Tom Bennett holds over these other men. Maybe we can convince the members not to play Bennett's game."

"Tom Bennett and our brother can't be allowed to set foot into the family's company again. They're most probably planning to finish what they started, but only over my dead body," Michelle said.

"Michelle, we need to alert the security team you hired. This is serious," Emilie said.

"On it." Michelle was already sending an email. "I think you're right. I'll have security send someone up here, too."

"We can't wait for them to arrive," Jackson said. "I need to get this book back right away."

Michelle nodded.

"We need a lot of answers, so we better get started."

Her voice sounded strong, positive, and even laced with humor. But on the inside, her nerves were jumping rope. Her left hand shook; she grabbed it with the right and stopped the trembling. Michelle looked around the room, relieved that no one noticed her tremble with fear. She hoped to maintain the façade and didn't want anyone to think of her as vulnerable, but everything seemed like a horror movie, like something was after her, and things like this weren't supposed to be real.

"So what's the plan?" Jackson said.

"I'll finish translating as best I can," Emilie said. "We need to know everything about the kind of group we're dealing with. There's a lot of names on that list to investigate, and if Tom Bennett convinced one of them to kill Frank Kain, what's to stop them from killing us?"

The room went quiet. Michelle swallowed hard, thinking about the danger implicated.

Jackson snapped his fingers. "Let's scan the book. We can each take a section to look up words for Emilie, to help her translate," Jackson said.

They got busy and concentrated on the work. Michelle welcomed the diversion from her pessimistic notions and by midafternoon, they had a clearer picture of what the Society was all about.

The puzzle pieces revealed the Black Wolf Society as an underworld multinational type organization, framed similarly to the Black Hand that once operated in Serbia. Years ago, the Black Hand conspired to liberate the Serbs from the control of the Austria-Hungary governments. They were a group of saboteurs who used propaganda and they organized a covert spy ring. The secret group had even implemented political murders. They used violence and any method necessary to forward their agenda. They were responsible for the assassination of the Austrian heir to the throne, back in 1914, one of the causes of the war. The Black Hand was responsible for one of the sparks, causing World War. The world was forever changed by their violence.

"So this new Black Wolf Society is a group of men who work in secret to play games with world politics," Michelle said.

"Yes, looks like that and maybe more. They use their influence for the financial benefit of the group members. Extremists for sure, it seems like they'll perform whatever task necessary to protect and promote each other, according to this book. They call them *Beneficial Acts*. To sum it up, they're a bunch of psychopaths."

Emilie pointed to the list Jeremy had found earlier.

"Each member listed here also has a crime listed near the name, but it was something done for them to get them out of a situation of some sort. *A Beneficial Act*. It's like a list of things being held over their head. Like an insurance policy, it probably secures that they do what was asked of them by the group leader.

"Right here, Silas's name is listed and it's noted that the society did him a favor by killing Frank Kain. Now that he had a favor done, he owes the Black Wolf Society his allegiance. Every other member has a similar mention to hold over them."

"So the secret message on the top says what?" Jeremy asked.

"The translation mentions favors done and how they're unique actions granted to each listed member. And it's to be written in this special book or holy book, no—not holy, but maybe more ceremonial book. Yes, ceremonial book. It's written after a special spiritual ritual. It's a foggy account, and I don't get the whole story yet, but it points to something that happened to Tom Bennett years ago. He discovered some kind of secret weapon, which he used for the Society's behalf. The words make no sense. I'll have to recheck the translation, but it doesn't sound like anything good," Emilie said.

"Sounds to me like the Black Wolf Society is something sinister that we need to stop."

Jeremy looked uneasy, his face pale.

"So someone in the Society murdered Silas's father. We need to focus our attention on the who, and that should lead us to the answers to other questions. It's more than just me now. There's something else going on here that's hurting other people, too. This is a big conspiracy," Michelle said.

"Tom Bennett is like a bad penny," Emilie said. "Oh, I'm sorry, Jackson. I didn't mean to be so cold. It's just . . . "

"No worries, Emilie. Believe me, all of you, I understand. I hate calling Tom Bennett my father because I know he's so evil," Jackson said.

"You have a heavy burden, Jackson," Jeremy said.

Michelle heard them all in the background while staring into space, dreaming up a plan in her head, her fingers tapping out a drum roll on top of the table.

"I'm going back to my original plan," she blurted. "I'll meet with Silas again and pretend I'm interested in him and try to get him to slip up with some information. I'll be his Mata Hari."

She smiled with a mischievous grin.

"Only my sister would think up something like that. You have an overactive imagination and too much energy," Emilie said.

Frustration showed on her face, one of her headaches from too much clairvoyant baggage was beginning to bother her. Jackson moved in front of Michelle, blocking the view of Emilie.

"I don't like the idea, Michelle. You have no clue what he's like anymore. Silas might hurt you. You said yourself he was plotting with Ramsey to frame you. Why on earth would you trust him?" Jackson said.

His face was red, and his voice more angry than concerned. Michelle knew Jackson had feelings for her, and he was probably being over-protective, or worse, he was jealous. Either way, Michelle always did what she wanted. No one was going to control her, ever.

"I don't trust him, not in the least. But he doesn't know that yet. I'll be careful. I'll act the part and try to get him to slip up, that's all. It'll be easy. He never was very bright when it came to women. He lives for his penis and doesn't understand any of the finer sides of manipulation," she replied.

"I don't like it," Jackson said.

That was the end of the discussion. Even Emilie couldn't talk her out of it. Michelle was going to call Silas and set up the date. She agreed to let Jeremy and Jackson be her backup, just to be safe, while Emilie and Aunt Victoria stayed at the house and kept translating the book. They all had a part to play out, and they had their phones to keep in touch via text messages.

Michelle's last words as they left the house were, "What could go wrong?"

Chapter 17

Michelle's emotions twisted inside her. The suspense of playing spy excited her, while another part deep inside was frightened. Leftover attraction to Silas exposed her vulnerability. Uncomfortable in her own skin, she pledged to control herself even with these lingering memories that haunted her heartstrings.

She arrived at Silas's stoop, like so many times in the past. Nights filled with wanton desire. The exhilaration she had realized when his fingers touched her secret spots beneath her breasts and behind her knees; his fondling fingers coaxed her body to quiver. His seductive eyes—his touch—desirable against her skin. He captivated her when he grazed her thigh with his hand, letting it roam up to her most sensitive place between her legs. Every time he had touched her, sensations surged her body and she lost control.

It was her deepest secret, his power over her body. Her worst fear—to be controlled by a man—was realized with Silas. She took a deep breath and hurried up the steps of the townhouse before she lost her nerve. She rang the front bell. Her heart pounded against her chest, palpations throbbed against her skin.

Silas opened the door, his expression an engaging smile.

"Hello, Michelle. I'm so happy you called and decided to come over. Please, come in."

Silas waved his arm, inviting her to enter his house.

"Thank you."

She brushed past him, his fingers slightly touched her arm zinging her with unexpected pleasure, and threw her off balance. Michelle heard herself chattering nervously and fumbled a bit unwrapping her scarf, finally pulled herself together as she tugged off her coat.

"It's been a while. Time has gone by so fast. The place looks great. How many books do you have released now? Are you teaching the same classes? How are you truly, Silas?"

Embarrassed, she prattled like a bumbling idiot schoolgirl and internally chastised herself. *Slow down the prattle and think up something clever to say!* She draped her coat on the back of a chair and glanced across the familiar room. Not much had changed, modern furniture, comfy and plump in light colors. There was a new mirror on the wall over the fireplace, but everything else seemed familiar. His reflection in the mirror distracted her while he answered the slew of questions.

"I'm the same as I was yesterday when you asked in the coffee shop," Silas said, chuckling.

"Surely there's more to talk about than what we said during our piddly meet-up in the cafe. Tell me, Silas, all about your books, the publishing, your triumphs."

Michelle turned around, tilting her head just a tad, and batted her eyes with her seductive gaze, pursing her lips just slightly suggestive. She flexed her charms, luring him in, despite her nagging internal struggle. She refused to give in to her fears and emotions, hoping to gain control of the scene.

"You look wonderful, Michelle." He sighed.

Silas looked her up and down hungrily and grinned. Just as she predicted, Silas was as horny as ever. The man lived by the seat of his pants, literally.

She told herself that the old flutter she used to feel for him was only a strong memory. The man in front of her now gave out nothing. While smiling outwardly the entire time, Michelle wondered how she was ever attracted to such a pig. She would still play. She planned to seduce him into her trap.

"Michelle, you look even more beautiful than all those years ago. Time has been your friend. How about a glass of wine?" he asked.

He poured without waiting for her to answer and handed her the glass. Michelle stuck her pinky into the glass and then slowly licked her finger clean. Silas's eyes grew large with excitement.

"Yummy, this is good."

He poured his wine, then tipped his glass to hers.

"To love reborn," he said.

How corny. I think I'm going to be sick. They tapped glasses and took a sip. Silas stared at her glossy lips; he looked mesmerized. A sudden brainwave jolted her, *had he poisoned her drink*? She moved the glass away from her mouth quickly and set it down on the coffee table. As she straightened back up again, he leaned and was about to give her a kiss. Michelle knew his moves, moved back a step, and turned. She started to chatter again, putting off his invitation of affection, half disgusted by his attempt, yet the other half of her questioned her own resolve.

She had reacted to his touch already and was fearful her willpower would melt against his tempting allure. *What would happen should their lips touch? Be strong.* She swallowed the lump in her throat and changed the subject.

"Silas, I read your books and you're brilliant. I did some writing myself when I worked at a magazine here in Boston for a while," she said.

"Yes, I read your articles. Informative and funny. You write well," he said.

"Well, that was a while ago. Now I'm working at my father's company, but you know all about that, right?"

He smiled and took another sip of his wine, but she could tell he was getting either frustrated or wary, or maybe he wanted to skip the niceties and jump right in to the sack, just like old times. *No wonder he goes after young students. The man clearly doesn't know how to have an adult conversation.*

"So all your dreams did come true. I remember you always wanted to be a respected author, and now you are. Well-deserved, too. You worked so hard. If your mother was still here, she would be jumping for joy and would be so proud of you, Silas. And she would want you to celebrate your fame. My mother died when I was young, too, so I understand how you feel about missing her."

Silas sat on the sofa, smiled, and accepted the compliment she paid him. Michelle always did a great job of boosting his ego; that hadn't changed, either. She had played with his heartstrings, too.

"Your mother died, too? I didn't know that," he said.

There's a lot you don't know. She sat in a chair across from him and smiled back.

"I hate to say this, but it's a good thing your father was killed. He would have sucked all your happiness away. Have you and your brother stayed close? Have you two gotten any leads about your father's murderer?" she asked.

He put his glass down on the table and sat back against the cushions of the couch. It was a cozy sofa, plush with soft pillows to sink into.

"No, no leads, as I said the other day. Milo and I do stay in touch, but we're both so busy. We don't see much of each other. You know how it goes."

"What does Milo do? As a career, I mean?"

Michelle didn't want to seem too obvious that she was digging for info on the murder case. She smiled and blinked a few times. So far it seemed to be working. She sat back into the cradle of the chair's cushions and met his gaze.

"Oh, my brother is doing great, too. He's teaching at a private school and simply loves it. He writes on the side; nothing major, just enough to keep him content. He never had an ambitious nature like me. But you know all about that; you recognized my ambition before I did. You said I would do anything to get published, and you were close to right. I would do almost anything. But I didn't murder my father," he said.

His forehead wrinkled, his eyes squinted as if from a headache. Michelle wondered what he had to do to become one of the members of the Black Wolf Society. They all had something held over their head and they had to do a favor for someone else.

"Of course you didn't murder him, Silas. You were with Milo making funeral arrangements for your mother, so how could you have done it?" she said.

"That's right, I was with Milo. They questioned you, though. That's the reason you never saw me again, isn't it? You blamed me for that episode. I understand. You were such a young thing, you must have been scared to death over the whole ordeal. Believe me, Michelle, I had nothing to do with that. I wish they never brought you in for questioning."

He sat quietly and looked so earnest, but Michelle knew him now for the liar he was.

"Yes, I was a bit traumatized. I needed to put the whole thing behind me and move on. You know how I don't like drama in my life. I like things to be happy. But now, looking back, I wonder what did happen to your old man. Do you ever wonder who killed your father? I understand that you didn't love him or anything, but aren't you curious in the least bit?"

Silas reached for the glass on the coffee table. Michelle looked down and noticed many other glass rings lingering on the glass top, probably from previous consorts with young students. He took a sip. She stared at the circles on the tabletop, watching how the glass top reflected the flickering candlelight as she listened to the nervousness in his voice.

"Not in the least. It was a blessing, not only for Milo and me but for all mankind. If I knew who did it, I'd shake his hand. Frank Kain was one of the anchors weighing society down. He swindled so many trusting souls, I'm sure. Worse than that, he hurt my mother beyond belief. He was probably killed over a gambling debt or something."

Was he angry or just nervous about the ordeal?

"Is that what the police think?" she asked.

She was pushing now, trying to get him to say something incriminating; hell, anything. He knew more than he was telling. *Why else would he agree to frame her?*

"I don't know what they think. Can we talk about something else, please? This is really tiresome." He rubbed his face and drew in a deep breath.

"Sure, no problem. I just wondered is all. You know yesterday, I tried to see if there were any updates, but apparently, that Detective Ramsey has moved up in the world," she said.

Michelle already knew that Ramsey had said something to Silas about her visit to his office. If she was upfront with Silas, perhaps she could gain his trust, then just maybe he would slip her some crumb of information.

"What do you mean?" he said. *Caught his interest.*

"I was thinking about things yesterday, so I dropped by the precinct just to see if a suspect was ever caught. I tried to see that detective who questioned me years ago, but he was promoted. He didn't have time to see little ole me."

She flashed him her hot smile, pretending she wanted nothing more than to change the subject and to be with him. Silas smiled back. His gray eyes captivated her own, hypnotizing her. He leaned in across the coffee table slowly, tempting her until he found her lips, then he kissed her. That's all it took, one kiss.

Michelle loathed this man and all he represented. Still, his kiss fondled her heart and allowed her own body to betray her. She floated, light-headed as he pressed his lips to hers. His touch sent her blood rushing to her head and she found herself lost, adrift on a wave of desire. Involuntarily, Michelle kissed him back, helpless, drunk with passion.

A floodgate opened after locked in place for years. He had a hold over her, she enjoyed the kiss and his touch, and yearned for more. Still, at the same time loathing him and herself.

Her vulnerability was exposed. Michelle kissed him back with compounded passion. She joined Silas on the sofa and slid close to him. It only took a moment for them to let go, responding to their basic urges. She pulled off his sweater. He unbuttoned her blouse. Their hands fondled each other, moving up and down, touching each other with frantic desire. He drew her tightly against his lean frame and caressed her. Their bodies pressed together in the heat of the moment. The touch of his warm smooth skin against hers sent sizzling sensations through the rest of her body; then the phone rang.

His lips froze and the firm hand on her thigh went limp. Silas pulled back, unable to meet her gaze, and hung his head. He let out a deep sigh when another round of ringing broke the thick silence.

"Excuse me, I need to take that," he said.

He got up with reluctance. Silas crossed the room to answer the phone on his desk. *Saved by the bell! What do you think you're doing? Don't forget the man's a jerk,* she reminded herself. Michelle brushed her hair back into place with her fingers and buttoned and tucked in her blouse, trying to regain her composure. She eavesdropped as she put herself together. He stood there listening to someone on the other end of the line but didn't say a word back. Silas barely blinked, only nodded, accepting commands like a brainwashed twit, then he said "understood," and hung up. *Get out now,* she said to herself.

"Listen, Silas, I just remembered I need to meet my aunt. I made plans with her and forgot all about it until your phone rang. I can be such an airhead sometimes," she said.

Michelle moved away from the sofa, still straightening out her clothes. Silas was lost in some other reality and looked right past her as he replied. "Don't worry about it. As a matter of fact, I've just been called to an emergency meeting myself. I have to go, too."

"Emergency at the school?" she asked.

"No—no, nothing like that. It's a group I belong to, and we take our duties seriously. I'm working on a project with a couple of other fellows and they need my input, that's all. Can we meet again soon? I'd love to finish what we just started."

Silas smiled that devilish grin. *What if the phone had never rung?* She gulped back her saliva along with regret.

"Of course," she said.

Secretly the idea repulsed her, but even worse, she didn't trust herself from sinning against her own best interests. *What was this man, some kind of libertine? Why am I so attracted to him?* Suddenly he seemed like a predator to her. No, he was a vampire. Silas was a perverted seducer, sucking her in only to feed off her affections. She questioned her own state of mind, being attracted to such a debauchee. She never wanted him to touch her again. *Never!* Embarrassed by her weakness, Michelle looked at Silas with changed vision; he seemed different to her now, he had transformed into something unrecognizable right in front of her.

Hurriedly, Michelle slipped on her coat, jerking her arms into the sleeves not nearly fast enough, and grabbed her scarf. She fled out the door, not even saying goodbye. Still reeling from the encounter, Michelle got into her aunt's compact and circled the block.

She parked down the street from his house and waited for

Silas to leave. She called Jeremy and Jackson while waiting. They were her backup, sitting in another car. They were ready to play surveillance tag. A few minutes later Silas emerged from his house. In a hurry he got into his vehicle and floored it, heading down the street. The guys waited as Silas's car passed them at the end of the street, then they pulled out and followed.

The days were short this time of year, and as dusk darkened into night, they took turns being the lead car behind Silas's beamer so he didn't notice he was being trailed. Finally, Silas exited an off-ramp and drove into a desolate area of the north shore, clustered with old warehouses.

Most of the buildings appeared empty, some vented with broken windows. Others were utilized, evidenced by security lights and the nearby dumpsters filled with trash. Silas turned down one of the side streets and parked his car behind an old factory that looked abandoned, or maybe just neglected. Under a lone street light, grass jutted out between the pavement cracks of the parking lot. Frost heaves pushed up long sections of tar that lay between the several parked cars in the lot.

Jeremy cut the headlights and Michelle followed suit. Jackson and Jeremy parked one street over. Michelle pulled in behind them. She got out and walked up to the driver's window.

"I'm going to sneak into that building. I want to find out what's going on."

Before either of the men could object, she ran off into the darkness.

"Should we follow her?" Jackson asked.

"Hell yes," Jeremy replied.

They both got out of the car and slipped into the shadows, hoping they caught up to Michelle before she did anything else impulsive.

Chapter 18

Michelle slipped into the silent darkness. The old warehouses appeared to be empty. She stealthily edged down
the alley, keeping close to the decrepit cinder block wall. Bits of
stone and grit rained from up above. She squinted and rubbed
the corroding building debris from her eyes. The brick was
crumbling, turning the warehouse into a decaying ruin. She
quickened her pace down the narrow passage. Fallen bits of
masonry littered the ground and scraped against the bottom of
her flimsy shoes, sending shivers up her spine. She wished she
had changed into sneakers. Her heels were low, but no good
for sneaking around in the dark.

When she reached the other end of the long building, she
peeked around the corner and saw Silas's car along with three
others. She found little comfort that Silas told the truth about a
meeting. She wanted to get closer to hear what was going on.
Her curiosity propelled her forward. She visualized Silas and
Ramsey discussing her future doom and needed to hear it all.
Acting on impulse, she ran across the small parking lot, maneuvering around potholes and puddles. She stopped herself short
and slouched beside one of the parked cars, suddenly realizing
that her eagerness could get her into serious trouble. She waited
a moment. All was quiet. Michelle peeked around the edge of
the car to gauge the situation. The deserted parking implied
they had gone into the building.

Michelle scuttled to the gray metal entry door just past
some loading docks. She went up a few cement steps and
pushed down on the handle. It wasn't locked, so she warily
opened the door and slipped into the building. The door closed
slowly, hissing softly as the compression arm collapsed. Holding her breath, she waited in case the noise from the door had

brought any unwanted attention. The sound of her pounding heart broke the silence. It was dark inside, with only the exit sign above illuminating the immediate area, urging her on. Beyond a nearby stairwell stood another door, which she also found unlocked. Gently pushing it open, she proceeded into a long hallway.

Amber light illuminated the long corridor, streaming streaks flooded the hallway from small, rectangular windows in the industrial doors that lined the hall. Michelle tiptoed and peeked through the first door window. A fluorescent light fixture in the ceiling hummed, and a couple of computers lit with screen savers scrolled the banner *Smith & Company Fencing*. One by one, Michelle looked through the glass of each door, searching for people or any sign of movement on the other side. She was confused. The outside appearance made the place look abandoned, yet there were signs of a working business inside, but no life stirred, no actual people operating the workstations. Why was Silas here? She kept peering into the rooms, making her way down the hallway.

At the end of the corridor, through the last door window, there was movement. She crouched, then cautiously raised her head again and peered through the glass. Silas stood there with his back to her, along with three other men. They gathered around an old metal desk. When he leaned to the side, she recognized Tom Bennett, his nefarious expression unmistakable, seated behind the desk and pointing to some papers sprawled across the desktop. He was instructing the others, or more accurately barking orders, his expression intent. She squinted trying to focus on the other men. Sensing her presence, Tom Bennett suddenly looked up. Michelle ducked quickly, afraid he had seen her. She held her breath for a few moments and kept still.

Squatting close to the floor, she hoped no one would come

into the hallway to check things out. Minutes passed like hours, her nerves tense. Sweat beaded across her forehead. Then a click sound sent a rush of adrenaline spiking through her body. The source of the noise was the whirring sound of the central air system as it began a cycle. A cool breeze streamed down from a ceiling vent above her. Relieved, she gulped, slowly moved up, and spied through the door's glass again.

They were still there. Michelle spied and tried to listen, but the metal door was thick and only bits of words penetrated through any cracks. Mumbles about planting evidence easily led her to guess at what they were conspiring. She realized this wasn't about her, but instead some other poor sap, and attempted to identify the other men in the room. Their backs were still toward the door and she couldn't make them out.

Frustrated that she couldn't hear more, she made an attempt at reading Tom Bennett's lips instead, speculating as they moved, but it was futile. She never realized how much Tom Bennett reminded her of an animal, like a sleek dog with a dark, mean, menacing face.

Michelle decided to retrace her steps since this wasn't getting her anywhere. Maybe Jackson and Jeremy had a better idea. She exited the building the same way she had entered and saw the men crossing the parking lot.

"There you are! Don't ever do that again," Jeremy said.

His face looked red even in the dimly lit parking lot. Jeremy didn't usually use such a strong tone of voice, obviously, he was angry with her. He would probably tell her sister how irresponsible she behaved by darting off on her own. Disappointing Emilie was something she tried to avoid, but she usually managed to do it anyway.

"Sorry. I just figured I could get in there more quietly on my own," she said.

"Next time let's discuss it first, okay?" he said.

"Okay," she said with resignation. "Now what?"

"Tell us what you saw," Jackson said.

Michelle pointed and they jogged over to the side to stand in the shadows. Still pumped with adrenaline from all the possibilities that floated through her mind, Michelle spoke quickly.

"I couldn't differentiate much of anything. The door was too thick to hear much. I tried reading their lips, but couldn't get the right vantage point, so I came back out. That's it, promise."

Jackson put his hand on her shoulder, compelling her attention.

"How many?" he asked.

"There was your father sitting behind a desk and three other guys standing around. One was Silas, of course. Another looked like Ramsey, but I can't be sure because his back was to me the entire time. I have no idea who the fourth man was, but he rather looked like my brother from the back. But that's impossible. He's in Memphis."

"Right," Jeremy said. "I have a sinking feeling about all this. I think it was Robert you saw."

"What in the hell is your brother caught up in?" Jackson said. "Robert colluded with my father once before, so it's not a big jump to assume he was the other person."

Michelle dropped her head and looked at the wet ground. She hugged herself, wrapping her arms around herself to keep warm from the cold evening chill. *My brother—Why he did these things?*

"What under heaven could they be scheming? How far will Robert go to bounce me from the board?" she said.

"Do you really want to know?" Jackson said. An expression of disgust changed his face.

"He wouldn't hurt you—his own sister, his own family," Jeremy said.

He sounded as if he wanted to make himself believe his own words.

"What are we going to tell Emilie? Knowing Robert's here—it will crush her. She had hoped everything was getting better with him," Michelle said.

"We tell her the truth. She may not like the fact that he's part of this, but no matter what's going on in there, she deserves to know the truth. We know they're up to no good, otherwise why meet in secret here in the middle of the night?" Jeremy said.

"Well, I hope it wasn't him," she said. "We still have no clue of what they're up to, and I'm not sure I want to know the truth; probably not."

"Let's get back to the car and discuss it there," Jackson said. "If my father was in there it means he might head back to the house sooner than I assumed. I have to get the book back quickly before he finds out and kills me."

Michelle turned, looked at his face, and realized for the first time just how deep his fear of his own father was. They retreated, walking toward the street where they had parked their cars. As soon as they passed from under the lone streetlight, barely hidden in the shadows, the warehouse door opened. The metal door squeaked, breaking the silence of the parking lot, sending them a warning. The men filed out, each going to their own car. They didn't seem to care about making noise, obviously aware of the area's isolation.

Alarmed, Michelle, Jackson, and Jeremy ducked and hid behind a large garbage bin. They spied from their concealment as the men got into their cars. They clearly identified Tom Bennett, Deputy Ramsey, and Silas Kain as they loitered, finding their keys and unlocking their cars. The car doors slammed shut, and the men started their vehicles and revved the engines to life.

Parked closest to them, the last man to leave opened his car door. The car's interior lights came on, and as he slid into the driver's seat, Michelle recognized her brother, Robert.

She gasped, shocked and saddened by the confirmation of his complicity to whatever bad mojo they had conspired in there. Michelle covered her mouth and ducked, quick to hide, but it was too late. Robert had heard her and paused, searching the parking lot for the source. He stepped out of the car and scanned the area. He leaned forward, heeding the shadows.

Michelle moved back farther behind the dumpster. Her foot kicked a beer can that littered the ground. It rolled backward, clinking against the tar until it hit the building and stopped with a ting. Robert stepped closer to check out the noise but stopped and turned around when Tom Bennett drove up beside him in his Lexus and unrolled his window.

"I'll meet with you later, let's say in two hours, your hotel. I have to deal with a few things first. There's another Black Wolf meeting to oversee as soon as I can get there. But I need to see you tonight, we have some serious things to discuss," Tom Bennett said.

"Will you be mentioning me to the group tonight in the meeting?" Robert asked.

"All in good time, Robert. All in good time. Don't worry, you'll get everything you deserve."

He rolled up his window and drove off without waiting for a response. Robert headed back to his rental car, climbed in, and closed the door. He started the vehicle and drove off toward the city. Once the coast was clear, the trio emerged from behind the dumpster.

Michelle was worried. Tom Bennett's words in the conversation with her brother sounded more like a threat from her viewpoint. She had no reason to trust the scoundrel and wondered how her brother could have been so taken in by the man.

Robert was wise to the ways of the world and not usually so naive. Clearly, he was blind and under the man's spell.

"How the hell did Robert get here, and what was he doing with those losers?" she said aloud.

"I understood you had security watching him. What happened?" Jeremy said.

She stomped back toward the car, walking ahead of the men, too angry to stand still.

"Don't worry, Michelle. Maybe it's just more money stuff. Maybe they're cleaning up some of those projects they worked out together," Jackson said. He was walking fast to catch up to her.

"No, all those accounts have been cleaned up and closed. There's nothing else going on business-wise between them, that we know of anyway. I have a surveillance company watching for stuff like that," she said. "Obviously, they aren't very thorough, or worse, he bought them off."

"Well, I think you need to give the team a call. Clearly, they let Robert slip out of their sight. They have some explaining to do and a lot more investigating. Come on now, time for us to go back to your Aunt Victoria's house, don't you think," Jeremy said.

Suddenly it down poured. Michelle's clothes soaked through to her skin and she shivered as they walked back to the cars. They drove to the house in a hurry because the book needed to be returned, and fast.

Chapter 19

Tom Bennett

Tom Bennett left the warehouse and drove twenty minutes, heading west on the Mass Pike, and took the Exit 8 ramp heading into the old town of Sturbridge. The Black Wolf Secret Society held their meetings here, in a secluded house nestled into a slice of woods, where the major highway arteries and local routes intersected.

He pulled off the highway and stopped at a nearby parking lot on the corner of River and South Road that belonged to a homemade candy shop, closed at this late hour. Driving to the back of the lot, he took notice of the row of cars, a few Mercedes, a couple of Corvettes and Hummers, and other luxury cars. He parked in his usual spot and got out of his Lexus.

Tom drew in a deep breath and bent his head back. He took in the redolence, the fresh fragrance of pine needles from the dense forest, mingled with the musty scent of dried leaves, and filled his nostrils. Sensing no danger, he walked to a path that led deeper into the woods.

He walked down the old trail and heard other car doors opening and closing in a distance. Then he heard a rustling of footsteps as someone ran to catch up to him. Tom shook his head in aggravation, weary of the other's need for his attention and approval. Grown men—acting like egotistical children.

Ramsey caught up to him, and a moment later Silas reached his side. They both had been with Tom at the warehouse just a half-hour ago, planting incriminating evidence against the owner of the business who had recently thrown his name into a local political race.

"So the *Beneficial Act* is done. Our new recruit now owes us a favor. Ramsey, do you have your plans ready?" Tom asked.

"Yes, all set. There will be an anonymous tip called in. Then I'll give the word, sending in a task force to raid the warehouse. Your friend, the judge, already signed the warrant. I just need to fill in the time stamp. The officers will discover the chemicals we planted, no problem. The guy will be labeled a terrorist. Our guy is a shoo-in to win the office."

"Brilliant," Silas said. "Then the owner will be forced to drop out of the race. It's a genius plan, Tom."

Tom harrumphed and shoved Silas to the side, thinking about how he had been too inept to handle his own problems with his father seven years ago. *Quivering coward*. He had to kill Frank Kain himself, and Silas didn't even have enough nerve to ask what happened, preferring to remain ignorant. The only reason Tom kept him around was because of his past with the de Gourgues girl, a relationship that had come in handy to bait her into the web. Tom didn't need Silas any longer; he had out-lived his usefulness.

"So, once this favor is done for the new kid, he'll be elected, and he's in our pocket. That's good. I could use some inside help. There are some areas of influence that I just can't reach from my desk," Ramsey said.

"Don't worry, more clout is on its way. There are other deals in the fire, too. Tonight we have a few new recruits. We'll show them a glimpse of how the Black Wolf Society works, a favor for a favor. The candidate we helped tonight will have his *Beneficial Act* marked in the book at the next meeting, after the arrest is made, then he'll owe us. He'll get elected—he knows the score."

Tom quickened his pace and walked ahead, bored with their company. Ramsey sped up to his stride.

"Hey, wait up. Tom, why did you bring Robert to the warehouse tonight? He's not one of us," Ramsey said.

"I asked him to join us because I wanted you to see the famous Robert de Gourgues face to face. You'll need to recognize him on a future mission, soon."

"How did you get him there? He didn't question anything we did? How much does he know?"

Tom laughed, mostly to himself.

"You have a lot of questions. Don't worry, Robert does anything I ask of him. He thinks we're considering him to join the society and craves the power. Of course, he won't ever be initiated, if all goes as scheduled."

Tom stopped and turned, glaring at Ramsey and Silas, who had caught up and was now at his side.

"The plans will go smoothly, without a hitch—right?" Tom demanded.

They nodded in agreement. Tom got a whiff of their fear. Yes, they were still in line, afraid to get on his bad side, right where he wanted them. Tom turned back around and together, they walked farther down the old trail.

The woods were eerily quiet at this late hour, only the squeaking of the trees as they bent in the wind and the pitter-patter of light rainfall onto the dry autumn leaves. A thick fog hugged between the dipping valleys and hills throughout the wet woods. Visibility was less than five feet ahead, but Tom knew his way by heart and walked the path by instinct alone.

The old colonial was hidden in the woods, wedged between the Quinebaug River and Hobbs Brook, and surrounded by the pine forest, cloaking it almost invisible year-round. The smell of smoke from the chimney was the only hint of its existence. They reached the house, fashioned with the traditional center entrance design. Covered with cedar shingle siding, it was stained dark brown and camouflaged with the surrounding woods. Four large rooms claimed the downstairs and were used for their meetings. The upper rooms were private, reserved for other activities that only Tom partook in. No one asked him for details. With no electricity nor modern conveniences in this place, it was intentionally kept them off the grid. The only outdoor light was a torch stuck into the ground by the entry.

"Put on your masks, gentlemen."

They each pulled on a mask that covered the upper portion of their face but left openings at the eyes. The white blank masks made them appear even more intent. Tom pushed open the front door.

"Wolfpoint," a voice shouted. Someone immediately moved forward and greeted him.

"Good evening, Grand Master. Please, sir, let me take your wet coat."

Tom gave his coat to the young member, who in return handed him a glass of whiskey. The member scurried away toward a back room.

Tom turned and strutted into the center of the front room. The members mingled about, all wearing long robes, mumbling among themselves. The room was just as dreary as the woods. The only brightness was a blazing fire, which cast silhouettes on the opposite wall. The walls were papered with an old-style print, yellowed with age, and faded over the years by the summer rays that streamed in from the front window. The furniture was strewn around the room without any sibilance of order, various chairs constructed with solid woods for the utilitarian purpose of Shaker and Craftsmen design filling the space.

Tom walked across the room, the men moving out of his way, bowing their heads, as he steered toward his favorite chair. The members seated themselves once Tom had passed.

Chair legs scraped against the varnish-bare oak floor, riddled with gouges from years of wear. Tom sat down and sipped his drink, admiring the rainbow cast by the light against the crystal glass.

"Tom, would you like another drink?" A voice behind him asked.

He turned around and saw Silas. *Poor Silas.* Drops of rain dripped down Silas's forehead from his thick dark ash hair, and he pulled a handkerchief from his pocket to wipe himself dry. Tom turned away and answered someone else's question.

"Sir, are you ready?"

"You can start by gathering the phones. Make sure they're turned off and stow them away. Then go to your seat. Wait for my nod then announce the beginning of the meeting."

The young man hurried to the corner of the room and picked up a wicker basket, then as he passed by each member, they dropped their cell phone into the well of the weave. Tom turned his attention to the others in the room, watching and recognizing their arrogance and greed. He soaked in the energy from the place, growing stronger. His dark eyes reflected the flame of the hearth, his face smoldered under his mask, so he turned away from the fire. The shadow of his profile on the opposite wall resembled a wolfish creature's shape with arresting definition as his head jutted forward.

Ramsey and Silas also masked and donned in their robes with their hoods pulled over their heads like the others in the room. Thirty men in total, half of them also wore purple sashes that draped over the shoulders against the black rayon gown. Like Ramsey, the men with the purple sashes were the older members and Tom's most trusted followers who had proved themselves many times over. Prominent in places of society, masters of their own world, they were egotistical and strong-willed men, and they were his to command. Tom admired their ambitions and positions to a degree. Still, the vital core of the society was known only to him in the room.

Only the heads of the various world groups who shared knowledge of the true nature of the Black Wolf Society knew of its grasping reach and ultimate plan of domination. They lived in a privileged world with their eyes wide shut. They knew things and kept secrets. An even more exclusive inner group existed, a few of the leaders who knew about Tom's secret powers. They supported his agenda with the full intention of taking advantage of his powers for their own sake as well. The others outside of the loop, of course, instinctively feared him, too. Just like the men in this room.

Tom was ready. He stood and dressed in his own red robe and purple sash that had been carefully hung on the back of his chair. His garment was far more elegant, with gold thread embroidery sewn into a Byzantine scrolling pattern that illuminated repetitive seven-pointed stars edging the robe and sash, along with jeweled embellishments stitched into a design.

He noticed Silas fidgeting in his chair, seated next to Ramsey. Tom gave a knowing glance in his direction. *Poor Silas looks particularly nervous tonight. He's afraid that he'll be found out. Too late, I know all about your visit with Michelle. Nothing gets by me.* Silas was becoming a problem that had to be dealt with soon. Still, his fear alone energized Tom beyond his need, as his muscles grow under his gown. His insides were turning him into something other than human. He consumed the fear of the others in the room growing. They sensed his danger but had no clue of what to name it. Tom soaked it all in, then nodded his readiness.

"The special meeting begins," the young man shouted. "Be silent and listen to our Grand Master of the Black Wolf Society."

The room hushed, the only sound was the crackling sparks from the dry fire logs being eaten by the licks of flames. Tom

Bennett stood, his frame extending over six feet tall, a body fit with toned muscles. He was a formidable presence. Everyone in the room looked up at his figure standing in the center of the room. Tom's silhouette cast on the wall opposite the fireplace, dominated all the other shadowy shapes.

He slowly looked at each of them beyond their masks, glaring directly into their eyes, mesmerizing, evaluating. He demanded their full attention and allegiance, and the monster in him sensed their pulses and smelled their fear. They understood his power over them and were ready for whatever he was about to say.

"Welcome, members of the Black Wolf Society," Tom said. "Tonight we're here because we have a few new members, and it's our responsibility to get our message across. This is also a good time for all of us to remember what we're about—why we're here. The purpose of the Black Wolf Society."

He took a few steps toward the fireplace, then turned.

"Each and every one of you who pledges to the Black Wolf Society has to be allegiant to the other members. No questions, it's that simple. We'll use any means necessary to ensure we stay free and clear from the restraints of this society. If anyone offends and gets in our way, we'll do whatever it takes to clear the path. We all want success and can achieve great things if we help each other with our *Beneficial Acts*, the cornerstone of our organization. Each favor is completed to uplift our members and will be written about in our most sacred book."

Tom looked over at Silas, nodding, smiling.

"People who stand in our way of achieving our goals will be dealt with and will pay the price; pretty simple concept. We have the power of our collaboration, and we will prevail. It's our obligation to pave the way for our own kind, our fellow members of the Black Wolf Society."

Tom looked about the room, heads were bobbing.

"Our group is all about support for each other, to do whatever it takes to meet our end goals. Whatever it takes," he repeated and waited a moment. "We need the power of control because we're the only reality of consequence on this earth. Other people exist only to serve our needs. The Black Wolf Society runs the show; it's our world. And you are the privileged few accepted into the fold. Wear that honor with loyalty to the brethren."

Tom cleared his throat. "New recruits, step forward."

Three men moved to the center of the room, unhooded their robes, and faced Tom.

"As a new recruit, you need to understand the importance of our anonymity. Our thriving survival depends on it. Now that your destiny with us has begun, you shall remain with the Black Wolf Society forever. You must pledge your loyalty to your brothers with your life."

"Do you pledge your lifetime loyalty to the best interests of the Black Wolf Society?"

"Yes, I pledge my loyalty," the pledges said in sync.

Tom lifted the men's hoods to cover their heads, then turned them around to face the group.

"Fellow Black Wolves, welcome the new pledges to the group. Each has an assigned mentor who's required to meet with them after this meeting. Discuss with them what will be done on their behalf as a *Beneficial Act* and the code words they need to commit to memory. The deeds for the *Beneficial Acts* will be written into the sacred book during the next meeting."

There was a flutter of hand-clapping, then the new recruits returned to their seats.

"Groups of the past who centered their energy in seeking power have tried to rule the world and failed. But the likes of the Black Wolf Society had never been seen before," he said.

"Friends, we're being blindly herded into the 'New World Order' an idea dreamed up and constructed by politicians and socialists of the day. They want everyone to work together for global causes, for peace, but it's all a lie. The reality of their philosophy is the same that has been practiced by the old Catholic church, as well as other religions, for centuries. They're herding the people. It's all about control. Control is power."

He made a tight grip with his raised fist, strangling something invisible in the air.

"The 'New World Order' intends to brainwash the public with humanitarian falsehoods, leading them to believe that they're more independent than ever, when in reality they've never been, nor will ever be, truly independent. They're mere sheep. Herded in whatever direction they were pointed to. Mindless people; they might as well be zombies."

Light laughter floated across the room. Tom extended his arms and continued spewing his words as his arms swiped the air back and forth across the group.

"Of course that excludes us. We're the Black Wolf Society and we follow no one. We will not follow the 'New World Order' dreamed up by politicians. We won't allow ourselves to be constrained by anyone or any philosophy. We're the true rulers of our fate, and by colluding together, able and willing to do whatever it takes, only then can we ensure our survival, on our own terms. Today, our Black Wolf Society stands together to create a strong power hold. I'm happy to say that earlier this evening we set into motion help for one of our newest recruits."

Tom placed his hands on the shoulder of one of the new members.

"His *Beneficial Act*, a planned action to ensure his leadership in politics, has begun. The Black Wolf Society will have another politician in our midst."

The crowd mumbled.

"That's right, men, we're the winners, the relevant, and the stronghold. In return for your fellowship, you'll be the recipients of power, and money, and a seat at the table of the most influential group in the world. Nothing happens without it being our intentions. We are the Black Wolves!"

The men in the room stomped their feet to the floor once, one thunderous sound of unity. Tom paused a moment taking in the thunderous worship.

Tweet. A lone sound chirped.

Tom stopped in his tracks, and turned his head; the Twitter sound from an iPhone. Everyone turned and moved away from a man in a black gown with no sash. His hand quickly fell behind his robe.

"Grab him."

Immediate action happened after Tom's shout. Two men grabbed the other's arms and dragged him front and center to where Tom stood. Tom pulled back his hood.

"You, Peter Brooks. What have you done?"

"Sir, I'm sorry. I forgot to hand in my phone."

The man on the left grabbed the accused man's phone from his right hand and gave it to Tom. He turned on the phone and scrolled, checking emails, then scrolling pictures.

"You videoed the initiation." Tom's face grew dark with his verdict. "What have you done?"

Peter Brooks began to whimper. "Nothing, Sir, honest; nothing."

"Who put you up to this?"

"No one. It was my idea. Thinking it would be good for me to have leverage."

Tom let out a chortled laugh.

"Leverage," he mocked. "You want leverage over the Black Wolf Society. Tsk tsk, that's not how this works. We'll show you how it works, Mr. Peter Brooks. You're well aware of the consequences of treason. If anyone did put you up to this, well, they'll never find you again for a conversation."

Tom snapped his fingers and a big man from the back of the room stepped forward. After Tom nodded, the brute punched Peter Brooks in the gut, and he doubled over and fell to the floor, lying at the feet of Tom.

"This will be a lesson for you all. No one crosses the line. We're here together, strong together, and you must do everything in your power for the Black Wolf. No one is to hold any secrets over me. It's I who hold all of your secrets. I must remain the stronghold, the wall, for this to work. You understand."

Hoods bobbed up and down.

"Take him outside to the post."

The brute of a man grabbed Peter Brook's arms, wrangled him up off the floor, and walked toward the door, pushing the man in front of him. Peter Brooks struggled.

"No, please have mercy on me," he cried.

They stepped outside into the cold night air. It was pitch dark since all torches had been doused. Stepping about fifty feet from the main house, the brute ripped off the robe and tied Peter Brooks to a charred stake already staged and protruding from the ground. The other members followed and gathered around the post, forming a semi-circle. Tom turned in front of them all.

"This is one way we handle traitors." He raised his arm, rubbed the flint in his lighter, then lit a torch. The sudden glow from the flame made the men wince and cover their eyes. Tom stood there, his looming presence even larger than before. He reached his arm straight out to his side, and the brute man took the torch from his grasp. In a fluid motion, the man bent and lit the ground around Peter Brooks.

Peter cried out, "Please give me another chance. I didn't understand. What I did wasn't treason. It was a mistake."

Tom took a few steps to the side, picked up a stake that had been laying on the ground, and drew close to Peter Brooks. In a hushed, deep tone Tom said, "There is no going back."

He thrust the stick into Peter's side. Blood gushed out and spilled down his body, his clothes painted red with blood.

The man groaned in pain. "I beg of you, please . . ."

The trail of blood let off a steam into the air and faded, along with his voice.

"This is taking too long." Tom grabbed a small gas can from the forest's shadows. He gave it to the brute, who opened the can and shook gas all over Peter Brooks.

His body was engulfed in flames and sizzled. The man's groans of agony were smothered by the furious sound of burning hot flames bubbling over his skin and burning him while alive. They all witnessed his body melting, the smell of scorched flesh overtaking the fresh pine scent of the woods.

The other members stood there motionless, watching a good ten minutes before Tom turned around and walked back to the house. All the men followed except the brute man, who watched over the burning body. Tom quickened his step and went to his place, sitting in the worn leather seat of the Mission Club chair. He soaked in the fear of the men.

Now, they all shared one more dark secret, a secret soon to be buried far, far away by a lucky chosen individual. Casually he picked up his drink and rolled the liquid against the glass, thinking about who to give the honor of cleaning up this mess. *Not Ramsey this time. I'm saving him to help with something much more important.* His calculations strayed to his own deep secret.

I'll have my revenge . . . Just like when I killed my parents for their inadequacy and brutality toward me. I'll have my revenge against Pierre—his entire de Gourgues family will be eliminated, then I'll gladly help myself to all his money. The Black Wolves will do as I request without question, and my justice will finally be served. The right time was near.

The other men filed into the room and seated themselves in silence, then a lone man stood and clapped. Tom bowed his head and accepted the praise.

Chapter 20

It was late by the time they returned to Victoria's house. The trio walked into the front hall, shivering from the cold night air. Aunt Victoria steered them into the dining room and served everyone a warm cup of tea. Michelle took a sip; the warm herbal brew chased away the chill in her bones as it slid down the back of her throat. Safe again, they drank and warmed up. The trio told Emilie and Victoria about how they had followed Silas and about Robert's unexpected appearance at the warehouse.

"Well, he's up to old tricks," Emilie said.

"Nothing Robert does these days surprises anyone," Michelle said.

"Well, I don't understand how your brother is involved in any of this mess," Victoria said. "He is usually so watchful over you girls."

Michelle held back tears and shook her head instead of doing what she wanted to do, cry. Emilie suddenly clapped her hands together, surprising everyone.

"Are you all ready for one crazy tale?" Emilie said. "I translated a good portion of the book while you all were gone."

"Of course, tell us what the book revealed. I need to get that relic back into the vault before my father gets home, which might be sooner than I thought," Jackson said.

"Here it goes, but remember, these are not my words, just what I translated. First off, we've already discovered that this book is about a secret society called The Black Wolf and that the group members have a pact to help each other. No, scratch that. Not to help, but to promote each other, so that they can each achieve their dreams. This society is all about power. The members become successful in their field and use the power and influence gained to benefit the group. Every member takes a vow of obedience and to help when asked, without question. Here's the tricky part. Once a favor is granted to a member, then he owes a favor. It's due at any time requested, no questions. Each member must be willing to do anything it takes, and I mean anything. I hope you understand the ramifications of this. It means they have to do and use any means necessary at their disposal."

Emilie's eyes were wide open, ensuring that everyone in the room understood her.

"Do you mean, like Ramsey and Silas have to frame me because they were instructed to do so? Even if they don't want to?" Michelle said.

"Exactly like that, but more. They documented the things the group members did for each other using that old Siksika language as code. The *Beneficial Acts*, as they call them, are listed on the pages. It's a long list, and most are criminal acts. I didn't believe it at first, but it reads like a hit list. One, in particular, jumped out at me, so I went back and re-checked the translation again, using the Ojibwe chart, to be certain. Plain as day, the murder of Frank Kain is listed. It was one of the *Beneficial Acts* and performed for Silas Kain's behalf."

Michelle froze, her heart pounding in her ears.

"Okay, Sis, I need to know. Who murdered Frank Kain? Who did it for Silas?"

Emilie scratched her head.

"That's the problem; it doesn't list who did the actual Act, only who it was done for. Of course, we already know who it was done for, don't we? It looks like your professor was a member of this group and someone else took care of his problem by murdering his father. So we haven't learned anything new, except that he was aware. Hell, he requested it. We also confirmed that Ramsey's a member, and the two of them have orders to bury you and implicate you for the murder. Ramsey must have questioned you seven years ago at the direction of the society way back then, too. Something else must have triggered because there are still marching orders against you, Michelle. So, what should we do now? Anyone have a suggestion of our next move?" Emilie said.

Michelle stood and crossed her arms.

"We're going to do nothing for now. Emilie, you and Jeremy should go back to Memphis and watch over the business. Please, don't even argue. I have Jackson here and Aunt Victoria. It seems The Black Wolf has had a mark on me for years, so nothing has changed," Michelle said.

"Chelle, I think this is happening now because you control our money. It all started again after Father died, right?" Emilie stood and faced her younger sister. Her expression was cross, unlike her. She pointed her finger to the floor as she spoke, her voice rang a bit raised. "There's no way I'm leaving you here, especially now that we know Robert was here, too. Come home with me and to hell with their threat to pin a murder on you. Let them try it. We have highly paid lawyers for that."

Emilie hugged Michelle, giving her a tight squeeze before letting her go.

"Okay, maybe you're right, Em. But please, just go back home tomorrow to watch the helm. Neither of us trusts Robert, and someone needs to be there. I'll follow shortly, I promise. There are just a few things I want to do with Aunt Victoria first; nothing dangerous, I promise."

She flashed her grin and pleaded with her bright blue eyes, nudging Emilie to give in. Victoria intruded into the sisters' squabble.

"Emilie, I promise I'll stay by Michelle's side and send her back home safe and sound. When this is over, I think I'll go to Memphis with her for a little visit, if that's all right with you, dear. I want to meet Rachael."

Emilie let out a sigh of surrender. "Okay, but Michelle, you promise me, nothing dangerous, right?"

"I promise," Michelle said as she held up her fingers like a solemn pledge.

"Oh pl-ease, Michelle, you were never a Girl Scout," Emilie retorted.

Michelle shot her a smirk, and Emilie was too exhausted to argue.

"Well, on that note, good night, ladies and gentleman," Jackson said.

He smiled and turned, leaving without delay, anxious to return the book to the secret safe. Emilie and Jeremy said their good-nights and went upstairs to bed, leaving Michelle and Aunt Victoria to clean up. They gathered the dishes onto the tray and headed for the kitchen.

"Michelle, I know you well enough to know you have no intention of leaving before you get the answers you need, but those men are dangerous, and not only to you. They pose a danger to everyone," she breathed deep. "I wish I had stopped Tom Bennett years ago. I should have shot him myself when I had the chance. The world would have been a better place without him."

She splashed the suds in the sink, taking her frustrations out with the dishcloth.

"Except there would have been no Jackson," Michelle answered.

Victoria turned off the water to the sink and smiled at her.

"You're right. I regret those murderous impulses, for his sake."

Michelle wiped her hands on the dishtowel and turned to hug her aunt.

"Let's stay cool-headed. I need your help. Together we'll

take on the most heinous man in the world. Tom Bennett will pay for his secret sins. I promise on my Mother's grave."

Chapter 21

Jackson

Jackson drove home, wondering what his father's recent activities involved, no doubt someone's financial demise. He wanted to stop him and bring him down. He was tired of his abusive behavior. First, he needed to place the book back into the safe before his father realized it was missing. He wasn't in New York City as he had said, and after seeing him at the warehouse, he could show up at the house at any time. Jackson wouldn't feel safe until it was back where he found it.

He worried he might be too late. His gut twisted inside. *What if his old man was already home?* There were no cars in the driveway. Relieved for the moment, he took the steps two at a time in a rush to get the book back into its hiding place. He walked down the hallway with fast strides, looking to his sides, making sure the house was empty. He caught a glimpse of a shadow cast into the hallway from one of the bedroom doorways.

Fear skated down his back, and he pushed himself against the wall. He swallowed hard and gasped shallow breaths. He watched and waited in silence. Out stepped the housekeeper, Lilly, carrying her dusting rags and supplies. She jumped and let out a yelp, startled when Jackson stepped out from the shadows. The bucket and cleaning supplies crashed to the floor and made a ruckus.

"Oh! Oh, it's you. Jackson, you frightened me. I thought I was alone in this big spooky house."

Jackson wiped his forehead. "I just got in. You startled me too. Is my father home?"

"No. Not yet, but I'll be leaving now before he gets home," she said.

They both laughed and went on their way. As soon as she descended the stairs, Jackson crossed the hall and quietly opened the door to his father's bedroom, holding his breath and praying for no squeaks to announce his entrance, just in case his father had sneaked into the room unnoticed by Lilly. The room seemed empty. He snapped on the light, relieved to find he was indeed alone. He walked directly to the mirror, lifted it from the wall, and leaned it against the bed. He entered the combination, opened the door, and returned the heavy leather-bound book into the safe, then closed it, snapping the lock tight. He placed the mirror carefully back on the wall hanger, then left the room as stealthily as he had entered.

He hurried back to his room, then closed and leaned against the door, breathing out his relief with a puff of air. His limbs deflated as the tension left his body. The last thing Jackson wanted was his father to know he was plotting behind his back. He was a dangerous man, and even though Jackson was his son, he didn't trust him nor feel safe around him. Family meant nothing to him.

A few hours went by then Jackson heard a car drive up. He went to the window and peered down.

His father parked his Lexus near Jackson's old Nissan compact. Tom walked up the front steps. He entered the house, slamming the front door closed, and clanged things about, making a racket. A wild animal was let loose in the house. Jackson went back to his desk, put on his headphones, and tried to forget Tom was even there. The escape didn't last long. Within minutes his headphones were ripped off his ears. Stunned, he looked up to see his father's hand coming down on him.

Smack! Across the face, his father's hand surprised Jackson and left a stinging impression. Then a sucker punch impacted

Jackson's jaw. Instinctively Jackson jumped up from the chair and pushed himself away from his father's grasp. Jackson's eyes teared and his face burned. He shouted back. "What the hell are you doing?"

He wiped the blood from his mouth, swallowing hard while wishing he hadn't said that, knowing it was best to keep from any confrontation with his father. Tom Bennett stood over his son, leering at him.

"What am I doing?" his father bellowed.

Jackson winced at his father's strong voice but pushed himself to stand up to the man. Looking up into his eyes, Jackson defended himself. "I didn't do anything wrong."

"Playing the innocent with me. Well, are you going to tell me?"

Jackson was scared. *Did his father know he took the book? Had he forgotten to move something back in place?* He played a cool hand and wouldn't give anything away if he didn't have to. His father often hit him for senseless things that popped into his head. Jackson braved his stance, forcing his voice to remain steady, though his legs shook.

"I don't know what you're talking about," Jackson said.

Tom made some guttural groans and growls in his throat.

"Michelle de Gourgues is what I'm talking about. Someone told me you were with her. Is that true?" he said.

Jackson swallowed hard. *Be brave,* he said to himself.

"Yes, it's true, but what's the problem? I see her whenever she's in town. I've known her for years. Why are you suddenly so angry about that?"

He kept his eyes on his father, just waiting for another slam to the head.

"How long have you known her?" he shouted.

"I don't know. Probably as long as I've known Robert, she's his sister. We were introduced, years ago, when she visited campus. You remember she even came to a few parties here, at the house. What's the big deal anyway?"

"You better be telling me the truth," Tom said. He pushed Jackson back with one last jab.

Jackson lost his balance and landed sitting on the bed.

His father stomped out of the room and slammed the door.

Jackson's trophies rattled on the shelves, one toppled over. All those awards he worked so hard for, to gain some attention from his father, but his efforts were never good enough for Tom. Jackson's heart sunk.

He was fed up with his father's behavior, acting like a crazed animal again tonight. For years, Jackson took the blows like a punching bag every time his father was angry. *If this is how angry he gets just because he spoke to Michelle, how would he react to them scheming together?* Jackson had no doubt his father would kill him if he ever discovered his recent moves. He had to get away while he still had the option to flee.

He packed a duffel bag, shoving in shirts and pants, not caring if they were wrinkled or if the colors matched. He threw in a few personal items, then headed down to his car, jumping down the stairs three at a time, unable to get away fast enough. He refused to stay in the house a minute longer while his father was still alive. Jackson knew the old family house was his legacy; his grandfather had told him many times when he was a little boy, but he wasn't around to protect him anymore. *Tom probably killed Grandfather, too*, he considered, as he left the house for good.

He ran across the driveway, slipped into his car, and drove off, gunning the gas pedal. The car tires spun on the loose stones, which flew into the air and landed on the lawn as he made his escape. As soon as he had some distance from the house, he pulled over to the curbside to call his mother.

"Mom, I know you're away. Please listen to me. Don't come

home. Dad just got back, and he's acting like an animal again. Stay away, Mom, as long as you can, at least until it's safe. Promise me." He left a voice message on her phone.

He hoped she picked the message up and would take heed of his warnings. He did what he could, and there was no other way to get in touch with her tonight. Still seething with anger, he put his car into gear and started to drive off again. It didn't matter where he was going, as long as it was away.

Chapter 22

Tom Bennett

Tom Bennett was alone in the house. *Finally, peace and quiet.* He dragged himself to his office and kicked off his shoes. His head was spinning; he needed to organize his plans. He sat on the floor cross-legged in the middle of the room and closed his eyes. Meditating, he went back to his place of power. Fear was what strengthened him.

Earlier, when he was upstairs, he had absorbed the fear that pulsed from within his son. Tom had sensed the vibrations that the housekeeper had left behind. He had soaked them in, gathering the fear of all those who had been in the house. Fear fed his strength and power at their best. He was the secret weapon of the Black Wolf Society and must be prepared for when he was needed, once again.

Something still bothered him, making him antsy. He jumped up from the floor and went to his desk. Tom Bennett sat back in his leather chair and gazed across the large wood-paneled room. His eyes landed on a picture at the corner of his desk. He stared at it. The photograph was taken so long ago. He remembered that night; it was the last party he was allowed to attend at college.

Bethany had been so beautiful then, wearing her tight designer blue jeans. They had fit her so snugly, and she wore a blue top with a V-neck. Tom Bennett closed his eyes, and the thrill he had gotten looking at her cleavage came alive again. His passion throbbed once more as his groin grew with illusions of her. He had claimed his love for her that night, but she rejected him. In anger, he took her virginity. It had been his right to have what he wanted. Since he was young, Tom Bennett always got what he wanted; he was a privileged young man. Of all the young women on campus, he had chosen Bethany. She should have been honored, but instead, she crossed him, betrayed his feelings, and dared to turn him away.

Tom Bennett relived that night in his mind.

He had driven her home in his father's Lincoln Town car after the dance and pulled into a dirt road on the way to her house. The area was isolated and surrounded by the woods, a good spot for necking. He had shared his feelings with her that night, wrapped his arms around her petite body, and told her he wanted her, but she pushed him aside. She struggled from his grasp, twisting her tiny body away from him.

The look of fear on her face had stirred him in a new way, and his excitement grew. He continued his advances, pulling her close and groping her. Her fear grew into terror, and he detected the raw edge of her emotions. Blazing desire engulfed him. Filled with lust, he hadn't cared if she submitted or not; he wanted her as his. His animal nature had taken over. She had become his marked territory.

He forced her down onto the front seat and pushed her legs apart. His weight had kept her in place, and all her squirming was fruitless. His right hand reached under her blouse, and he grabbed her breast, the bosom she had tempted him with; he groped their plumpness as he squeezed them tight.

With closed eyes, Tom Bennett recalled more details of his memory.

He remembered how, in his excitement that night, his mouth had watered, and he drooled all over her face as he slobbered kisses on her cheek and neck. So sensuous to him. He worked his way down to her breasts. That's when she had screamed the loudest. She wiggled under him, her arms and legs pushed up against him, which only heightened his desire. He was erect and hard. Nothing she did could have changed her fate at that point. He had morphed into a monster already. His left hand slid down her firm, flat stomach, and he forced his way into her tight pants with zeal and tore the zipper open. He touched her soft pubic hair; the sensation plunged his lust into a place of no return. He'd submerged into a haze of unbridled raw emotion.

He had her pinned down with one arm and yanked her pants away, down to her ankles with the other. She screamed as her panties followed. He shifted his weight and moved his right hand to grope her pelvic area. His fingers probed her, shaking with excitement. Bethany cried out in a blood-curdling scream, maybe even louder than before. Shivers ran down his spine at the sound of her cries, and he had consumed all her fear. He experienced its strength, then, that first time.

He covered her open mouth with his cheek and pushed down, crushing her face with his. Using his weight, he lay on top of her and shoved his hardened penis into her. He remembered how her insides had been dry, but soon everything was hot and wet from his surging release. He thrust into her again until he had been satisfied.

When he had finished, he pulled his face away and looked into her eyes. Bethany lay quiet, her eyes wide open with horror, her face bleached. He was in awe of those wet blue eyes and had watched as the red veins in her eyeballs burst and became bloodshot pools. It was life, growing there in her scarlet eyes. The fear in her had thrilled him and turned him on more than he'd ever imagined possible. It had been nirvana for him.

He got off her and watched as she curled herself up against the passenger front door. She had cowered there, with her arms wrapped around herself like a cocoon. She slowly pulled her pants up, whimpering and shaking in convulsive spasms.

He turned on the ignition, pulled out of the woods in reverse, then drove her home. He had dropped her off at her parents' house. She franticly pulled the door open and got out of the car, running with a limp straight to the front door. Without saying a word, not even a glance back, she had fled inside.

He had wanted to see her again, taken by her raw emotional edge, but that had been the only time he would ever have her. After that night, she was never seen again at any social gatherings. She never came back to campus.

That experience with Bethany had been the most exhilarating of his life. His time with her had felt so energizing and natural for him. He had wanted Bethany, and only she could give him that heightened sensation to satisfy his animal urge. She had opened doors into his real self that night; doors that would never close again.

Tom Bennett shook his head with disgust. The past made him angry. Consequences had arisen from his actions because no one understood his true nature. After that night, unfortunate events followed Tom. Things happened that changed his life forever.

First, Bethany's sister, Victoria, had stormed into the frat house and had screamed his name aloud for all to hear. Tom could still hear her shrieks in his head, *Tom Bennett, you coward, you rapist! People should know what a mean son of a bitch you are! Everyone stay away from Tom Bennett. He's a rapist.* He had become a pariah on campus after her outburst, and people looked at him with disgust. He hated Victoria and still had a score to settle with her as well.

Pierre de Gourgues had decided to play the hero, threatened Tom, and demanded that he stay away from Bethany, but he couldn't help himself. He sent her letters, flowers, called the house, leaving messages. He had even considered apologizing to be with her again. *No one had understood his need.*

She had refused every attempt he made.

Later, the police visited him, another unfortunate event.

Changes to his life had been unrelenting. Harvard had requested that he never return to campus. Tom was booted out of school, and the draft board had been notified of his updated status. His parents were made aware of the rape complaint against him but never had asked him about it. Instead, they pushed him onto a plane, to a god-forsaken place, a camp in Montana. His mother had said it was a place where he could *heal his soul.* His father had been ashamed of him and never spoke to him again. Tom hated his parents and never forgave them. After all, he had only followed their lead.

Since college no longer had been an option, he agreed to go to the retreat camp and hide from the draft board. In the end, the trip to the reservation in Montana had proved to be the greatest experience in his life. After Bethany, of course. Tom had walked into the reservation a troubled boy, humiliated and hurt like a wounded animal. After his Vision Quest at Medicine Grizzly Bear, he had walked out a monster with a secret weapon, capable of wiping out all his adversaries.

He dedicated his entire life to revenge. For years he'd been patient, savoring every small step of the way, like jumping from stone to stone in a riverbed, waiting for his payback. Unfortunately, Bethany and Pierre de Gourgues had both died unexpectedly, much too young. They escaped the full power of his wrath, too little torment for Tom's sadistic pleasure.

So his plan altered and he would have to settle for the demise of their children instead. They had to be erased from the face of the earth. He planned to send the final push soon and watch them all descend into hell.

Tom's face burned with fury. The images of old memories, lost lust, humiliation, and rage haunted his reflections. Tom's only recompense were plans to ruin what remained of the de Gourgues legacy.

The plan was set into motion. Soon all three of the offspring would be killed, starting with Michelle, then Emilie, and even Robert. The Black Wolves would help him; not that he needed them, only to set things up. No one knew his true secret power or would ever find out the entire truth about his secret sins. *They wouldn't believe me even if I told my story.* Who would ever believe that Tom Bennett was no longer a mere human? He was a new creature, capable of vanquishing anyone who got in his way. Tom Bennett was a monster.

He laughed to himself, amused with his final plans.

Chapter 23

Tom Bennett

Tom was tired of stewing in his anger. Instead, he preferred to concentrate on the events that happened after he left Bethany. His strength emerged and grew from his Vision Quest. It had been his rebirth after all, up there on the mountain.

Almost a century after the Ghost Dance was banned across the country authentic lodges had begun to spring up again for those who sought religious enlightenment or awakening with mother earth. Sweat lodges had always been a major part of tribal life, and they had become popular with the masses during the 1970s. He was sent to Montana to a spiritual retreat directed by a young tribal priest, who claimed he could help troubled young adults back onto the road of redemption, using the old ways.

Avoiding unpleasantness with the law and the draft, Tom had agreed to go along with his parent's devised plan. He had hoped the rumors about the use of peyote heaven were true. He wanted to try it out first-hand and figured the obscure camp in the wilderness taking part in the use of such hallucinogens while cleansing the soul.

Like previous dwellers on the threshold, Tom was told that he would connect with his spiritual familiar for guidance. During a sweat lodge, as a seeker, he would open his channel to the other world. He would be a dweller on the threshold. Calling up his individual familiar, who would teach him how to go beyond the conflicts and experiences of this world. Free him from the shackles of previous worlds, away from the things that held him back from reaching true knowledge of self and soul.

They all had hoped he would finally learn to be good.

It was a rainy day when Tom Bennett arrived at the retreat site in the summer of 1972. He could have walked away, could have disappeared into the bleak rocky mountain terrain, never to be found, but instead agreed to stay and wait things out. One of the camp leaders met him at the drop-off area. They shook hands, then hiked a path until they reached Grizzly Lake. The camp leader's name was Chief Black Wolf, a tall young man over six feet and lanky, who behaved more like a kid than a man, showing insecurities right from the start with his weak handshake and wavering voice. The Chief and a shaman priest who ran the Medicine Lodge had explained to Tom the purpose of the rituals and ceremonies.

"Before you venture on this quest, you must become the dweller. First, you must outcast doubt so that you can seek the knowledge that leads to good. A positive outlook will help you as a dweller on the threshold. Reach beyond your personal experiences and find good, then become selfless," Chief Black Wolf said.

The Chief bent closer to Tom and squinted into his eyes, peeking inside, looking for Tom's soul. The Chief darted back, an uneasy expression washed across his face. Tom bit his tongue, holding back his laughter. This kid wanted to be a great leader, but he was the naïve one. Tom was aware of his nature already, and it wasn't good. He had a unique thirst for terror. His heart would never be good. His quest for his familiar was a sham, but regardless, he resigned himself to go along for the ride and scheduled the sweat lodge purification, then a Ghost Dance to open channels before his Vision Quest.

"We need to prepare you right away so you can connect with our ancestors. They'll give you the peace you're missing in your heart," Chief Black Wolf said.

Tom shrugged, not concerned about his heart or soul.

"You need the quest badly before you lose yourself completely," the shaman said.

The words didn't faze Tom, all junk religion to him.

"We'll do a sweat to prepare you and make you clean from the inside," the shaman said. "And then the dance ceremony to open your channels. Then you'll be ready to hike into the wilderness by yourself on your Vision Quest journey. There are no supplies allowed. Expect to be visited by your animal power in a dream. He'll come to you as a familiar, to show you the way," Chief Black Wolf said.

Tom listened to the old tales and spiritual hogwash, realizing the truth—he would be dumped in the middle of nowhere south of camp past Oldman Lake with no food or water, stuck on his own away from any glimpse of civilization. *A dream, yes that's right, a dream would show him the way*, he had internally ridiculed. Tom hated all the bullshit that the religious leaders dished out, and this young band of wannabe spiritual leaders was no better than the rest of the zealot.

"This journey must be taken alone. You will see things out there that may frighten you. Your past lives and experiences will confront you. They will try to block your way from moving forward, but you're the dweller. You must keep your heart clean and open the channels to your familiar. Only then will you find your true path.

"The animal familiar will be your supernatural link and guide you to your soul's true enlightenment. You'll see a different world vision beyond this life. Tom, you will become mighty with the guidance of your animal power and become master over your future path."

Those last words were the only ones that made sense to Tom. He liked the idea of becoming master over his future.

Tom suffered in a sweat lodge for four days, sitting in the rigged dome, covered with animal hides, filling up with smoke and the heat generated from rocks cooked in a fire, all for the sake of his purification. The first hours he complained, but no one listened.

There was one woman who brought the stones in. He liked to watch her as she flexed her muscles while maneuvering the stones into the pit. Lust filled his loins, but she never reacted to him, only looked away as she walked past him.

He sat vigilant for days as the heat pulled the moisture from his body, and he almost passed out a few times. He was given a small dose of peyote and experienced some crazy hallucinations, feeling invincible. The colors of the rocks, the glow of the coals, were all bright and shiny. Everything seemed more intense. Animal skins covered the sweat lodge dome and rippled in waves when a wind blew. It was all drug-induced, and no magic hocus-pocus happened. When they finally opened the tent's flap, a crazy pleasure overtook him.

Dazed as he stepped out into the mid-afternoon sun, he noticed dancing going on and heard the slow pounding of a drum melting with the soft chanting. The dancers stepped in circular movements, softly going around an open fire. Chief Black Wolf handed him a drink, and Tom sipped the bitter water and soon experienced an outer body sensation. A surreal calmness rushed through him as if suspended in air, while the ceremony kept going on. He was lost in time, enjoying the rhythm, drifting, floating, separated from the real world. Tom participated in the Ghost Dance ceremony with his channels opened to other worlds. His mind swirled as he danced in circles for hours.

When they finished the ceremony, Tom was escorted across a rocky trail. He avoided the rugged cliffs beyond the edge of the mountain. Released on his own to find his unique familiar guide, he embarked on a journey in the wilderness. They gave him one last instruction.

"Avoid any ceremonial or burial grounds and carcasses."

The first day of his Quest had been horrible, the air dry and hot in the afternoon sun. He found water in Oldman Lake, then traveled along the dried-up creek bed named Dry Fork, searching for any shade under the occasional tree or jutting cliffs on the outlining mountainside. He couldn't remember how far he had walked, but by dusk, he was on Rising Wolf Mountain on the north side of Two Medicine Lake.

He stumbled upon an old burial ground, that area was known as the resting place for many ancient graves. Chief Black Wolf had warned him to stay away from any area of death because ghosts sought out to haunt seekers. Tom was brought to the edge of the dead world during the Ghost Dance, now an open channel waiting to be filled.

He laughed to himself at the idea and put no stock into the nonsense and folk tales. He understood the practical side of the matter; this place offered some protection from the coming cold night air. With no tent for cover, he made his night's resting place there, behind a large stone used as a marking monument in the old burial ground.

Tired from hiking, he loosened his bootlaces and realized his feet were sore and blistered. Leaning against the stone, he tried to relax. His senses were heightened, still feeling the effects of the ceremony. He listened to the sounds of the wilderness, owls, and faraway coyotes. His vision was enhanced as well, and he stared as a snake crawled by into the darkness. A shroud of energy hovered around it, glowing as it slithered away.

An eerie feeling crept into his mind's eye as he searched the area. Shadows stretched across the stony field as the sun's last rays hit the ground. Twilight morphed into the night sky as he lay hunkered against that old stone, trying to stay warm. He worried about possible scavenging animals, not wanting to be night prey. He planned to sleep through the remaining days of the quest, then get away as fast as possible from the desolate area and never return to Montana.

Tom dreamed about his bed back home in Massachusetts and pondered his mother and how stupid she'd been for letting his father hit her all the time. He fantasized about his father and how someday, Tom would hit him back with retaliating hard blows. His mind was filled with hate.

Bethany's face popped into his mind's eye, and he relived the night he had her, her screams, her lovely cries for mercy. She had been under his power for just a short time, and he needed more. His lust for her filled his head with self-indulgent gore. He concentrated on the smell of fear and allowed the essence of that memory to linger in his nostrils. Memories of Pierre de Gourgues and his meddlesome good deeds invaded his psyche, too, filling Tom's entire being with a deep black hole of hate.

Tom vowed he would get his revenge. It was at that moment, when he was loathing Pierre de Gourgues, that a sound roused him from his reverie. Something in a distant tree rustled. *Shriek,* a nearby owl hooted, then a loud crazy call filled the night air with a shrill, then . . .

Everything went silent.

A spike of fear replaced his hate. He cowered, wide-eyed and awake in the darkness. The moon was full that night but hidden with intermittent clouds. Slivers of light illuminated the area as whimsical winds blew the feathered clouds about in the night sky, casting dancing shadows.

An awful feeling crept into Tom's head. He wasn't alone. *Was his animal familiar out there?* Something was out there. He couldn't deny it even if he didn't believe in the Chief's ancient tales about power animals and familiars, who dwelled at the edge of the threshold. For the first time in his entire life, Tom was afraid. Fear speared through his being.

Suddenly it appeared as if by magic, staring straight at him. The creature, a monster of the night, loomed in front of him. It was larger than any animal he ever imagined. It grew larger as the shadows cast down across the ground. A growl from the creature's throat, low and guttural, filled the air with an echoing menace. It was a gigantic wolf and stood not ten feet away from him.

Drool dripped from its teeth. It growled and twitched its head from side to side. Tom sensed the monster measured him with its keen dark eyes. Positioned like a predator, the creature was a dark shadow in the charcoal night. The beast's ivory fangs, sharp and ragged, stood out stark against its midnight black coat. It absorbed Tom's emotions; he weakened. As the wolf consumed Tom's fear, its eyes smoldered from the emotive hostility. The monster thrived on his terror and appeared to grow larger along with Tom's mounting horror.

He heard its breathing, the sound of the exhaled air, and saw the steam leave its nostrils and mix into the cold night mist. He heard the rumble that vibrated from deep in its throat. The beast's wet fur smelled wild, a feral wreak.

The clouds moved and cast light across the beast. This creature was worse than anything Tom had ever imagined. He understood that his natural tendency leaned toward a psychopath; he had never been afraid of anything in his life. Petrified, frozen with fear, he wanted to flee, but he couldn't move his muscles, the message was lost in the delivery somewhere between his brain and limbs. Without additional warning, the beast lunged forward and attacked.

Teeth gripped Tom's entire shoulder blade, digging in deep as it gorged his flesh. The beast wrestled him to the ground and the two bodies rolled about, kicking up stones and dry dirt.

Tom grabbed a rock, yanked it up to the wolf's head, and pounded it over and over again against the monster's skull. There was a brief yelp of surprise, but the monster never loosened its grip for a moment.

Searing pain shot through Tom, every nerve ending jumping out against his skin. The fangs pierced through to his limbs. Blood oozed out from his wound and dripped down his arm. The rust smell of blood filled the night air and melded with the stench of the beast's wet fur. In a final attempt to survive, Tom grabbed the monster's coat with great force, but nothing registered with the animal; it just kept chomping away at his shoulder and arm, devouring Tom's meaty muscle. The more panic Tom generated, the extra blazon the beast's attack grew. It was futile to battle, any attempt to protect himself from the deadly beast failed.

Terrorized, Tom gave up. His aggressor penetrated one last deadly bite into his neck. Tom lost consciousness as his blood rushed out in a river, and his spirit floated away from his body. At peace, his soul rose into the sky. He was between the world he lived in and the other world on the other side of the veil.

A flash of lightning filled the sky, and his being vanished. He became part of the burst, and everything became visible in blinding illumination. A ghostly white animal, that had once been the dark wolf, was now holding Tom's limp body in his arms. The massive wolf had somehow become a walking creature and carried Tom's corpse to a place high up, into the sky, toward the bright light. Another streak zapped through the ether, booming a thunderous explosion. The streak burned through him, scorching his insides and cauterizing his skin closed. His internal organs were singed, blackened.

It was his turning point—that night of the bite. He transformed, and his new life had begun. He turned into his new supernatural being, filled with animal instincts that surged throughout every cell in his body.

Tom awoke back on the ground and realized he changed and was no longer merely human. He was a skinwalker, a shapeshifter, a wolfman.

The black werewolf creature no longer gnarled at him. Instead of fearing the beast, Tom felt a bond to it. This creature was his animal power, his supernatural link, and he intended to keep it near, always.

Tom had transformed into a transcendental creature of the night, a supernatural beast from the other side of the dweller's threshold. His primal instincts were strong. He could smell everything with a new sharpness, the rocks, the dirt, everything. When he lifted his head, he smelled human fear in the breeze. This would be his secret weapon to use for his gain. That night Tom embraced his renewed evil nature, his true destiny all along.

Fear, his favorite new heightened sense, made him a bigger and stronger human monster. He was a bloodthirsty wolf, craving a chance to vanquish anyone sufficiently juiced up in their fear. His muscles burned and grew, his blood rushed through his veins in explosive pulses. Excited with this realization, he rushed back to the Medicine Lodge.

Tom told Chief Black Wolf and the shaman what happened, and as they listened he smelled their fear build. His strength grew, and Tom was intoxicated with the abundance of the terror; anything he desired was for the taking. No one could stop him; he was invincible. Fueled and ramped up with his youthful heightened lust, Tom stormed his way to the women's barracks.

Grabbing the first pretty face near, Tom ripped her clothes off her frail body and raped her as she cried in horror. Her screams only strengthened him.

Chief Black Wolf barreled toward Tom, determined to

knock him down and protect the women. Despite his bravery, the man was no match for Tom. He fought him, along with all the other men at the camp. All who dared to try to stop Tom were mauled with his newly formed claws. They had been helpless against his evil, and he eventually knocked them all out cold.

Still, he needed more, so he sought another. The woman who carried in the stones for the heated lodge was in his sight. He raped her with gratification, knowing his lustful dreams had come true, then he took more women. His addiction to fear was insatiable. The screams were heard throughout the camp.

For two days, he traumatized the remote group. They were stranded and helpless to stop him, most of them young and unaware that such evil had existed. The screams and pleas for mercy, and their fear, had only made him stronger.

On the second day, when it no longer seemed a sport for him, Tom left the camp and returned to Massachusetts with a new handle on life; however, things weren't exactly what his parents had envisioned. His parents soon feared him, and Tom used his new nature to overtake his father's affairs. Before long, Tom ran the business and all financial family concerns. Tom Bennett left his father penniless and shamed; he became a recluse living in the backwoods of the family estate, a man afraid of his son. His parents were still around somewhere, lying under the ground in an unmarked grave. Tom wasn't sure of the spot anymore, nor did he care.

Sitting in his leather chair, pushing back with his weight, Tom closed his eyes and saw images of the men and women overwhelmed with fear and terror, reflected in his victims' eyes. He remembered the smell of fear, the taste of the sweat and blood. These flashbacks of horror filled him with supernatural power. Reliving the cries from long ago gave him power and drove him forward on his path of revenge.

He rolled his eyes and gazed up at the ceiling, savoring his old memories, swallowing the saliva gathering in his mouth. He smiled.

Tom's final revenge was near. He smelled fear in the air. Killing off any memory of Pierre de Gourgues and Bethany, the woman who betrayed him—this was his primary goal. Tom Bennett would have to settle with getting rid of their offspring.

The chance to torment Pierre and Bethany personally had been stolen from him in the end, because of the deadly curse that took them first before his chance. Soon, very soon, he would get rid of the last de Gourgues, and his deepest darkest need would be fulfilled. Every de Gourgues family member would be dead.

Chapter 24

Victoria

After Emilie and Jeremy left the old house to return to Memphis, things seemed eerily quiet. The floorboards groaned under Victoria's feet as she padded across the room. She sat across from Michelle at the kitchen table. She was spreading homemade jam on her rye toast and stopped to sip her coffee. Victoria made small talk. She had resided in Cambridge all her life and knew everyone who wasn't a transient connected to the college. The conversation soon turned serious.

"We both know who murdered Silas's father. It was Tom Bennett, his way of owning your professor. He has leverage over Silas, so Silas is forced to help Bennett ruin your good name. You know I'm right," Victoria said.

She stirred her coffee and stared out the window. Sad memories of her sister's rape haunted her. Even though Bethany ended up married and in love, nothing took away the bitter scar and pain she had been through. Victoria never got over watching her sister in such pain.

"Should I try to get information from Silas one more time? Before it's too late?" Michelle asked.

"No. I think his usefulness is over. Besides, he's a traitor to you, yet he still makes sexual advances toward you. What kind of person does that? He has no morals, and you should stay completely away from the idiot."

Michelle sighed.

"You're right, of course. So what's the next step then?"

Victoria stirred her coffee, thinking with her eyes half shut.

"Aunt Victoria, you have a sneaky look about you this

morning."

"Let's try Detective Ramsey again," Victoria said. The idea roused her to life and she sat straight up in her chair, alert now. "I know Tom Bennett has some hold over Ramsey, and he owes a payment of some sort, but still, he's a police officer at heart. I've found that most cops, even the ambitious types, still believe in good and evil. I think we can reason with the man if we can just get him to listen for a moment."

Michelle nodded in agreement. "Okay, let's go back to his office."

"No." Victoria shook her head. "This time I'm going to his house, alone."

Victoria smiled.

"I play bridge with his wife, and there's a game today."

Michelle's eyes widened as she snickered.

"Aunt Victoria, you've been holding out on me."

"I didn't place it until yesterday when we were going over the list of names from that old book. I saw the address, and the bulb came on," Victoria explained.

Michelle laughed as they cleared the table. Another big day and time ticked away.

Later in the afternoon, Victoria left for her bridge game. She planned what she would do at her friend's house, snooping for anything that could help. She would discreetly check the bedroom on her way to the washroom and, if she was lucky, look in his office, too.

She arrived at the house and parked. It had been a while since the last card game at the Ramsey house. She closed her eyes a moment and tried to remember the layout. *Maybe there was a secret room.*

Laughing at her over-active imagination, she got out of her car and slammed the door. It felt good to blow off a little of the tension. Victoria was determined to behave natural while peeping.

After Victoria walked through the doorway, everything rolled into place. The four women sat across from each other, slapping cards down on the table for almost an hour.

"Excellent. We take it again," Victoria said.

She reached the center of the table and gathered the cards. She packed them together and started to shuffle.

"We're having a good afternoon," Claire said.

Claire was a wiz at cards, and she smiled a lot, especially when they won. They had been playing Bridge for years, and Victoria never made the connection that Claire's husband was the same detective who questioned Michelle all those years ago. Claire Ramsey never spoke about her husband all these years, always too involved in the game. Victoria was glad for that because now no one would suspect when she left the table to snoop.

Victoria pounded the deck against the table, snapped them in one last shuffle, then laid them down and rose from her chair.

"Okay, ladies, before we start another hand, I need to visit the powder room. Excuse me for a moment."

She grabbed her purse and discretely headed for the bathroom. Her friends' laughter drifted down the hall; she was confident they didn't suspect anything. She scooted into the bedroom, went to the dresser first, and rummaged through the drawers, but found nothing. She searched the nightstand next, only finding the basic things expected, reading glasses, a few books, and magazines, some aspirin, Kleenex, but nothing incriminating. *What did you expect? A secret file he read at night?* Victoria rejoined her friends.

The cards were passed out, and they all picked up their hand.

"You know, Claire, you have such good taste in furniture," another woman said.

Victoria chimed in as she arranged the cards in her hand.

"Yes, I agree."

Claire blushed, her face lit up with excitement.

"I just redecorated my husband's office. He didn't want me to fuss, but I was so tired of the old desk he had. And the walls needed something to liven the room up," Claire said.

"Oh, Claire, how about a tour?" Victoria said.

She laid down her cards, thankful for the turn in the conversation. *A lucky break.* She followed the other women. They discussed draperies as Victoria searched the room, her eyes roaming from corner to corner, looking for anything questionable or out of place. Everything looked normal. *Where would secret papers be?* she asked herself. Victoria walked behind the desk and covertly opened the drawers one at a time. No one seemed to notice. There was one last drawer on the right side. She tugged at it, but it wouldn't budge. *Locked! A secret drawer!* She grabbed the letter opener from on the desktop and intended to jimmy the lock. Just as she slid the pointed end into the keyhole, Deputy Detective Ramsey stepped into the room.

His eyes shot across the room to her, standing behind his desk. She melted from his stare. He noticed her hand on the drawer. She jerked it away and hid the letter opener behind her back. He glared. Victoria begged herself not to look guilty, but it was too late for the innocent look. Her face burned; it was probably bright red by now. She hoped he often saw red-faced middle-aged women, since his wife was experiencing menopause herself, and wouldn't make anything of her appearance. Victoria's head was going to explode. *Did he know who she was?* They never were properly introduced after all, and it was years since that night in the precinct office. *Would he suspect why she was there behind his desk?*

"Okay, ladies, I think the tour is finished. My wonderful husband is home early."

Claire walked over to her husband, pecked him on the cheek, then started to herd everyone out of the room.

"Sorry, Dear, I couldn't help showing off your newly decorated office."

While he was distracted by Claire, Victoria placed the letter knife on the desk, moved away, and joined her friends as they marched out of the room. They all left his office, following Claire back to the living room, like waddling ducks following their mother. He stared as they left, not a word spoken. Victoria sizzled from his glare as she paraded past him. *He must have remembered her.* That was a night no one could forget. Mr. Ramsey didn't take his eyes off her, even after she passed him. His stare burned her back.

Victoria had often been told that she was a woman men couldn't forget, with her tall frame and natural blonde hair, which she had styled feathered around a young face for fifty-something, but more often, it was her demeanor of confidence that men complimented her on. Being a single woman all her life, she had no concrete idea about the full effect she had on men. Right now, Victoria wanted to be oblivious to Mr. Ramsey's physical reaction to her. He stared at her heatedly. She felt guilty because her friend Claire had noticed his stare, too. Claire probably got the wrong idea.

They sat back down to their game and played a hand. Victoria sensed her friend's eyes watching her, but she played the game, nothing was amiss. After just a few minutes, Mr. Ramsey walked into the room. He stood near the card table smiling, but it didn't look sincere.

"Hello again, ladies," he said.

"Claire dear, this woman." He nodded toward Victoria.

She wanted to vaporize and disappear into a puff of smoke.

"I believe she came to my office looking for an appointment yesterday. She stopped by with her niece." He turned his gaze at her and tilted his head down a twitch. "Unfortunately, I was tied up all day. But I was told it was urgent, so maybe we can discuss it now if you don't mind?"

Claire gave Victoria the evil eye. "Oh, where are my manners, please, forgive me. Dear, this is my Bridge partner Victoria. Vicky, did you need to see my husband? What's wrong? You never mentioned any troubles?"

Victoria stood and walked around the card table.

"Oh, it's nothing serious. Claire, I had no idea that your husband was 'the' Deputy Detective Ramsey. My goodness, you kept him a secret all these years. Yes, well, my niece wanted to talk with him about a matter. What a surprise to see him here. So nice to meet you."

Victoria held out her hand, and the detective shook it amicably.

"It would be lovely if you could spare a moment, Detective. Thank you for giving me your time. Claire, I'll be right back."

Claire gave Victoria a weak smile, then dropped her eyes back to the cards. He led Victoria into his office and closed the door.

"What are you doing here? And in my house? I think you're going way over the line."

Victoria raised her eyebrows, injured by his tone.

"I'm so sorry, Detective, but I think you have the wrong idea. I've been coming to your house and playing Bridge with your wife for years. I had no idea she was your wife until now."

He cleared his throat.

"Oh, I'm sorry; guess I'm just a little jumpy lately. So much is going on these days, long hours. Sometimes it gets the best of me," he said.

His face turned red, which looked pleasant against his dark

peppered hair. He was a handsome man. It was too bad he was married and planned on framing her niece.

"Of course, I understand," she said.

"So what was it you two needed? I know who your niece is, I remember."

"You're going to think we're a little crazy after all these years, but my niece and I just wondered if there was an update on that old murder case. You remember, the man named Frank Kain, murdered years ago."

"Seven, but who's counting. The guy was a loser," he said.

"Anyway, we were talking about it, and curiosity got the best of us. Was the case ever solved? We didn't mean to cause trouble, just an update, if you have one you can share."

Victoria spoke softly and calmly, even though her nerves skipped rope. His presence was electrifying. What are his intentions and what did he know? She remained skeptical of his motivations. Clueless as to any other way to proceed, she appealed to any goodness he had left in his heart.

"I'm sorry to say that the murder was never solved."

"That's a shame. Well, at least we know my niece wasn't involved. She was with me the night of the murder."

"What, she was with you?" His voice leaped up an octave.

"Yes. Didn't you ask her where she was?" she said.

"Yes, we did, but she never said anything except that she often slept at her professor's apartment."

"Yes, well, you see, she was upset and mixed up. That was a confusing time. The professor had a temper, you see. I think he was anxious over his mother's illness, and he wound up losing his self-control the night before. My niece called me in tears, and I picked Michelle up. She was distraught over the whole ordeal. Of course, she could have easily pressed charges against Professor Kain, but Michelle refused and instead decided to stay away from the man. I believe you picked her up on campus the next day?"

"Yes, you're correct," he said.

His square jaw tightened, and his forehead scrunched into rolling hills, revealing his discomfort. Deputy Detective Ramsey's muscles in his cheeks pulsed in angst.

"Well, I dropped her off myself, you see."

Victoria smiled, trying to hide her glee over his unease, pleased with herself for coming up with the instant alibi for Michelle. *He should worry, now that she has an alibi, and no one can prove otherwise.*

"Anyway, I just wanted you to know she had an alibi that night. Oh, we went out to eat that night, too. Even though it was years ago, I know the restaurant owner will remember us there. We go to the same place every year on that day to celebrate my birthday."

Her smile broadcast her glee. *Touché.*

"Oh, I see. Well, that's good to know," he said.

The lump in his throat moved up and down. That knot was hard for him to swallow.

"Yes, well, thank you for your time, Deputy Detective Ramsey."

Victoria left the room and returned to the living room to finish the game with her friends. She noticed Claire's stare. She most probably wondered what the drama had been about, but Victoria remained poised and played a cool hand. There were no troubles in the world.

The rest of the evening dragged by. Victoria couldn't wait to get back home and tell Michelle all about the card game.

Chapter 25

Michelle promised to stay at home while Aunt Victoria played cards but abandoned that idea as soon as Jackson called. He wanted to meet right away, his voice sounded urgent. Michelle wrote a note to her aunt and left it on the counter. She called for a cab, grabbed her coat and scarf, and flew out the door, heading to the same place where she had met Jackson the other day, Finnegan's Pub.

The cab pulled up to the curb and Michelle got out, running to the entrance to avoid getting soaked from the pelting rain. Standing under the awning, she brushed off her coat and shook her head. Drops of rain flung off her hair. Stepping inside, she bee-lined past the tables straight to the back room and slipped into the booth across from Jackson.

She smiled. "Hello there. We have to stop meeting like this."

Jackson laughed at her playful attempt at a sultry voice. A candle on the tabletop glowed, its light reflected in his blue eyes. He brushed back his sandy blond hair, exposing his forehead and strong jawline, now covered with a city-chic five o'clock shadow. Jackson was handsome and looked inviting. Michelle wondered about his feelings for her. He liked her, and she could easily fall for him, too. She considered her recent interactions with Silas and realized she fell too easily. When she gave her heart, it left a trail, and she couldn't afford to lose sight of her objective. She decided to dismiss any hope of developing a romantic relationship, and wouldn't allow herself to be impulsive again. She drew in a deep breath and exhaled.

"So, anything more about the book?" he asked while she slipped out of her coat.

"Nothing new that I know of. Emilie took the copies with

them, to read on the plane back to Memphis. If anything else comes up that looks important, I'm sure she'll let us know."

A waitress in a green plaid skirt came over to take their order.

"I'll have an original Irish flu shot," Michelle said.

"One Jameson with a shot for the lady. And you, sir?"

"Make mine a draft." Jackson squeezed his eyes half shut. "A shot and beer, really?"

Michelle giggled. "I feel like a college girl again."

The waitress left to get their drinks.

"So how about the Patriots' game last night?" he said.

"I missed it. I was translating some secret book for a friend." Michelle rolled her eyes.

"Well, I caught the sports highlights on the morning news. It was excellent."

"Of course, they always deliver for the fans," she said.

He waited a moment, then added, "Well, he delivers most always. Hey, I think I can get Bruins tickets for this season. You up for a game or two?"

"I'd love to, but as soon as all this secret business clears, I'm heading back to Memphis. I have a company down there that needs my attention."

"Since when are you all business?" He snickered, his cheeks blushed.

"I have to be. No kidding, it's not easy being the youngest and the person in charge. Not to mention I'm a woman, too. You might think that's not a big deal, but down Mid-south it is."

"All I know, Michelle, is that they're lucky to have you. You're the smartest person I've ever met."

"Thank you, Jackson. You're so kind." She fluttered her lashes, then stopped herself. "I have no idea how you turned out so nice. You certainly didn't get it from your parents."

"Right. Let's change the topic. We can talk about anything other than my parents and the Black Wolf Society."

Jackson took a sip of his beer and wiped the foam from his upper lip with his sleeve. Michelle giggled, then out of leftfield, she blurted something even she didn't know was bothering her. "Do you ever feel someone is watching you?"

"Why, do you? Is someone stalking you?" He turned and looked around the room.

Michelle grabbed his sleeve to get his attention.

"No, I don't think so. Yesterday someone stole my camera."

"I'm sorry to hear that. Maybe you should file a report."

Michelle frowned. "No, I don't think that will do any good. It's just that with all this stuff going on, with your father's secret society and all, well, I feel like eyes are on me. I know it's probably my imagination," she said, "but it feels weird. A few months back, before my father died, Emilie and I were followed when we took a trip to New Orleans. I assumed it was Robert's doing, but he claimed to be innocent."

He choked on his sip of beer and chuckled softly. "Innocence and Robert don't go hand and hand." Smiling, he said, "It's not your imagination. You're a beautiful woman. Of course, there are eyes on you."

Blood rushed to her face. "Thank you."

"Michelle, I hate bringing up my father again, but . . . well, he came home just minutes after I returned the book."

"That was a close call," she said.

"Talk about just in time. He stormed into my room, and I don't mind telling you that I was afraid. I figured he found out that I'd been in his stuff. Instead, he tore into me about seeing you. I reminded him that you were Robert's sister and that we're friends. God! I hate him. He's such a brute."

Jackson took the last sip, thumped his mug down, and lowered his eyes. He stared at the tablecloth, circling his finger around the design in an absent daydream.

"I called my mother and told her to stay away for a while. I left the house and plan on never going back while he's still alive."

Michelle reached out and touched his sleeve again.

"I'm so sorry, Jackson. You can stay at Aunt Victoria's if you want."

He shook his head.

"Thanks, but I made arrangements with friends. I'll be okay."

Relieved that Jackson planned to stay away from his father, she had less to worry about. She cheered up Jackson with more small talk. They kept each other company until the hour grew late and the last call bell rang. She called for a taxi. Jackson escorted her out of the bar as the cab pulled up to the curb. Michelle moved into the back seat, and with a last look over her shoulder, she waved goodbye.

A creepy feeling seized her attention. The same awareness she had experienced before when eyes were watching her in New Orleans, then again the feeling she had at the house in Memphis. A shiver ran down her spine and she pulled her coat snugly. She definitely sensed eyes spying on her. In a rush, she gave the cabbie the address.

"Hurry, please, take me home."

She needed to feel safe again and hoped Aunt Victoria was home so the house wouldn't be empty. Her phone rang.

"Michelle, where are you? I just got home and guess what? You're not here like you promised." Victoria was agitated.

"Sorry, Auntie. Jackson called, and we met at Finnegan's. I'm in a cab right now, heading home."

The cab swerved, and Michelle was thrown from one side of the back seat to the other.

"Yikes! What the hell." Michelle lost her grip and her phone flung from her hand.

"What is it?" Victoria's voice was muffled, coming from the phone that was lying on the back seat. Michelle leaned forward, tugging at the cab driver's jacket, and yelled.

"Are you crazy? What are you doing, trying to kill us?"

"Sorry, lady." He swerved the cab again, his dark eyes popping out of his bony features. He scoured the road and his rearview mirror.

"There's some kind of crazy guy behind us, trying to push me off the road. He almost slammed into us. He's probably some drunk driver. Sorry, lady."

Just then there was a thump against the rear bumper and the car lurched forward.

"Oh my God!" the cabbie shouted.

"What the hell!" Michelle shrieked into the phone, panicked. "Someone's trying to run the cab off the road. Auntie, do you think they're after me? What do I do?"

"I'll call the police," Victoria said. Her voice was calm.

"The cops can't be trusted. Hell, most were on the list. For all I know one of them is following this cab right now."

"Don't panic, Michelle. Where are you?"

Michelle searched for a street sign.

"I'm in Hudson, at the corner of Main and High Street."

"Good. Have the cab stop, then you jump out and run to High. Run, then hide in the closest alley. I'll be at the other end as soon as I can. Just sit there and stay hidden until I get there. Do you understand?" Aunt Victoria said.

Michelle shook her head as the car behind them slammed into the cab again.

"Did you hear me, Michelle?" Victoria repeated.

"Yes. Yes, I heard you. I'll be there," she said.

Slipping her phone into her pocket, she leaned over the seat to talk with the cab driver. She noticed his nametag.

"Listen, Roger, turn at the next intersection and let me out. I think the car behind us will leave you alone. Can you do that?" Michelle said.

"Lady, if I stop the car, they could shoot us both," he said. "It's probably some kind of street gang trying to win points or something."

"My, you have a vivid imagination, Roger. It'll be all right. There are street lights at the intersection and businesses. No way will they do anything crazy like shoot in plain sight. It's better than having them follow you and push the cab off the road, causing an accident, isn't it?"

Michelle reached into her purse and pulled out a wad of money.

"Here, this is all the money I have on me, but it's more than enough to cover your time. Just pull down the street now, while we have a short lead. They had to stop at the last light."

She stole a look back and saw they were going through the light.

"Now Roger!" she demanded

The cabby took a sharp right, then stopped the car. Michelle jumped from the vehicle and started running. The cab pulled away from the curb, back into the street. She looked over her shoulder as the car accelerated and sped off. She was on her own.

Whoever drove the chasing car must have noticed her getting out of the cab. Michelle heard the screeching of tires as the chasing car came to a halt and pulled to the curb. She kept running.

Ducking into the first alley available, she hid in a corner, catching her breath. Michelle realized she was blocks away from the intersection of Main and High Street. She would have to go back two or three streets to get to the meet-up spot. She heard two car doors open and slam shut.

Michelle stayed hidden in the shadows, pressing her body as close to the building as possible. She turned her head, squeezed her eyes, and peered down the alley toward Main Street. She made out the silhouette of two men standing under the light, too close to her position for comfort.

One of the men said, "You go that way and I'll go down here." She waited until they split up and went in opposite directions down the street.

Desperate, feeling like a trapped rat, she needed to find a way out. She spotted a door off the alley. Michelle took the opportunity, ran to the back door, and turned the handle. "Please be open, please be open," she whispered to herself. She pulled the handle and pushed. The door nudged open, and Michelle ducked in. Familiar smells of wasabi, cabbage, garlic, and soy sauce filled her nostrils. She had stumbled into the kitchen of a Chinese restaurant. *Thank goodness they stay open late.* A man who worked there walked in, noticed her, and started talking loudly at her in what she trusted was Mandarin.

Michelle didn't understand a word but knew she needed to get out of there. She ran through the kitchen, passing stainless steel prep tables and gas ranges, and made it to the front of the restaurant. She passed by an aquarium filled with angelfish, hustled to the front window, and looked out between the curtains to see if she could spot either of the men who had chased the cab. The street appeared empty. She could see the corner of Main and High just another street sign away. She turned around and faced the restaurant worker.

The man repeated his rant of words she couldn't understand, adding body language with arms flying.

"Thank you," she said while smiling and bowing her head, then she took off.

She didn't run, but instead strode at a brisk pace down the

street, then turned into the alley between two buildings just before High Street. Slowing her pace, she let her eyes adjust to the darkness. The alleyway was dingy and eerily quiet. The rain had stopped, but the pavement was still wet, and streaks of light from the neon business signs reflected off the puddles on the blacktop. A car passed by on the main street and blinded her with the glare of headlights. She raised her arm and shielded her eyes, then waited as they re-adjusted to the gloom. Standing there, in the center of the alley, made her a target. So, she bolted to the edge of the old building and worked her way down. There were trashcans, crates, and junk edging the brick wall. She maneuvered around them, careful not to make a sound. Her heels clicked against the tar, and she cursed herself for wearing the wrong shoes again.

Michelle halted near a large dumpster and used it to hide from open view. She waited a moment, listening for signs of her pursuers. Instead, a couple of cats mewled, yowled, and yelped. The noise haunted the space. Another noise, from farther down the passageway, stole her attention.

An indistinguishable scratching sound came from the dumpster and sent a shiver down her spine. Stories by Poe jumped to mind, and she remembered how people were tormented by the sounds of the night that dared to play against the guilty conscience. She had nothing to feel guilty about. Nevertheless, she felt guilty.

Suddenly, garbage fell over the dumpster's top edge. Junk fell to the ground with a crash and sprawled across the road. The racket echoed between harboring walls as a lone metal trashcan rolled across the alley clinking. A rat scampered from the pile of rotten trash; its claws grating against the pavement.

Michelle jumped back, away from the bin. Her hands flung up to her chest. She held her breath, afraid that the rodent might turn around and scamper toward her. A split thought;

178

the noise could have attracted the wrong attention.

She froze and listened. All was quiet again, except for the water that dripped from a nearby drain spout. And, of course, her beating heart, banging against her chest so hard that it threatened to jump out of her rib cage. Standing still shivering, not because she was cold, but out of fear, Michelle wondered who was chasing her and why. She didn't dare make a sound.

Chapter 26

Michelle pressed against the wall, silently catching her breath. Calmer now, she slipped to the far end of the alley and hid behind the last dumpster, which also overflowed with garbage. The sour smell of fermented fruit and vegetable peelings reminded her of the New York City garbage strike back in the summer of 2006. She had met up with some friends for a shopping spree, and the smells of the city had been horrid. The fetor in this alley was horrible, too, but worsened still when a breeze blew down the alleyway and wafted in the stench of urine.

She gagged and covered her mouth. Her reflux burned the back of her throat. The more she contemplated the horrible smell, the more she wanted to vomit. She needed to think of something else because she was stuck there until her aunt arrived. The trip down memory lane proved a distraction only for a moment. She kept scrunched down and remained motionless while waiting for Aunt Victoria to find her.

The minutes passed like hours, and Michelle found it hard to stay still. She was antsy and fidgeted, trying to get more comfortable. Her foot slipped and collided into a bottle, sending it rolling across the alley, clattering. It knocked into some unstable garbage on the other side, toppling the junk over in a crash. *Why do I keep wearing shoes with slippery soles?* She peeked around the corner toward Main Street, hoping the noise didn't attract attention. Too late, a man stood under the streetlight at the other end of the alley.

Dread tightened her throat, and fear welled from within her. Her heart pumped fast, her pulse vibrated against her skin. She dared not move a muscle, so squinted to see better. His shape stood out like a dark ink spot on a white sheet of paper.

As she stared, the lamppost cast an illusion around him. He looked like a phantom or monster. Michelle imagined him as an incubus waiting to consume her. She shook her head, *stop imagining things*. The last thing she needed was to panic.

The silhouette grew and spread across the alleyway, creeping closer to where she hid. The long arms grew and bulked. *Were those claws?* Sharp pointed tips extended from the end of each finger's shadow. The man bent his head back, and Michelle heard it inhale with a snort, sniffing the breeze like a feral dog hunting its prey. The cold night air blew down the alley, away from him. Thankfully, she was downwind. She held her breath, petrified the thing would find her still and kill her.

The soft hum of a car approached. It turned, and a bright light illuminated the alley. The car's high beams faced Main Street. The headlight lit the passageway and exposed the figure that originated the shadow, Tom Bennett. He raised his arms and shielded his eyes from the unexpected harsh light.

Michelle jumped out from her hiding place and ran to her aunt's compact, squinting through the blast of light. Victoria sat behind the wheel, reached over, and pushed the door open. Michelle hurried into the passenger seat.

"Thank God you're here."

"Are you okay?"

"Just get out of here quick," Michelle screeched.

Victoria shifted into reverse, and the car zoomed backward. Then she shifted into drive and stomped on the gas pedal. They barreled down the street until she put as much distance as possible between them and that alley.

"I'm so glad to see you!" Michelle said. She wiped her brow; her hands were shaking.

"What was that about? I could have sworn that was Tom Bennett at the top of the alley," Aunt Victoria said.

"He was going to kill me. That was too close. I think he

tracked me, like hunted prey. It was so weird. Thank you for coming to my rescue, Auntie."

Michelle tried to make sense of the image she witnessed in the alley, her imagination stressed to the max. *Maybe it had been an illusion.* No one could turn into a monster, not even Tom Bennett. She almost fainted by the sheer horror of the idea.

"Good thing I know my way through the back streets and got there in time." Aunt Victoria gazed over and gave her a tap. "Now, take a deep breath and calm down. We need to keep a cool head. Maybe I should drive to the police station?"

"And say what? Tom Bennett hunted my niece? I don't think that will fly. Technically no wrong committed, he didn't do anything—yet." Michelle crunched her lips, disgusted with the possibilities running through her mind.

Chapter 27

Tom Bennett

The other man who joined Tom Bennett was a young lawyer who wanted to become a politician. He had pledged his allegiance to the secret society, after asking for help to win the election. Of course, that meant he was obliged to play foot soldier. Tom summoned his help to surveil Michelle de Gourgues. The new recruit never questioned the master, only followed his orders. When the girl jumped out of the cab and slipped into the night, the chase became interesting. Tom ordered the new recruit to search the northern direction, and the recruit would soon return to the car without the girl.

Tom Bennett slid out from the driver's seat and followed Michelle's trail down the dark alley. Her scent ended near one of the back doors. He tried the handle, but it was locked. He went farther down the alley to pick up her scent again, but the trail went cold. His animal instincts told him she had ducked in that locked door. He went back and pounded on the door. The door opened a sliver, and someone yelled to him in Mandarin.

No time for this. Tom Bennett kicked in the door with his foot and pushed the man aside. The man fell back into a stack of crates filled with cabbage and onions. They knocked over, spilling across the floor. Two other young employees, maybe the older man's sons, rushed to the back kitchen to see what happened. When they saw Tom, they raised their arms and hands and started making martial art movements. Tom Bennett shoved them aside with hard punches, blazing through the kitchen, to the front of the restaurant. A young, thin woman, playing hostess to an empty room, froze when Tom stormed into the room filled with small tables. He advanced towards the front window. She turned and disappeared through another side door.

He found Michelle's scent again by the door and followed its path into the street. She was nowhere in sight, so he rushed to catch up. He rushed past the alley, then stopped and backtracked from the corner of Main and High.

Tom Bennett stood at the curb, sniffing the air, lifting his head toward the sky, searching for her scent, and listening for the sound of her heartbeat. His shadow loomed down the alley, his silhouette stretched across the pavement, haunting the road. The wind against him, he lost the scent.

Tom heard cars in the distance, a cat calling out to the night, and the scurrying of rodents. Then the soft rhythmic thumping of her heart.

A car's high beams blinded his eyes. Tom raised his hands to block the glare. He recognized Michelle's long legs running to the car. She got in, and the car sped away.

Seething with anger over losing his prey, Tom punched the brick wall nearest him. *That wasn't supposed to happen.* Michelle wore on his nerves like a true de Gourgues, a thorn in his side. Tom had promised Robert he would get his sister out of their way, and the poor sap never dreamed the true meaning of the intentions. A more deserving plan for Michelle sprung into Tom's mind. He wanted her dead, of course, but now more was warranted. She dared make a fool of him in front of one of his new recruits.

It had been a while since he indulged in bloody carnage. He'd been saving himself to gorge on Victoria, but Michelle would do nicely as a first course. His mouth watered as he envisioned tearing that troublemaker limb to limb. He would avenge the insult he endured because of her.

If he had caught her tonight, no one would have been the wiser nor associated her disappearance with him. He was supposedly in NYC for business and had the alibis standing up, nicely in a row. That was the beauty of the secret society. When he needed the law to overlook things, it was convenient having the Deputy Superintendent of Special Affairs as a foot soldier. Ramsey had said from the beginning that he couldn't do anything brutal. Hiding paperwork and planting evidence was a great asset, too. Soon, he may be required to do more.

Years ago, Ramsey had contacted Tom.

"Someone from Montana called my office. They told me all about the damage you caused while visiting a retreat. I hear you have some sort of power now."

At first, Tom assumed he was being threatened.

"Who called you?"

Ramsey went on. "Don't worry. You haven't done anything to get in trouble, yet. I have someone I want you to meet. He's the local leader of the Black Wolf Society. The old guy's dying and the group needs a new leader. I think with your secret talents that you'd be the perfect fit."

How could Tom have refused? Since then, the Society helped him throughout the years, and he returned the favor by using his gifts to get things done. Recently, however, Ramsey had been challenging some of Tom's decisions and making him second-guess his moves. He needed to think, hating when things didn't go as planned. He drove home after impressing upon the new recruit that the situation was still under control.

Tom stepped into his office, ready to calm down so that he could plan his next attack on Michelle. Of course, that meant he would have to find her again.

Immediately something seemed off. A human scent lingered in the house that didn't belong. He searched the room in a frenzy, sniffing everything in the room. It didn't belong to the help or his son. The scent smelled like his prey, Michelle, mingled in with other smells.

Tom raced up the stairs and barged into Jackson's room. It was empty. He went to his desk and picked up the jacket that hung on the chair. Jackson's coat reeked like Michelle de Gourgues. Tom's temper flared. He threw the jacket onto the floor, then tore the room apart like a wild animal, shredding even the drapes and wallpaper.

Chapter 28

After driving a few miles, Victoria slowed the car and merged onto another street. "We need to think. I don't think it's safe to go home. If that was Tom Bennett chasing you, he'll be watching the house."

"Agreed. So let's stay off the routine."

Aunt Victoria drove aimlessly for a while, heading east. "How about we go to the shore? We're heading in that direction anyway. Besides, some fresh air will do us both good."

Michelle nodded, not in a talkative mood. They drove until they saw the ocean. Victoria parked the car and got out. Michelle grabbed the car blanket in the back seat and followed. Together they covered up with the blanket and took a slow walk along the beach in quiet company. Michelle had a lot to sift through in her mind.

The cold Atlantic breeze stung Michelle's face, but it felt good. She was alive. Shivers ran through her from the cold damp. She pulled up the collar of her coat and tugged the blanket closer. The sound of the waves beat with even tugs and pulls, humming in her head and calming her jagged nerves. She needed this time to clear her mind. It had been a long night. Drinking until closing time, then scared out of her wits, and with no sleep—it was all taking its toll.

Frazzled, Michelle had too many unanswered questions plaguing her intellect. It was high time to answer the worries. She did something she hadn't considered doing for a long time. She prayed. *Lord, please give us a sign. I need your guidance. I need your blessing.* The sky began to lighten in the distant east as dawn drew near. The seagulls squawked and flew around in groups as they pillaged the leftover garbage along the beach line.

"Now what, Auntie? Tom Bennett is gunning for me. I guess framing me wasn't enough. He wants me dead."

"Yeah. Something like that," Victoria said.

Her voice trailed off, she was in another conversation somewhere else.

"Great." Michelle swallowed hard and held back tears that lingered close by. She vowed to remain strong; it was the only choice.

They left the beach and found a small place that just opened its doors and served morning coffee. They sat outside on the patio at the Gallery Cafe, enjoying their Starbucks and the sounds of the city waking up. They needed to contemplate their next move.

"We need backup," Aunt Victoria said.

"Ya think?" Michelle replied. "Should I call my sister? My brother? Call the police? No matter who, they'll all think we're nuts."

Victoria stopped talking and put her arm around Michelle.

"You and I are the only ones who truly understand this situation. Even your sister doesn't know everything about him, what a monster Tom Bennett is, and why. He hates your father, wants revenge, and now he's using your brother to get you out of the way. All so he can get his grubby hands on your family's money. Next, he'll go after Emilie, then Robert, too, I'm afraid for us all."

Michelle sat back in the chair and looked out at the ocean. The faint line of dawn grew brighter now as the sun stretched its rays like tired arms, edging higher into the sky. She turned and watched her aunt. Her face seemed pensive. Victoria stood and stared out across the water, mesmerized and far away in her memories. "I should have had him arrested years ago. Or maybe I should have shot him dead myself."

Michelle dropped her head. She hated hearing her aunt's

regrets. Victoria had been nothing but a pillar of strength when Michelle needed her most. She had been a rock for her mother, too. There was no blame to be put on Aunt Victoria.

"I'm sorry, Michelle. I know it's crazy to talk this way. Please forgive me."

"Auntie, please stop blaming yourself. You did nothing wrong. Besides, there was no way of knowing he would turn out to be such a psycho. We don't know that he actually wants us dead. We're assuming things. He might just be toying with us, like some deranged jerk. Maybe it's just about the money."

Victoria seemed hesitant, she had more to tell but was afraid to share any more bad news. Michelle wondered how much more there could be. *How much do I want to know?*

"Listen, Aunt Victoria, if you have anything else, know anything else, now is the time to share. Full disclosure seems the wisest way to roll, considering the danger we're all in. This affects us all."

Michelle looked at her aunt with a stern stare, waiting for her to share.

"I'm assuming nothing. I know he wants us all dead, and that includes me, too. He threatened to kill me and I believe he will someday."

Victoria pulled a letter out of her pocket.

"This was folded and hidden in part of that book your sister translated. Go ahead, read it," she said.

Michelle took the piece of paper from her hands. It was a letter, held together by shreds, worn where it had been folded and unfolded many times. Written years ago and signed by Tom Bennett, the scribbled letter was addressed to Victoria, and it spewed hateful threats of murder and vengeance. The last sentence jumped off the page . . . *"I will tear you to pieces."*

Michelle swallowed hard and folded the paper back up with trembling hands.

"He's crazy. What if he discovers this is missing from the book?"

Michelle's stomach turned. The danger that taking this put them all in, especially for Jackson, troubled her. She turned away and stared blankly, then noticed Victoria's face fade.

"Oh my, I'm so sorry. I never considered the consequences of keeping the letter."

Michelle reached out to steady her aunt, who seemed a bit woozy, swaying while still on her feet. "Let's sit down a moment." Michelle guided Victoria to a bench seat. She took a deep breath, pulling her bearings together, not wanting Aunt Victoria to realize how afraid she was. She swallowed hard, clearing her voice. "Are you all right, Auntie?"

"Yes, I'm fine now."

"Hopefully, the man won't miss the letter." Michelle didn't believe that for a minute. It was obvious that Bennett read that letter as a frequent ritual; he was obsessed. Still, she didn't want to scare her aunt, so she tried to shift away from any blaming. "It's pointless to regret taking a letter. There's so much more to consider right now."

"Yes, that man is crazy and dangerous. We're also dealing with the evil society he leads, and we have no idea how deep the society goes. We can't even depend on the police for help. Half of the members listed are involved in law enforcement in one form or another, beginning with Ramsey, who's now in charge of criminal investigations!"

For a while, they sat quietly on the bench and pondered the situation as they sipped their coffee.

"There has to be someone else besides Ramsey, someone we can trust." Michelle blew her coffee, thinking about who they might be able to trust, then turned to Victoria, raising her eyebrows. "You never said what happened at the Ramsey house?"

"Nothing helpful. I'm not sure if he has a conscience left." Michelle wrinkled her nose.

"I hate asking my sister for help, but the more people we have nearby whom we can trust, the better. No one else is going to believe this craziness or that Deputy Ramsey is a bad guy. Hell, I have a hard time thinking that of him myself, even though I heard what he said with my own ears," Michelle said.

"Maybe we can still reach Ramsey's conscience and try convincing him this has gone too far. I don't know what Tom Bennett has over him, but it can't be that bad. He seems decent enough. Maybe I can get his wife to talk to him with me?"

Michelle scowled. "I don't think that will work."

"You know, I'm proud of how well you've taken all this weird stuff. It's a lot to carry for such young shoulders. Why just a few hours ago, you were chased down an alley. Who knows what could have happened if that monster had caught you." Victoria shivered.

Michelle drew in a deep breath and exhaled slowly.

"As much as I love walking the beach and drinking coffee, we need to get moving. They'll soon figure out we aren't going home and will start expanding the search. Who knows how many eyes Tom Bennett has and how many people owe him favors."

Victoria slipped her arm through Michelle's and kissed her cheek. They walked back to the car huddled arm in arm.

Chapter 29

Emilie

Early in the morning, Emilie and Jeremy had left Aunt Victoria's house and headed back to Memphis. After spending the previous day translating the book that Jackson had found, they uncovered information about the Black Wolf Society. They learned the group existed as scattered clusters throughout the world and discovered that Tom Bennett's little piece of the Society seemed to be operating in a realm of its own. They engaged in illicit activities, and their mission veered from the main, often committing serious infractions with the law. It was all listed in the book under Beneficial Acts. They planted incriminating evidence, bought political candidates, and the list progressively got worse. They performed sinister acts of torture and even murder.

As they sat on the plane, Emilie and Jeremy reviewed the translated pages they had copied. Emilie found a passage of interest. "Jeremy, look at this. It seems Bennett is more of a mad man than we supposed. Look here." She pointed to a passage. "It says he has a secret weapon that he found while at a tribal retreat back in 1972."

Jeremy took the notebook from her and read where she pointed, shaking his head in disbelief. "This isn't possible, is it? Are you sure this was translated correctly? My God, knowing this puts us all in danger. What exactly is this referenced secret power?"

"And what does it mean to us?" Emilie shivered.

"Emilie, are you all right?"

"Yes, I'll be all right if you stop worrying, please. I can sense that you're troubled."

"Of course I am, but I'll work on it," he said. "First, we need to alert the authorities about this group. They sound more dangerous than we imagined. Maybe they're terrorists. It sure reads like it," he said.

"I think we should check this out first and see if this information is for real," she said.

"Yes, I agree. Besides, the police will need to see proof, or else they'll never believe us, especially since Ramsey is one of them. And just how would we explain these translated pages from a book that's locked away? We would have to tell them how we got it, then Jackson would get into trouble, too."

Emilie covered her face with her hands, then looked up at Jeremy almost in tears.

"Jeremy, you're right. We should check it out. This is dangerous, and we can't fool around. But, we need to get Michelle away from these people right away. Aunt Victoria, too, especially since her name is on this list."

Jeremy nodded.

"I have an idea. Let's turn this jet around and go north to Montana and find out what happened up there back in 1972 when Bennett found the secret weapon. We need to know what Bennett's secret is and understand what we're up against."

Jeremy turned the pages of the notebook. She reached over and pointed to a page.

"We need to visit the Blackfeet reservation to see if anyone remembers what happened back in 1972. Someone must know something. Horrible things, and men as evil as Bennett, don't happen in our lives every day. They leave scars behind," she said.

Emilie got up, walked to the front of the plane, and spoke with the pilot, instructing him to change course. They flew to Montana, hoping to find someone who had answers. The plane landed at the Glacier Park International Airport. They rented a car and began their trek toward Chief Mountain.

It was a sunny autumn day. They drove an hour and a half, following Route 2 through the mountain valleys of the Flathead Range. Later they reached the prairie, spilling across the horizon with dried sweetgrass as they got closer to Browning. Emilie opened the car window to smell the dry swath, burnt from the summer days gone by, now dormant and ready for the winter cold. It smelled like the good earth and filled her soul with a sense of belonging to the relaxing tempo of nature. Miles away in the background stood the majestic peaks of East Glacier Park and forest. The leaves of the trees had turned, for the most part, leaving the mountain edges with only a soft glow, a shining gold rim of foliage that edged its purple stony peaks.

They arrived in the small town of Browning, the Blackfeet reservation hub, which sat in the middle of the wide-open terrain. Blue skies feathered with random clouds softened the town's lonely streets, and the mountains made an illusionary backdrop. The area seemed more like a painting than a real place, Emilie mused, *if there could be magic it would be here.*

"It looks like Central Avenue is the main drag in this small town," Jeremy said. "Look, it's lined with retro motels, souvenir shops, and stands dotting the street."

They drove east, then back again until they found the Blackfeet Heritage Center.

"Jeremy, this is the place. Pull in here to the right."

When she got out of the car, the west wind blew down from the mountainside and tinged her cheeks with a burning sensation. The air smelled fresh, crisp, and indicated snow was soon to visit the area. They weren't dressed for the weather, but they didn't mind the cold. Emilie pulled her arms tight to keep herself warm. She drew in a deep breath, appreciating the refreshing clean air.

They went inside and viewed the exhibits, impressed by the varied displays of cultural artwork and fossils. They asked for directions for the tribal offices. They got back into the car, drove a short distance, and found one of the office sites. They went in and asked to speak with one of the leaders or historians of the tribe.

Moments later, they stood face to face with Chief Flying Crow, a handsome man in his early thirties. He was tall with dark shiny hair pulled back and a muscular yet lean body. His face was bright and honest. He wore designer jeans and a blue Oxford buttoned shirt covered by a corduroy sports jacket that fell loose on his frame.

"Hello there, my name is Chief Flying Crow, but please call me Fred."

He extended his hand and they all shook acquaintance.

"Please be seated and we can talk."

"Thank you kindly, Chief Flying Crow. My name is Emilie de Gourgues and this is my friend Jeremy Laughton. We came here today to research some history."

The Chief smiled. It was an irresistible smile, with bright teeth and a strong face. He appeared professional. His aura reached out to Emilie, and she intuited his goodness of heart and smiled back at him. Emilie turned and smiled at Jeremy to let him know Chief Flying Crow had passed her clairvoyant test.

"We're happy to discuss our history with travelers. As you may know, it's a continual challenge for our tribe to spread the truth. We're currently in the process of reviving our culture's language, and any support is appreciated."

"We understand, and I'm sure that I can help in that effort with a donation."

The Chief smiled and nodded his thanks.

"The thing we're searching for is a particular truth that probably was never written down. It's not an ancient custom we seek, but something that happened."

His left eyebrow shot up, and she sensed his skepticism.

"Chief Flying Crow, we're looking for information about something that happened back in 1972. We wonder if you have any records of the campsites that participated in Medicine Lodges back then, with white people as customers or anyone who came and took part in a treatment center," Jeremy said.

The Chief sat upright with his back straight.

"Yes, we do have some records. I thought I recognized your last name, Emilie. Is your mother Bethany de Gourgues?"

She dropped her head, not expecting the reminder of her mother. No matter how much time passed, Emilie still reacted with deep feelings every time her mother's name was mentioned.

"Yes. Bethany is . . . was my mother. Why? How do you know of her?"

"Your mother and the friend she came with were the only other people who knew about the incident besides those involved."

"A friend? Who?" Emilie asked.

"Eddie was his name."

"You mean Father Eddie? He was a priest?" Jeremy said.

"Of that, I'm not sure. It's true though, there was an awful incident that occurred in 1972 at a nearby camp. Years ago, your mother came here to ask questions. She met with my father, and he told her the truth, but she had already known some of it somehow. I think your mother was a powerful woman and had a special mystic ability. I wonder. Do you have her ability, too?"

Emilie smiled, happy that for once, her clairvoyant gift

wasn't a subject of ridicule nor denial, but looked upon as a gift, as it should be.

"Yes, my gift is empathy. I feel things."

Fred's brow went up again, and this time a grin flashed, too.

"I can help you in two ways," he said.

Jeremy leaned forward. "Tell us. Flying Crow, what two things?"

"The first thing I can do for you is to reveal facts about the incident that happened. It was before my time, but my father was there, and he passed the knowledge to me." He chuckled. "I considered it just another tale he dreamed up to warn people until the day your mother came to visit. I was just a small boy, but I realized the story was real and that we needed to keep vigilant against the evil that was unleashed back in 1972."

"You know what happened? Tell us, please," Emilie said.

"I will, and I can show you where it happened if you need to see it."

"What's the second thing you can do for us?" Jeremy asked.

"The second thing is for Emilie alone. I can help her develop her special gift. She'll need it sharpened, in preparation for the probable assault."

Emilie saw Jeremy's face turn pale. She took his hand and gave him a gentle stroke with two fingers, and he returned a faint smile.

"We're in your hands, Chief Flying Crow. Please, tell us everything you can. We want to be as prepared as possible," she said.

The Chief delved into the story entrusted to him by his father. He spoke with reverence, and Emilie trusted his word as truth.

"In my role as Chief, I practice the old ways. I perform ceremonies to help strengthen and heal my people. I practice the Medicine Lodge, in the tribal sense of the word. I heal through nature and spiritual rituals. We still use the sacred Sweat Lodges and Vision Quests to help people find their soul's true path," he said.

"The Blackfeet believe there's a magical veil that separates our world from the time of our ancestors. A pathway between the two dimensions in time becomes available during our ceremonies so that we can communicate with the ghosts of our ancestors. We channel over to their side of the veil to remember our culture and learn the old ways from our ancestors to keep the tribe alive. There's a native prophecy, *we shall return in your children's children*. That was the promise of the Ghost Dance, but unfortunately, that practice led to a path of destruction and hurt our people. But there are other ways. We have many ceremonies.

"Some ridicule our beliefs, but our future world depends on the ghosts of the native peoples returning. The ghosts of our ancestors will view this modern world through our eyes, the current dwellers of the threshold, then are the spark of the tribe's future. We have ceremonies like the Sun Dance and the Giveaway Dance, which practice communicating with the ancestors. But sometimes it's not safe, like what happened back in 1972. You see, it's not just the tribe that can traverse time to the beyond, then return to the present. It could happen for anybody, even a white man like Tom Bennett."

Emilie gasped. "You know his name?"

He nodded yes.

"Let me explain. The ceremony opens a window in time and space. Some rules should be followed to keep everything safe, and we must avoid taboos, to prevent unintended travel of evil between the veils. First, there's a sweat lodge to cleanse our spirit, which helps to keep any corruption from occurring between the veils. When an exchange happens between the two sides, it can be fatal if the wrong energy passes through the veil. So we have rules to prevent corruption, for example, cleansing first, fasting, then staying away from burial grounds. That's to prevent evil ghosts from passing through."

Jeremy asked, "Is that what happened? Bennett corrupted the veil?"

"Exactly. Our existence here is an unstable state that we need to keep in balance. Our immortal being, or should we call it our soul, lies between what went before and what will come. As long as we understand the power and respect the possible danger of that power, our knowledge can open the window to our ancestors. We enter their time, hear their teachings, and learn healing powers. Everything that was lost can be accessible again through that window. This is how our tribe will survive. I learned the healing power and use Dream Medicine to sustain the health of the community. We use the power of the open window to learn our ways again, to save our people."

The Chief was smiling, but his stare remained serious. He seemed to be assessing their reaction to his claims. His eyes were keen and intelligent. Emilie was touched by the ideas he shared and the plight of the Blackfeet and their struggle to get back their heritage and traditions. His critiquing eyes searched for her response. She grew warm under his scrutiny and had to move. She stood.

"I understand this magic has deep roots of power and that Bennett had perverted that power somehow, and a catastrophe erupted. But I want to know more about this power and how I can use it wisely. Chief Flying Crow—"

"Please call me Fred," he said.

"Fred, please explain the second thing you can do for me alone. I want to be able to control and use my gift to help."

199

"Emilie, I sense that a horrible event stands in front of you. I wasn't surprised to see you here today. In a way, I expected you. Over the years, I've tried to keep tabs on Tom Bennett after my father told me what happened. I know something evil is fringing. I can teach you how to control your power, and you'll be able to use it when needed. Come, you two; let's go back into my office. I'll show you on the map where the incident happened back in 1972."

Chapter 30

Emilie

Chief Flying Crow led them to a private office at the end of a long hallway. A large window streamed light into the room, warming the space. The table and chairs were plain but new. The wall opposite the window displayed a large map of the local area, marked with points of interest, mountain peaks, trails, and rivers.

"Have a seat," Fred said. He took a pointing stick and circled an area on the map. "This is where the camp was back in '72, located at Medicine Grizzly Bear near the south side of the lake. It's a beautiful place and a popular hiking spot today, but back then not many visited.

"A young tribesman who knew some of our ceremonies and medicine led the camp up there. Unfortunately, he was still naïve and didn't understand the depth of our magic, or the consequences of corruption. My father was there as a helper, just beginning to learn the medicine ways himself."

Fred went to a desk in the corner of the room and pulled out a file. Turning, he slapped it onto the table in front of Emilie. The contents spilled out. She picked up the papers and started reading. A jolt of revulsion shot through her body when she spotted the pictures. She swallowed back reflux that burned the back of her throat. She made noises while clearing her windpipe.

"Here, take a sip of this water."

Fred handed her a bottle and she unscrewed the cap and took a sip.

"Thanks." Emilie's attention returned to the files.

She picked up the file with trembling hands. Evil permeated the pages and she bore the horror of what had happened years ago. She leafed through the documents sensing the emotional pain attached to the event.

She closed her eyes and envisioned the young women crying in pain with their faces cut and bleeding. Images filled her mind. She touched the photos, tracing the lines of the faces and the injuries with her finger. Emilie felt the sting of a sharp razor's edge.

The trauma of the people's experiences weighed heavy on her soul, the fear and horror. Her own spirit dropped into sadness so intense, she worried about becoming entrapped in its mire. She dropped the folder; the pages splashed out and littered the tabletop. She pushed them away. Jeremy reached over and grabbed her hand, then rubbed her arm, soothing her back to balance again.

"You'll be alright. It's over now," Jeremy said.

Emilie feigned a smile.

"You already have a strong understanding of what happened," Fred said. "Everything will work out as it should." The timbre of his voice calmed her. It was an odd thing, like a misty layer of hope crept back into her soul at the will of his words.

"You feel these things, even years later," Fred continued. "I understand that these lingering echoes of emotion can get your soul out of balance. That's where I can help you. I can show you how to use this power to stay in control. You can use it as a strength and healing power, instead of a force pointed against yourself. I've noticed you react to Jeremy's touch. He calms you. Just like his touch brings you back to perspective, you can delve into your own power, and with some added old magic, you can use the energy as a shield to protect yourself and those you love."

She searched his face. His dark eyes glimmered with honesty, he was right.

"Yes, it's critical that I am armed with whatever power I can find because the evil pulsating from these pages is more than deadly. The evil used against these poor people sought to trap their souls. The more fear they showed, the more powerful the evil force had become. It was a cyclone of fear and rage," she said.

"Tom Bennett was a troubled man and needed much help, the retreat leaders understood that much. So the camp directors shared a sweat lodge with him, right here just south of the camp, and tried to cleanse him." Fred pointed to the place on the map.

"They performed a sacred dance, then sent him into the wilderness alone on a Vision Quest. They told him about the ancient spirits, and about how they would try to enter our world through him since he was an open channel. They didn't know that he was still so troubled, even after the sweat lodge. They dropped him off somewhere south of the camp, here near Oldman Lake."

Fred pointed to another area on the map.

"As best they figured, he traveled here along Dry Fork Creek bed, then up toward the north side of the ridge and ended up here at the foot of Rising Wolf Mountain, which is close to Two Medicine region. The Blackfeet consider that place sacred ground. The peak is named *Mahkuyi-opuahsin*, which means *The way the wolf gets up*. Tom Bennett left to find his spiritual familiar, but he came back from the journey no longer a troubled young man, but a monster. His mind and soul had been taken over by an evil spirit hidden in wolf form, and there was no way to return the evil to the other side of the veil once the window closed."

Emilie had experienced the other side of the veil once before when her father had taken part in an ancient ceremony just before he died. She had never been able to explain the experience to anyone else, and hoped that Fred would be a great teacher for her and that she would finally be able to understand her gift.

She shut her eyes and envisioned the scene. She experienced in her mind a troubled soul in the wilderness stumbling over loose rubble and rock. She could feel a strange entity shadowing him; an entity not of this world, but of another that had crossed the veil. Evilness lurked and then had engulfed him, smothering him with a dark force. Her body shook for a moment, then the vision left her. She opened her eyes wide. It took a moment to reorient her eyes to the light. Both men were watching her.

"I'm okay, guys," she said. "Fred, what exactly do you mean by 'he was taken over by an evil spirit'? I want to understand what he is now. There was a dark force presence, but I didn't envision any wolf shape or form."

"I can only say what was told to me. I wasn't there Emilie, but my father said Tom Bennett came back a monster. He returned to the campsite possessed by a demon. Some call it a wolfman, some a shapeshifter, still others a skinwalker. Whatever he was, he appeared wolfish and acted like a monster. He raped a girl, but his lust ran deep, so he raped another, and again, and again. He touched his evil shadow on every young girl there," Fred said.

"You mean he was a serial rapist?" asked Jeremy.

"He's worse than that. He's pure evil. No one could stop him. He was too powerful. Each time the men tried to save the women, he tore at them, ripping off their flesh. He scratched and pulled off the skin of their arms and backs with his claws. He threw their bodies across the campsite like they were rag dolls. All the men and women who were there during the carnage were left with massive injuries and scars. Check out the other pictures."

Chief Flying Crow pulled a manila envelope from under the folder, which contained more photos.

"Here's a photo of my father." He pointed to the top photo, revealing a forearm with scars across the muscles. "And here are pictures of others from the camp with their sleeves rolled up. Look at the thick scars up and down their arms, and check out here their scarred backs."

Emilie examined the photos. Shiny pink embossed skin exposed on film, the scar tissue had formed and covered the wounds. Deep cuts, the gruesome results of the monster's claws. Emilie touched the photos and again shut her eyes and suffered the emotion behind them. Pain and carnage, the fear that had welled up inside of the people . . . then she realized something more. Their fear had been food to the monster. Her mind's eye saw a young Tom Bennett standing in the center of camp, in the middle of the mayhem, soaking up the energy from the other's fear. The intensified emotion turned him into an evolving monster, an ethereal wolf, yet still a man.

The strong image haunted her until she couldn't endure it any longer. Emilie forced herself to return to the present. She jolted and swung her head back and forth, shaking herself out of the hallucination.

"Emilie, are you all right?" Jeremy said.

"Em, come back to me." His voice sounded edgy.

She struggled to pull herself together. Breathing hard, she found her balance point again.

"I'm fine, thank you. You have no idea how much you help me through all this supernatural stuff just by being there for me."

She smiled at him and his mind relax a bit.

"Sorry for the interruption," she said. "Please go on, Chief Flying Crow."

"Please call me Fred, it's okay. Where was I? Oh yes. The camp leader wanted him arrested and put on trial, of course, but the victims were traumatized and afraid of his retaliation; they just wanted to go home and forget what happened. Besides, they couldn't contain him anyway. But when Tom Bennett walked away from the Lodge, the oldest shaman placed a curse on him and outcast him, to never return to Blackfeet. Tom Bennett returned to his own people, back in Cambridge. My father was still a teenage kid, but he phoned Tom Bennett's parents and warned them about his true nature. He alerted the Massachusetts police, too, a Detective Ramsey."

Emilie and Jeremy turned and shared an aha moment.

"Of course, no one believed him," the Chief continued. "Still, my father wanted to do as much as possible. Our tribe only wants healing, so it was his duty to pass the information along. I guess it didn't do much good. I assume the monster managed to hurt your mother and who knows who else."

A shiver ran down Emilie's back, her face cold, all the blood had drained away. "What do you mean, him hurting my mother?"

"Sorry, I figured you knew and that's why you're here. We don't have time to go into that now. Besides, I was just a little boy when Bethany came here to learn the truth. You can ask her friend. He might know more about that than I do. There's something more important to deal with right now. You need to prepare for what's about to happen," Fred said.

Emilie stood and paced the floor.

"Emilie and Jeremy, do you want to go to the mountain? We can get there by following Starr Road," Fred said.

"No," Emilie said. "We need to get back to the family right away. My sister is in danger. This monster wants to hurt her. I can't let anything bad happen to her."

Fred closed his eyes and shook his head, looking defeated.

"I understand. But Emilie, you need to train yourself first. You need to strengthen your gift so you'll be ready when you're face to face with this monster. I saw it. The monster inside Tom Bennett will return."

She reached out and touched his arm. "Fred, I need to leave. I want to learn more, too, but time is running out."

"At least hear the basic aide before you leave."

"Yes, you're right. Please, tell me what to do," she said.

"When you begin to sense the monster's emotions, you'll feel him eating his way into the fear. You'll sense his appetite and his growing strength. When this happens, open yourself up."

She gasped, her hands flying up to cover her mouth.

"Don't be afraid. You know what I'm saying. You underwent that power when you held that folder and saw those photos."

Emilie shook her head, her eyes tearing.

"When you feel the monster's magic creeping in, open yourself up. It's the only way. Open your channels to the other side and you'll see. Your gift will turn to magic, too. You'll have the strength to soak up all his energy, and your gift will turn it into powerful healing. Then you can transcend it outward to everyone around you, including the monster, like a medicine to heal the evil. Think about it. Concentrate, so that when it happens, you'll be ready."

Chief Flying Crow reached his hands out to hers and took hold. She sensed his healing strength from his Dream Medicine and discovered in her heart a truth she had never seen before. In the minutes that passed, he guided her to the right path. Emilie entered another realm, a place that resembled home, a place where she understood all that she needed to know. Chief Flying Crow opened the door and brought her into a place of light. He showed her the way to use the gift of empathy as a shield from this monster and a means to salvation. Time froze. Minutes seemed like hours, then days. Emilie became the student, then the gifted master.

"Thank you, Fred," she said.

He smiled. "One last thing. Take this."

Chief Flying Crow handed her a man's ring. It was gold with a center ruby stone. The ring displayed the Harvard emblem, and the embossed side bore the year 1972.

"This was his class ring. Even though they tossed him out before graduation, Tom Bennett kept his ring. It got lost, or he didn't care any longer, after the incident."

Emilie was confused. "Why give this to me?"

"Maybe when you confront him, he'll notice this trinket and lean once again toward being a man. Maybe not; he might choose to walk away and have it left behind him forever. Either way, it just may give him a little push, a jolt of humanity. Memories can be strong influences."

She took the ring and tucked it into her purse, then Emilie wrapped her arms around Fred and hugged him. Now they shared a bond, both of them exposed to the healing medicine of the ancestors. This new knowledge could save her family; she owed him her life. Emilie knew she could never repay him.

She humbly said goodbye, and Jeremy and Emilie both promised to come back with an update when everything settled. They drove back to the jet and headed directly to Boston. There was no time to waste. During the return flight to Boston, Jeremy called Aunt Victoria, but no one answered at the house. He tried the cells, but no response from Victoria or Michelle. Toward the end of their return flight, he finally got through to Michelle and asked that someone pick them up at the airport.

He kept the conversation short.

Emilie was in meditation, preparing herself for the encounter. With her eyes closed, she went back to the experience she had experienced with the Chief. She practiced pulling the shield that she had recognized. It seemed easier now to maneuver its flexible boundaries. She concentrated on how to control her energy, her empathy, so she could use it as a weapon of good against Tom Bennett. *Just open your channel and absorb Bennett's evil intentions. Sure, no problem!*

Emilie planned to use more than her own power. She would implore her ancient relatives to join her spiritually and assist in this stand against evil. She had undergone their energy once before, the day her father had died, and traveled into the other realm. They had helped her father then, and she needed their help now.

Something bad had begun, and they were about to go face to face with pure evil. Praying to God, she asked for His blessing and His permission for the spirits of her ancestors to assist her. She needed their power released so the energy flow from them could join hers to strengthen the odds.

Chapter 31

Jackson

Jackson crashed at a friend's apartment, but he'd been too nervous to sleep. He slipped out early in the morning, without waking his friend, and drove aimlessly for a while, trying to clear his mind. His thoughts were about his father, as usual. Everyone who did business with the man or knew him personally recognized that his father was a bad guy and needed to be stopped. The question was how to expose him without proof or evidence that proved the society existed.

He pulled to the curb and speed-dialed Michelle. It went to voice mail.

"Michelle, are you home? Can I stop by? Call me as soon as you get this."

He left the message on her cell. Too anxious to wait, Jackson drove to Aunt Victoria's house on Washington Avenue. He was no farther than the porch's top step when someone caught him from behind, twisted his arm, and screamed into his ear.

"Where are they? Your father wants to know. Tell me, and maybe I won't break your arm."

The pungent odor of garlic and stale beer assaulted Jackson's sense of smell while a sharp pinching pain shot through his shoulder.

"What the hell!"

He tried to free himself, but the man only pulled his arm higher, and Jackson winced in pain. Tears stung the corner of his eyes.

"I have no time to play games, kid. Where are they?"

"I don't know. I just got here, for Chris-sakes."

The man swung him around and punched Jackson in the face. He fell back, and the man knocked him in the face again, harder this time. Jackson landed in a white wicker chair. Dazed, he tried to stand, and the man pushed him down again as he fumbled through his pockets.

"Sit down." The man yelled as he pulled out his cell. "Yeah, got the kid, but there's nobody here."

Jackson wondered why his father hired this muscle guy. *Now he has creeps pushing me around. Wasn't his physical abuse enough?* The man returned his phone into his front pocket, leaned forward, and stared at Jackson, two inches from his face.

"Listen, kid. Where are your friends? Call them now and make a plan to meet."

Jackson glared at him, tightening his muscles, ready to fight.

"Now, you brat. And put it on speaker."

Spittle hit him in the face as the goon spoke. The man stepped back and pulled a gun out, then pointed it at Jackson's chest.

His heart pounded, thudding so hard against his ribs that it hurt. The pressure made it difficult for him to breathe. Jackson gasped for air while searching the area, looking for anyone who might be around to call out to for help, but no neighbors were in sight, no one peeking out of a window, no help. He hung his head and closed his eyes. *Think, think.* He didn't know what else to do, so he pulled out his phone to call, with the hope that Michelle didn't pick up, just like before.

"Hi, Jackson," she said.

His hopes sunk when he heard the sound of her voice. Jackson's fear rose, his throat tightened. He tried to think of a way to warn her, a special message or clue, but his mind clouded and didn't catch up to his automatic words of response.

"I'm at your aunt's house and no one is home. Is everything

okay?"

The man gave him a thud to the head.

"Stay away." Jackson's voice cracked and his hands trembled, as he tried to hang onto the small phone with his sweaty palms.

"We aren't going back to the house; your father is after us. I know it sounds paranoid, but we won't chance it. Jackson, he followed me last night after I left you. He chased me. Long story—I'll tell you later."

Jackson's face hung along with his sinking heart. "I'm so sorry."

"It's not your fault," she said.

The man shoved the gun against Jackson's chest again, nudging him along. Jackson wilted. *His father was poisoning everything in his life, and he hated him.* Before he could utter another word, she blurted instructions to him.

"Jackson, meet us at Frank Suffolk Diner in Revere, on the 1A just south of Revere Beach Parkway."

Jackson shook his head no, wanted to warn her. "But—"

Michelle hung up. Jackson was leading the goon directly into her path. Horrified about what he just did, he tried to think of a way to change this course.

The guy with the bad breath pushed Jackson forward, and they marched toward the street. He considered running but then realized they knew where Michelle and Aunt Victoria would be. He thought of all the things he should have said to warn them.

"Listen carefully, kid, no funny business. You jump into your little car and meet your friends. Don't even think of bolting because we know where they are. We'll be following you there. Once you get there, go in and bring them out. Simple plan. If you do as instructed, no one will get hurt. You understand, brat?"

"If I do as you say, we'll get hurt. Who do you think you're kidding?" Jackson said.

The goon smacked him in the back of his head. At the street, a black sedan was parked behind his Nissan compact. Another big guy sat behind the wheel. With one more shove to his back, the goon said, "Remember what I said, kid. We're right behind you."

Jackson got into his car and drove to the diner, unable to call back with a warning since the goon kept his phone. He wondered how he could ditch them, drive to the police station somewhere, but then feared they would get to Michelle and Victoria before he had the chance to explain to the police. Besides, the police wouldn't believe him. He took a deep breath and swallowed. With no choices, he drove to the restaurant and parked.

Jackson walked into the diner and spotted Victoria and Michelle. He slid into the booth intending on telling them right away what was happening.

"My goodness! What happened to your face?" Victoria said.

His bruises from the blows to his face made him look as pathetic as he felt.

"Don't worry about that. I need to tell—"

"Jackson, we had no idea he hit you," Michelle said.

She reached across the table and took his hands. Jackson shook his head and took a deep breath.

"Turns out he's upset that I was talking with you at the pub. Anyway, I took off, but I need to tell—"

"I hate that man," Victoria said.

Jackson was surprised by her conviction. Victoria looked angry, her mouth drawn down and her blue eyes hard as cold steel. He had no idea about her past run-in with his father, but her reaction spoke volumes.

"I need to tell you something important—"

"Here we go." The waitress interrupted their conversation and placed the food on the table.

Jackson drew in a deep breath, shook his head, and glanced toward the door. Time was running out, he only had a few minutes ahead of those thugs. Michelle smiled and tapped his hand.

"Calm down and eat something. I ordered the Airport Special, eggs, bacon, and banana chocolate chip pancakes," she said.

His lead eaten up, he chastised himself for his feeble attempt to warn them and smirked. Frustrated, Jackson gave up and slapped his hand onto the table. Michelle and Victoria looked up with a question mark written on their expressions.

The two men entered the diner and looked straight at them. Jackson paled as the goons walked toward their booth. Another waitress stopped them midstream and escorted them to another booth about ten feet from theirs. The men took a seat but leered at the three of them.

"I think they're here for us," Michelle said.

Jackson swallowed the lump in this throat. He hated himself for being such a coward and leading them straight to Michelle and Victoria.

"I've been trying to tell you, it's my fault. They were waiting at your house. They heard you on the phone when I called."

He felt small and had no clue what to do next.

Michelle signaled the waitress over.

"Hold up the menu to hide my face."

Her command was directed to Jackson. He obeyed, pulled the menu up, and pretended to be reading while hiding her from the goons.

Michelle whispered to the waitress.

"Those men have been stalking me since the highway. I think it's a case of extreme road rage or something. Can you please call the police?"

She slipped some cash to the waitress and asked if there was a discrete way out.

The waitress nodded toward the restrooms and pointed with her eyes, then whispered, "The window opens easily."

Michelle smiled her thanks. A few moments after the waitress left, Michelle and Victoria went to the ladies' room.

Jackson stayed seated and ate some of the pancakes, relieved the women would soon be out of harm's way. He hoped the women would have enough time to get some distance from these goons before they got wise to the ploy.

The men kept a wary gaze on the empty bench across from him at the table, and they repeatedly checked the parking lot. The men looked cagey, checking their watches after a couple of minutes went by and the women hadn't returned to the table. Jackson gave them a cool glance and asked the waitress for another cup of coffee when she walked by.

Hopefully, the police would be there in a few more minutes, the usual response time. The first goon ran out of patience, stood, and walked over to Jackson's seat. The man leaned and placed his face right in front of his. The bad breath nearly knocked Jackson over.

"Excuse me, but the women with you, well, I need to speak with them, now. They're coming back out, right?"

Jackson held the man's stare.

"Do I know you?" He spoke loud on purpose.

Heads turned and everyone got a good look at the intimidating man. At that moment, two police officers rushed through the front door of the diner. The patrons turned to see what was happening, and another waitress pointed to the two men.

The goons looked at each other with searching eyes, and one jerked his head toward the back. Compromised, they ran through the narrow aisle between the booths, heading for the doorway with EXIT lit bright red, shoving a man who just walked out from the restrooms, unaware.

Jackson got up, leaned on the booth bench, gaped out the window, and watched the two men dashing for their car. They got into the black Nissan, started the engine, then tromped on the gas pedal, dark smoke polluting from the tailpipe. They took off down the street. An officer ran out of the diner and jumped into a police car where his partner waited, and they followed the goons. Every customer in the place talked at the same time and hummed with speculation.

Michelle and Aunt Victoria strolled out from the ladies' room as if nothing happened. They looked down at Jackson, who was filling his face with bacon.

"What? I'm hungry now that they've left."

"Do you think those good ole boys took theirs to go?" Michelle said.

She laughed at her own joke, but Victoria had lost all humor and looked shaken up. Michelle thanked the waitress for her help, and the three of them gave a statement to a lone police officer who remained at the diner's counter. Jackson explained the men had been waiting at Victoria's house and threatened to hurt them. The officer promised to call the Cambridge police department to give them the heads up and watch over Victoria's house. They went back to the booth, exhausted by the experience.

"A lot of good that will do," Michelle said. "Ramsey will get the heads up before anyone else will be able to help us."

A waitress brought warm food and smiled at them—they were famous in this small diner. They ate their breakfast and drank more coffee without talking much. Jackson spun his cup around on the saucer and watched the coffee swirl. His head leaned into his raised right hand and bent arm.

"I'm so sorry I brought those guys here," he said.

He sat up and looked at them. "I'm so sorry."

"Don't be foolish—you saved us. If we had gone home while those thugs were waiting for us, Lord knows what could have happened," Victoria said.

"Come on, let's get out of this joint already," Michelle said.

They left the diner, piled into Jackson's small car, and discussed their next move.

"I think we should go back to that warehouse and check out what Tom and the gang were doing there the other night. Maybe we can find something incriminating to give to the police—someone other than Ramsey, of course," Michelle said.

"We need to contact Emilie and give them an update," Victoria said.

Michelle pulled out her phone and called her sister, putting it on speakerphone. Her leg twitched with a nervous, up and down, spasm. She cursed under her breath for her sister to pick up.

"Hello, Michelle?" Jeremy answered. "We're almost there."

"What do you mean, you're almost here? How did you know we needed you; Em's a mind reader now, too? You're on your way back to Boston?"

Jackson watched Michelle; her expression of surprise was cute and made her look almost vulnerable. He liked her, but she was so damned cocky most of the time, holding the tiger by the tail and never worried about any backlash. Jackson worried that would catch up to her someday, probably soon.

"We have a lot to tell you," Jeremy said. "We took a detour and researched some information we discovered from the copied pages of the book. We're coming back from the Blackfeet Reservation. We spoke with someone there who knew about an incident with Tom Bennett back in '72. Michelle, he's not what he seems. He's a monster."

"We already know that, Dear," Victoria said.

"No, that's not what I mean. For real! He's a real monster," he said.

Michelle burst out laughing in the back seat. Victoria and Jackson turned around to see why she cracked up so hard. She laughed so hard, she was holding onto her side. Michelle grabbed the phone, stumbled out of the car, still holding her side, and almost dropped her phone onto the sidewalk. She took a deep breath, contained herself again, and said, "Jeremy, you're kidding, right? I mean, there's no such thing as monsters."

Her amusement wasn't shared. *Monster?* Jackson unrolled the window and craned his head to listen to the rest of the call.

"Right, just like you thought there was no such thing as curses," he replied.

Michelle stopped laughing and her face lost its frivolity.

"Listen to me, Michelle. It's worse than you could imagine. There's more going on with this man, more than anyone realizes. Can you pick us up at the airport?"

"Sure, no problem. When?"

"In half an hour, and be careful."

"Don't worry, we'll be fine. See you soon."

She hung up the phone and climbed back into the car.

"Okay. We have two small cars, and neither will hold five adults."

"You're counting yourself?" Jackson said.

He smiled and Michelle punched his arm in play.

"Just trying to relieve some tension here."

Victoria rolled her eyes.

"Okay, when you two are ready, let's figure this car situation out," Victoria said.

Michelle snapped her fingers.

"Aunt Victoria, please go with Jackson to the airport and pick up Emilie and Jeremy. Show him the shortcut to the hangar for our plane."

Victoria turned around and faced the back seat.

"And what, pray tell will you be doing?" She glared. "Or dare I ask . . ."

Michelle flashed her innocent smile.

"I'll take your car and go back to that warehouse to look around in the daylight. Maybe I can find out what they were up to the other night and we can use it as leverage against them," she said. "Can I use your car, Auntie, please?"

Victoria shook her head. "I don't think you should go alone."

"You and Jackson will follow and meet up with me as soon as you get Emilie and Jeremy at the airport."

Jackson cringed. He brushed his hair back away from his face, then hid his frown with his hand. He was lost for words. *Why doesn't she want me to go with her?*

"No, Michelle, that's crazy. I won't let you go to the warehouse alone. We'll wait and go together," Victoria said.

Jackson turned and put his hand onto Michelle's shoulder, pleading to her with his eyes. She brushed his hand off, and her face took on a stern look. Something he said or had done made her angry.

"Oh my God! You two, don't worry about me; I'm not a baby." Michelle huffed. "First, you should get some ice on Jackson's eye. He looks like a blooming punching bag. Besides, it's in the middle of the morning. Nothing will happen in daylight. And you'll be following me with backup, right? It's best if we get a jump on things before someone decides to hide the evidence. Now that they don't have us, they might try to hide any evidence. I promise to be careful, scout's honor."

Michelle raised two fingers on her right hand.

Victoria smiled and said, "Please, we went through this already—remember, you were never a scout."

Jackson reached over the seat and awkwardly hugged Michelle. This was a mistake, but she always managed to get her way. Once her hooves dug into the ground, there was no arguing with her, and he didn't want her to stay angry with him.

Michelle got out of the back seat, closed the door, and waved as Jackson drove away. He watched in the rearview mirror and saw her get into Victoria's car. She drove away in the opposite direction.

Chapter 32

Michelle took Aunt Victoria's car and drove north toward the warehouse district they had visited the other night. The bright morning sunlight streaked through the barren branches with only patches of color remaining. A crisp wind blew the last of the foliage from the maple trees that lined the street. The leaves floated down in a stream of color, spinning to the ground in twists. The wet leaves scattered across the street, still covered with morning dew, adding to the slippery pavement condition.

She drove while admiring the last of the foliage, gazing into the rearview mirror. Michelle noticed a black sedan. She turned down the next street and checked the rearview mirror again — the same sedan followed. Another quick turn and check to see if it kept trailing her; the mirror reflected the black sedan still following a short distance behind. She sped up.

Making one last attempt to lose the car, Michelle gripped the steering wheel and swung an impromptu turn to the right. The car squealed as it maneuvered the sharp turn. The two right tires balanced the weight of the vehicle, with the left tires catching air, then they landed back on the pavement with a jerk. The slick street, littered with wet leaves, caused the car's traction to slip. The car fishtailed as it recovered from the sharp swerve. Michelle pressed the gas pedal and propelled the car forward. The car hydroplaned on ice. Afraid, she applied the brakes. *Big mistake!*

Aunt Victoria's small compact spun out of control and formed donut circles down the center of the street. She took her foot off the brake and straightened the steering wheel, but it was too late. She sideswiped the only parked vehicle around — a truck and the momentum of the impact sent her head-on into an old wooden, oil-slicked, telephone pole. The car's front hood crushed.

The thrust from the crash released the airbag. The pillow pushed against Michelle's face and chest. Her breath punched out of her, she gasped for air. It took a few moments of her panting before her lungs filled with air again. Spiked sharp throbs of pain vibrated in her head, the worst migraine she ever experienced. She remembered a car had been shadowing her and hoped they hadn't followed down this street. She scrambled out of the wreckage.

Swaying, she leaned against the side of the car to get her balance. The world looked dizzy. Michelle felt nauseous. She bent down and heaved, then raised her head in time to see the other car just as it entered the street. *Too late.*

Panic gripped her body; adrenaline pumped through her veins. She turned and ran. Looking for help or a place to duck for cover, she searched, but nothing on this street looked hopeful. It was desolate here with only a few decrepit houses that stood on cracked foundations. The driveways were heaved and had wild grass growing in the pavement grooves. This place oozed depression, a rundown neighborhood near the warehouse district and close to the waterfront.

The next block consisted of commercial buildings and held hope for a slight possibility of life. Michelle ran past a metal plating storefront, now an empty broken-down building closed for business.

The smell of scorched oil and old fish permeated the air. The seafront was nearby, with old fishing boats docked, stinking from yesterday's catch. That direction led to a dead-end unless she planned to swim.

She ran farther down the street. The next building looked like a battered garage. A dash of hope, until she noticed a lock on the door and the whitewash smeared the windows.

Michelle glanced over her shoulder and saw the car following her was getting closer. She ducked down a narrow pathway between the garage and the next warehouse. The black sedan screech to a halt. Looking over her shoulder, two rather large men got out of the car and followed her on foot. She used her slight lead to her advantage. Michelle turned the corner at the end of the path and ducked into a door crevice in the back of the building. She pushed herself flat against the metal door, hoping the wide doorjamb would give enough cover. Michelle held her breath. Her pursuers ran past her without slowing.

She stood quiet for a few minutes, afraid to move, and listened to every sound and strange noise; drips in the gutter, electric buzzing from the electric poles, and muffles from unknown motors that seemed far away. Spellbound, she listened to the pitter-patter of the squirrels and birds on the metal roof, looking for bugs and nuts in the crevasses. The wind blew. The glass of the windows high above rattled.

Michelle turned the doorknob, surprised when she found it unlocked. She pushed the door ajar and stole into the warehouse, hoping to find safety. Iron beams supported the huge open space, and metal stairs led to a mezzanine above that covered about half of the open area. A light shone from a window in one of the offices above, but no other evidence existed of life or work; a huge open space with no place to hide.

Michelle's heart raced. She drew in a deep breath, which only emphasized the pain from her bruised chest. The door on the upper mezzanine opened. She froze and held her breath. A moment later, she gasped as the shadow of a man appeared.

He stepped out from the doorway light and stood at the top of the stairs. His form was large and dark. Michelle couldn't make out a face, but she recognized the stance as he moved his head back and forth, his face raised toward the ceiling, smelling the air for a scent. *Just like in the alley.* Michelle's heart sank. Tom

Bennett!

Panicked, Michelle opened the door and bolted. The clatter of boot heels stomping down the metal stair rungs resonated from behind her. She ran toward the warehouse that she had intended to explore, hoping that her sister, and the others, were there by magic and waiting for her in the parking lot. She prayed she could run faster than Tom Bennett. She stole a peek behind her and saw him running at high speed, straight after her.

His body was sleek and he ran fast as lightning. Tom Bennett moved like a wild animal chasing its prey, sprinted with ease, and gained stride. He pounced. Michelle ducked, and his grasp missed her by inches. She kept running for her life.

Michelle's chest ached as she breathed in deep gasps. Hot steam blew out of her nostrils and mouth as her breath mingled with the crisp outside air. Her gait staggered as she zigzagged to avoid potholes in the gouged pavement. Michelle's heartbeat pounded against her chest.

"Don't look back, don't look back," she said aloud.

Something hard slammed into her from behind and knocked her to the pavement. She fell hard. Her knees scraped against the unforgiving tar, and pieces of sharp pebbles ripped her skin with stinging bites. Then she somersaulted from the momentum. Michelle endured everything in the toss—obstinate stones, protruding sticks, old cans, bottles, all hitting her body as she tumbled across the blacktop. She stopped, landing on her stomach. The smell of oil burnt her nostrils when she inhaled. Tears stung her face. She wiped them and smeared grime onto her cheek from the grease on her dirty hands from the filthy ground. *This isn't happening.*

Michelle stretched her neck and looked up. Tom Bennett stood over her, smiling. He kicked her hard in the side, and she rolled onto her back.

"Stop, please stop," she cried.

He peered down at her and kicked her again. His boot slammed into her gut, then Tom Bennett knelt down and took her face between the palms of his hands.

"Your eyes are like your mother's," he said.

Terror flooded her entire being. Michelle feared this monster was going to do more than kick her. Her imagination went wild with images of her mother's fate.

He picked her up, flung her over his shoulder, and carried her away. She came to her senses, found her voice, and pounded her fists against the small of his back.

"Put me down!" she screamed.

Michelle hoped someone would hear her cries and come to the rescue, but then she remembered where she was, a desolate ghost town of shambled warehouses, most abandoned for years. She closed her eyes a second and stopped beating her fists. Nothing seemed to work to her advantage.

Tom carried her to the building that she had spied on the other night when she followed Silas. *Maybe there would be help after all.* The place wasn't completely vacant; there had been desks with computers still working. Maybe Aunt Victoria, Emilie, Jeremy, and Jackson would be there soon.

An unexpected memory flashed in Michelle's head, of herself at church with her parents during Mass, kneeling with her hands clasped and covered in Rosary beads. Michelle took it as a sign and started praying. *Please help me.* For the second time in two days, she reached out to her higher power.

Tom kicked open the metal door with his booted foot and carried her down the long hallway. He opened another door into a large room that looked like an old test lab. The door squeaked as it closed, then shut with a final bang that echoed. The ceiling was high, with humming fluorescent fixtures that hung down from metal rafters.

She smelled something metallic in the air. Racks flanked the walls, filled with inventory. Boxes labeled with bar codes, metal cans, and sacks filled the shelves. Michelle read a label as they passed by—the chemical White Phosphorus. Recalling an article about the Boston bombing that she wrote while still working for a local magazine, she had discovered in her research the elements used for making bombs. White phosphorus topped the list. Her fear and imagination went wild, gripped with the fear that he was a terrorist. *He keeps getting creepier.*

Tom Bennett dropped her into a chair. Her back slammed into the cold hard metal seat. Pain pulsated through her entire body, and she moaned.

"Stop making that racket."

He kicked the chair and remained standing close by, a barrier between her and the door.

Michelle chanted prayers in her mind while she looked around hoping to find a way out of this mess. Determined not to lose her way, she fought to control her pain and fear.

Michelle heard noises in the room and leaned her body to the side to try to see more. There were others in the shadows, but they stood far off and she couldn't make anyone out. Tom Bennett blocked her view with his massive form. He stepped a few feet away from her and started a conversation with someone. She mumbled another prayer under her breath.

"Are you ready? We need to get this done and over with. She's a pain in my ass already," Bennett called out.

Shuffling movement in the space verified someone else was there.

"We only needed her fingerprints, not the whole girl! For Chrissake! How are we going to deal with this now?" a man said.

Michelle thought that she recognized the voice—*Deputy Detective Ramsey?* So, he was Bennett's heavy man. It figures.

She wanted to be wrong about him and wished Aunt Victoria's idea of the police being good deep down was accurate.

"Don't worry about her. Silas, you'll take care of her, right? You know what to do," Bennett said to someone else.

Silas? Michelle stretched more and almost tipped the chair over to see around Tom Bennett's frame. She spotted Silas across the room, her professor. He stared back at her without expression. Disgusted, she shook her head and looked away. She recognized that look, that blank stare. The same expression he wore seven years ago. His gaping eyes and mouth wide open, wordless, and with no life in his eyes.

Silas was a coward. Michelle hoped for a brief moment that he would muster the gumption to stand up for her, talk with Tom Bennett and convince him to let her go. *A girl can dream.* How futile that idea; he had no backbone.

"Listen, the two of you. We need to improvise our plan. We'll leak the fake evidence against Michelle as originally planned, but let's add a suicide note and seal her deal. That should get the job done, boys. Ramsey, you take care of part one, and Silas you have part two."

Bennett's voice bellowed into the lofty space, then he slapped his hands together and rubbed them, washing himself of the deed.

"Now, you idiots!"

Michelle swallowed hard as his words sunk in. *He plans to kill me.* She froze, her body numb again.

Deputy Ramsey stood. The metal legs of the stool he'd been sitting on, dragged and scraped against the floor, the sound sent shivers up her spine.

"No, this is not what I signed up for," Deputy Ramsey said.

A glimmer of hope filled Michelle's thoughts. *Finally, someone is talking sense. Thank you.* From the far end of the room, another small voice peeped.

"Tom, let's discuss this new plan. You know I care for Michelle. I can't hurt her like that. Let's talk about this and find another solution."

"Oh, I see." Tom Bennett spoke in a soft serpentine voice.

Michelle's knight in armor awakened, but it was too late. She understood the evil intentions that Bennett's voice suggested; he lured his prey. She wanted to scream to Silas, *run, Silas, run*, but she stayed quiet, tongue-tied, and paralyzed with fear. She chastised herself. *Warn him.* Nothing came out of her mouth.

Silas drew closer to Bennett, ready to deliberate like in one of his classes. His long fingers twitched, his face showed a faint glimpse of comradery and goodwill, but his timid body didn't match his brave words.

"Thank you for being reasonable, Tom," Silas said. "I'm sure we can complete the mission and keep this entire situation quiet without any extreme measures. I can hide her away, keep her captive, and we can stage her death somehow."

"Sure, whatever you say, Silas. Come here and we can discuss this in private so the girl doesn't hear us. Tell me your suggestions."

Tom Bennett gave Michelle a quick glance and smirked, then motioned for Silas to join him. Silas walked across the room closing the space between them. He walked with Bennett, who hadn't taken more than ten steps forward. Bennett faced Silas and grabbed him by his shoulders with chummy bravado. He smiled and moved his right hand to Silas's back, and gave him a pat.

In a flash, Tom Bennett moved his hand and snapped his friend's neck like a twig. The crunching click of the breaking bone echoed.

Michelle gasped. It had happened so fast.

Silas drooped in Tom Bennett's right hand as he looked

down at him with disgust, then let go. The limp body fell. Silas landed on the ground in a clump, the look of surprise and horror engraved on his face forever.

Michelle gawked at the lasting vision destined to visit her nightmares. Silas's dead face stared back at her; her Silas, her professor, her womanizer who claimed to love her. Her hope of surviving died with him, and fear overtook her, afraid to meet her own death. She whimpered, her body shaking with uncontrollable tremors. Her mind struggled to process the scene that just happened. His neck laid in an awkward position from his body, the cervical vertebrae was broken in two, displayed on the cold cement floor like some freaky sideshow, his eyes open, bulging, popping out, but blind to everything. Silas was dead; her Silas dead.

"For God's sake! What did you do that for?" Deputy Ramsey screamed from across the room, walking closer to them.

"I told you both, no questions. We can't ever forget how our society works; an act for an act, no questions, no matter what. Was something not clear?"

Tom Bennett's face darkened, and his body changed. He grew in size, right in front of her. She rubbed her eyes and looked at him again. His reddened face darkened more, his body bulkier, his shoulders broader, and his frame taller. The Incredible Hulk loomed in front of her, spare the ripping clothes.

"Ah!" she gasped in horror. *This isn't possible. I'm going crazy,* she told herself between chattering teeth.

"No. This isn't what I signed up for," Ramsey said.

He pulled out his gun, a Glock 30 slim, and pointed it at Tom Bennett in defiance. Michelle recognized the gun, the same kind she had practiced with at the shooting range—a 45 with a standard ten in a clip. Unshaken, Ramsey bellowed orders now.

"Down on your knees."

Tom Bennett turned his back to him and laughed as he walked closer to Michelle.

"Stop. I said down on your knees."

"What are you going to do, arrest me, or shoot me in the back?" he said.

Michelle zoomed in on Bennett's eyes. They changed to black pitch, like shining pools of oil, pure evil. He spun around and faced Deputy Ramsey, who swore something under his breath.

Is this the first time Ramsey realized this psychopath was over the edge of normal? The surreal scene played out in front of her, detached, suspended in a drug-induced reality.

A brief look of confusion unfurled across Deputy Ramsey's face, but then he gained control. Michelle wondered if any hope survived. *How could a man like Ramsey get involved with this lunatic in the first place?* She remembered Ramsey's power trip while he interviewed her; he shared that emotional need for power with Tom Bennett. Clearly, the detective hadn't planned for it to be like this. Ramsey must have been blinded by ambition, taking one small step then another, leading himself down a road but had gone too far.

"Go ahead, shoot me," Tom Bennett said.

He laughed and teased Deputy Ramsey on with his gruff voice, a wild sounding gnarl. A shot rang out. She witnessed the bright flare that sparked from the end of the pistol. The noise from the backfire billowed up above, reverberating in the high steel-beamed ceiling. The sound hurt her ears. She covered the side of her head with her hands, trying to muffle the ringing that shook her nerves. Tings, like jabs, caused her to shiver like a chalkboard had been scratched. A booming voice broke through the resounding noise.

"You can't kill me, you fool. I'm already dead!"

Tom Bennett lunged at Ramsey and pulled him down to the ground in one swift swipe. He raised his arm then struck, landing him a hard blow. Ramsey's body slumped, and his head hit the ground and bounced from the impact. Michelle could hear his skull crack against the hard cement. Blood ran down his head, pooled, then created a small garnet river that spread wide across the floor's canvas, creating a pattern that looked like a tree. His pulse drained the life from him, and Deputy Ramsey's face paled. Michelle watched Bennett hover over the motionless body, taking pleasure in Ramsey's demise.

Before Michelle could register the impact of the events that just unfolded, a loud noise boomed from the other side of the room. The heavy metal door slammed into the wall with a crash, then shut again, slamming closed. Her brother Robert stomped across the room, full of energy and life.

Chapter 33

"Hi, Tom," Robert called out. His happy tone evaporated quickly as Robert stepped closer, confronted with the bodies on the floor. A quizzical look washed over his face. "What's going on?"

Robert is clueless, Michelle thought. I wonder if he can help us out of this situation?

"Robert, run!" Michelle screamed.

Robert turned, his gaze locked on hers. Shock gleaned in his eyes.

She begged her brother for help, implored him with her expression. He returned a look of confusion, tilting his head.

Any adrenaline boost she might have experienced faded away, and the bruises on her body ached and began to swell. She was ready to explode, a balloon pushed to the outer limits.

Tom Bennett moved away from Deputy Ramsey's body that lay still on the floor.

"They failed to do their job, that's what's going on. Robert, I hate to bother you with trivial tasks, but I need your help to finish this ugly episode. As part of your initiation into our society, you must do a beneficial act. You must do as I say. You requested that your sister be removed and out of your way so that you could run the company again." He kicked the detective's body. "Unfortunately, Ramsey here is no longer available to plant the evidence at the police station. We need a plan B; find another way to get rid of your sister. Any suggestions?"

Robert's face melted into a ghostly mask. Michelle watched his eyes move back and forth as he calculated the situation and considered the bodies lying about the room. She was unsure of her brother's true intentions and wondered, *would he want to get rid of me no matter the cost?* Her brother never hid the fact that he wanted her out of the way, but surely Robert would never do anything as drastic as killing her?

Robert stuttered, trying to respond. "W-w-what do you mean? I won't hurt my own sister. I'll have to think of another option. I need a minute."

"As usual, I have to do everything myself," Tom Bennett said. He turned and walked toward Michelle. He grabbed her around the waist, pulled her up from the chair, and flung her over his shoulder again.

"Put me down, you monster. Ouch! What the hell do you think you're doing? Rob, help me! Robert!"

As Tom Bennett carried her across the room, his hard body brushed against her bruises. Michelle ached physically and in spirit. Her mouth sputtered obscenities, as anguish from the pain throbbed. Her knees stung, her hip and thighs were marred with red contusions, her chest hurt the most. Had she broken a rib when the airbag went off in the car? She smarted with every touch.

A faint mumble refocused her attention. Deputy Detective Ramsey roused. Somehow, he survived the brutal attack and the massive loss of blood. *Maybe he could still help her.* She was desperate for a miracle. From the corner of her eye, she noticed him reaching for his gun, his hand groping the floor, searching left, then right, until he finally found it. Like a match made in heaven, his hand and fingers fused to the Glock. The security of his firearm must have filled him with a sudden burst of strength because he stood.

"Drop her now," Ramsey said.

Michelle's heart beat faster, thumping hard and loud in her chest. She hoped this newest development would work, and she was relieved that Deputy Ramsey remained alive, of course. Even though she hadn't liked the way the man had treated her in the past, the sight of him lying on the floor in a puddle of his own blood flooded her with regrets for her ill will. If he could help her get out of this situation, all would be forgiven, and then some.

"Robert," said Bennett. "Take care of him."

Tom Bennett dropped Michelle unceremoniously. She landed on the cold hard floor with a thud; her pain seared again and her heart started racing. Obviously, he changed his mind and planned to take things into his own hands. He rushed toward Ramsey, who stood pointing the gun directly at Bennett.

Michelle saw that Ramsey's hands were firmly gripped on the piece, his aim straight and still. She could tell by his stance that he was an expert shooter. *Awards must fill the walls of his office.*

"Stop or I'll shoot," Ramsey warned one last time.

Tom Bennett kept barreling forward; his body grew in size at the same time.

She had never imagined anything like this. Tom Bennett turned into something else right before her eyes. Michelle rubbed her fists on her closed eyes, then looked again. No longer just a man, Bennett morphed into some kind of other-worldly beast. He was similar to a wolf in appearance, with his dark hair, now resembling fur. A new smell wafted in the room like a wet dog. His new barbed sharp teeth reflected the fluorescent light and drool dripped from his fangs, spilling wet slobber all over the floor. The monster lunged at Ramsey.

Michelle covered her face with her hands and took a deep breath, holding it. She couldn't believe her eyes and was too afraid to speak, her words froze.

"Holy shit!" Robert screamed aloud.

Ramsey fired the gun. Bright flashes filled the air repeatedly, but nothing put the Bennett monster down. He didn't stop or flinch for a second.

The noise from the Glock rung loud and Michelle's ears

pulsed. An acrid smell drifted across the room, her nostrils assaulted by the metallic burn. She counted as Ramsey discharged nine rounds.

"Dammit," he said. Ramsey pulled the magazine out and slid another clip into the slimline in seconds.

Michelle heard the metallic click. Bennett was only a few feet away from Ramsey and would reach him in seconds, before a chance to aim again. The gun flew from Ramsey's hands as the beast flung at him. The Glock skidded across the floor toward Michelle.

More voices echoed from across the lofty space. Michelle hoped it was someone who could help; the police, Jackson, her sister?

"Someone help!" Michelle found her voice and screamed with all her energy.

"Good," said Bennett, stopping for a moment. "Company. The gang's all here; magnificent."

His words hissed, then rolled into a rumbled growl that came from deep within his throat. The monster's eyes grew darker until they lost the whites completely and melted into the deepest black of midnight on a moonless night. All traces of the man named Tom Bennett were hidden, shrouded in darkness, gone from sight if the man had ever existed.

Robert slid closer to Michelle until he stood by her side. She turned and searched his blank face, wondering what he planned to do.

He whispered, "Michelle, what's going on?"

Confused by his question and his perplexed tone, she questioned his motives. *How could he not understand what's going on? Tom Bennett, his adored mentor was a monster!* Robert dropped his head; her brother never looked more vulnerable. The monster was pacing back and forth, taunting them. It worked. Fatigued, she followed his path with her eyes, safeguarding the distance between them.

"What are you doing here?" Robert asked.

"Trying to stop this monster, what else? I could use your help, Robert," she snapped.

Did big brother finally get it? She was on his side, had been all along. Robert had been fooled by Bennett's twisted mind conditioning, but her brother apparently, still couldn't raise a hand against the monster. *Was it out of fear or out of loyalty?* No time to care right now, Robert obviously provided no help. Her spirit sunk, and she questioned how much more she could take. She was on her own. Her survival threatened, she took action.

In a split second, she made a decision. Michelle ducked low and ran toward Deputy Ramsey, who was now a lump on the floor. His gun had slid closer to her. She grabbed his Glock and raised her hands, aiming it at Bennett. She pulled back the slide, making sure it loaded another round into the chamber, just like she had done hundreds of times at the shooting range. The clicking sound droned in her ears as the gun's spring left a round in the chamber. A sense of bravado filled her for a brief moment.

"Robert, I'm going to kill this man-beast. Please listen to me now. I need your help." The gun shook in Michelle's hands, but she still managed to keep it pointed straight toward Bennett, or more accurately, at the monster.

It bellowed a response. "Don't listen to your sister. She is nothing but a pain in our ass. Look at her standing there; she dares point a gun at me. Remember the plan. We are getting rid of her so you can have all the money. Remember? It's all for you, Robert."

Michelle kept her eyes on the target. Swallowing hard, she stood her ground.

"No, Robert, don't listen to him. Listen to me. He hates you. He despises the entire family. Rob, he used you for his own evil vendetta. You can see he's not what you thought. He's a monster. Move away from it before it's too late, before he kills you, too, like he tried to kill Mother."

Tom Bennett laughed aloud. Michelle watched in horror as his body bent back, revealing his broad chest, now shirtless, and grown into a massive canvas of muscle. Like a demon, he had soulless eyes. His face no longer looked human, with teeth protruding from a wolf-like snout, a changeling. Michelle's fear soared.

"Michelle, stop this craziness. No one is going to get hurt today, I promise. Put the gun down," Robert said.

Her anger matched her fear. She held the gun firm and pointed it at the monster, no longer shaking. She found an inner strength and knew she wasn't about to let this beast win.

"Look around you, Robert! People are dead. He killed Silas with his bare hands. For hell's sake! I saw him snap his neck like it was a chicken wing." Tears streamed down her face and she tasted their saltiness. "Then he mauled Deputy Ramsey, you saw, too. He killed a cop, Robert. Can't you see the beast in front of us?"

The monster paced about thirty feet away, staring at them. Robert shook his head in denial.

"Why can't you see him for the evil monster he is? Look at him," she said.

"What the hell are you saying? This can't be happening. There's no such thing as monsters," Robert said.

Michelle seethed, fed up with this madman's games. This supernatural beast had tormented and screwed up her family's lives long enough. Her poor mother, and the fear she had endured at this man's hand. Michelle wanted to kill this freak of nature, now.

Bennett the monster crept closer. He breathed in and out deep gasps, growled horrific bestial snarls meant to scare them.

She heard the rumble of his throat, now twenty feet away. The sound shuddered and reverberated down to her bones. She glanced sideways and saw her brother's back.

"Turn around and see the real Tom Bennett. Robert, face him dammit!"

Robert turned with reluctance and saw Bennett. Robert's body visibly trembled in fear. The monster's eyes deepened in darkness. Michelle noticed how Robert's grim emotions fueled the monster's strength. It was then she realized the creature gained strength from their fear. Emotional trauma was its food. *Calm down,* she coached herself. *Not going to happen!*

She saw Robert, frozen in place.

He stared straight ahead at the monster. The dark creature snarled. Robert backed up his steps, moving away from the thing that had now drawn closer. The beast paced fifteen feet away from them and within reach of them both. Robert turned and ran to the other side of the room toward the door, but slipped on Ramsey's blood. He fell and slid backward, stopping near Michelle's feet, with no hope of reaching the exit. His face looked frantic; she bent down, grabbed his arm, and pulled Robert up with her left hand as she kept a steady aim at the beast with her right. It was now or never time.

A thud broke the silence. The metal door behind them opened with a hardy push and banged the wall with force. Michelle half-turned to see her sister Emilie and Jeremy walking in, with Aunt Victoria and Jackson following close.

Michelle and Robert stepped back and slowly inched toward the others, the beast followed. Michelle never took her eyes off the monster as Bennett swayed left, then right, smiling at them, taunting them. Caught in a mousetrap.

"Go back! Call the police," Michelle screamed.

The monster lurched forward. Someone screamed. Michelle thought it might be her own voice, but she was too afraid to reflect. The beast was closer and circled them, then stopped. Together they moved around, too, while protecting their backs. He placed himself between the tiny group and the exit.

"Finally, the gang is all here."

The monster's voice growled, building up power. He stood tall on strong legs, still like a human, and his enormous new frame, filled in by a bulk of muscles. The monster intimidated them all.

"What is that?" Aunt Victoria said. She placed her hands on Jeremy's shoulders.

"I'm your worst nightmare," he said at her, baring his fangs. Spittle flung from its mouth, flinging between the space between them. Victoria leaned back.

"Don't be afraid. That's what gets him off. This beast feeds on our fear. He gets stronger as we become more afraid. I saw it grow and get darker right in front of me," Michelle said.

Jackson moved to her side and wrapped his arm around her.

"Where did this monster come from?" he said.

The monster laughed, sounding like he had smoked a ten-pack-a-day habit.

"I'm your father, don't you recognize dear ole dad, Jackson?"

His sinister voice shook up Michelle's nerves, despite her own warning. Shivers shot down her back. They all witnessed the monster's reaction as it grew bigger and stronger, feeding off their fear.

It bent his head down and glared directly at Jackson.

"You're such a fool, just like your mother."

Michelle noticed her sister, Emilie, standing still, mesmerized in a Zen-like trance. Her face was empty, a look Michelle had seen before. She shook Emilie's arm to wake her back to reality. This wasn't the time to have a clairvoyant episode. Emilie turned to Michelle and smiled.

"Don't worry, I can handle this beast," Emilie said.

"What does that mean?"

Jeremy wrapped his arm around Emilie. Michelle had noticed he often did this to give her strength and keep her empathetic talent balanced. A bulb went off and Michelle understood.

"Of course, you can absorb our fear and keep it away from the monster. But wait; if you do that, won't it just feed off you?"

Emilie turned and looked at her. "Michelle, you're sending out your fear again. I can feel it, and so can it. Don't worry, his day is done. I've got this one, trust me."

Emilie stepped forward, closer to Tom Bennett.

"What's this? Are you offering yourself? No deals." The monster snarled.

She raised her arms into the air, summoning a force. The floor shook under their feet. A strange sensation filled Michelle, a divine spirit swelled in her most private corners, opening her deepest dreams and desires, and a lump formed in the back of her throat. Michelle forced back emotional tears and swallowed hard.

Then the room fell silent, except for horrid sounds coming from the beast. Michelle grabbed Jackson's sleeve and twisted the material in angst. He tightened his hold around her. The monster paced in frenzy, a wanton attempt for their gut reaction.

"Jeremy, what is she doing?" Michelle said.

"Shush. Hold on, wait and see. Emilie practiced in the plane while on the way here. She knows what she's doing."

Emilie stood still in the center of them, her long brunette hair flowing down her back. A noise hummed, low at first, then gaining strength. It seemed to emanate from within her, like the sound of a tuning fork vibrating and growing stronger. A pale angelic form, almost glowing, she lifted her arms and reached toward the skylight. She immersed herself into a deep meditative state. Her heart-shaped face beamed.

She waved her arms out, then forward toward Tom Bennett the beast, a gesture so gentle and serene, like a ballet dancer performing Arabesque. She folded her hands together and prayed. She raised her head, faced the sky, with eyes closed, and a miraculous thing happened. As she opened her hands, beams of light filtered down into them from above, and she absorbed the rays like she was catching falling drops in her hands.

For the first time in her life, Michelle experienced happiness brought on by faith. Her mind floated in a peaceful state, and joy surrounded her with love and safety. This was the feeling she had with her mother when she was a child, so warm and happy. She turned and watched the faces of her Aunt Victoria, Jeremy, and Jackson, and they all glowed from the same vibration that Emilie radiated.

Michelle looked over her other shoulder and saw her brother. Robert's face dropped as he stared down at the floor. She regretted that he was unable to fathom what was going on. He didn't appear to feel the goodness that filled the room, and she pitied him. This electrical magnetism shrouded the space, and Michelle soaked in as much as her heart could embrace.

Moments later, Emilie opened her soft brown eyes, her attention on Tom Bennett, the monster. Her face pinched up, and she winced reacting to the pain she must have suffered as she absorbed his emotions into herself. She continued pulling them from his body, and Michelle saw a mirage-like stream flowing from the beast to her sister. The toxic fumes swirled in a fast undertow.

The monster growled in discomfort. Tom Bennett's form

changed even more, no longer resembling a man at all, but morphed totally into some kind of supernatural creature. All traces of his human form extinct, he took the form of a true black wolf, the fangs protruding from his opened snout. He groaned as his bones crunched and snapped. His agony soon turned into howls, guttural and deep. No human words were spoken, only animal yelps reverberated in the space.

Emilie stayed vigilant and kept her arms out toward him and drew more out until light started to stream from the creature, then its body fell to the floor.

Emilie walked closer and stood over his slumped form. She dropped a gold ring with a ruby center near his side. Its ting echoed. She stretched out her arm, and with her open hand toward the beast, she drew out even more from his body. A strange sucking sound filled the massive room, echoing like a drain emptying. Emilie's body shook as she depleted the monster's aura. He lay on the floor, limp and lifeless.

She stopped when there was nothing left to pull, and Emilie wrapped her arms around herself and rested.

After a few moments, she pointed her hands at the beast again. Light beams flashed from her palms and targeted the monster. Torrents of bright illumination beyond anything Michelle had ever seen filled the room with a cleansing effect. Everything was white-washed. Seconds passed. She stopped and dropped her arms.

Emilie's body crumpled to the floor from exhaustion.

Michelle ran to her side, dropped the gun, and cradled Emilie's body into her arms. "Wake up, Em. Are you okay? Please wake up, Emilie."

Michelle sobbed as she rocked her sister back and forth in her arms. Confused by everything that happened, she tried to focus on the real things in the room. Her sister's heartbeat throbbed and Michelle took solace knowing that Em was alive.

Michelle suspected her brother's stare. She turned her head and saw Robert looking down at his two sisters, but still speechless and without expression.

Chapter 34

Robert

Jeremy rushed over, pulled Emilie into his arms, and cradled her. He held Emilie, rubbed her arms until she revived and the color returned to her face. Aunt Victoria joined Michelle, and the two stood close.

Robert mumbled to himself.

"God, what just happened? What have I done?"

He glanced over at Tom Bennett's body. It was no longer human; it looked like a real monster, just as his sister said. He walked closer to him and eyed the body on the floor. He shook his head, troubled by the creature sprawled out in front of him.

"He was a demon wolf," Robert called aloud.

Overwhelmed, he doubled over and held his stomach like he was about to puke, then he noticed movement. The monster twitched, roused back from the dead.

"Oh my God!" Robert screamed out in alarm. They all turned to look.

"No, Robert, don't be afraid. It feeds off your negative emotions," Michelle said.

It was too late. Robert's dark emotions gave the creature a flicker of strength, and it pulled itself up and stood on its own. Swaying for a moment, it let out an angry howl. Using Tom Bennett's voice, it said, "You can't beat me. I'll kill you all. The de Gourgues family will be expunged from the face of this earth."

The creature stood then lunged forward, with all the energy remaining in its body. Robert jumped back, missing its grasp, then moved and stood in front of his sisters, blocking them from the beast. The creature tore at Robert, and this time scratched him across the face with his razor-sharp claws.

Robert winced from the stinging pain. His face bled and dripped all over his shirt and the floor. Robert moved his foot back and slipped on the blood; Deja vu. Again, he fell to the floor, knocking his head hard on the cement. He swore, then crawled on hands and knees toward Michelle. She had put the gun down by her feet. Robert grabbed it and got up, turning toward the monster.

Guarding his sisters, he raised the gun and shot into the beast's head, just as it pounced. It toppled forward and landed on top of Robert, the beast whimpering in pain. Robert shoved it off him and rolled away. He stood and kicked the creature away from his sisters.

A howl of pain echoed as the half-wolf, half-man pulled himself up and managed to stand. It turned and cast a piercing stare at Robert. The dark eyes paralyzed him. Then the monster's face morphed back to Tom Bennett; it returned to human form. The fur fell from its skin. He struggled to pull himself up from the floor, then he stood up like a normal man. Naked, he pleaded. "Robert, please, don't hurt me. It's me, Tom. I'm your only friend, remember? I'm the only one who truly understands you."

"Shut up!" Robert screamed. "What the hell are you?"

"I'm your friend, Tom. Together we're going to make our own empire remember?"

"I already had an empire. I had a family. You took it all away from me. Look at me now; I have nothing. You corrupted me!" he said.

Tom Bennett laughed at him. His face started forming back into the wolf, right in front of his eyes. It growled and grew stronger as it fed off Robert's pain and hatred. It walked closer to Robert, reaching out, ready to strike him.

"No, Robert. Don't believe in it, for God's sake! It's a monster. Shoot it!" Michelle screamed.

Robert pulled the trigger. A flash exploded. The creature kept moving forward. Robert shot it again, and again in the head. Bright strobes of light flicked on and off as shells landed on the floor and bounced, ringing shrill notes, until he pulled off all the remaining nine rounds and the magazine was empty.

The monster stood with blood oozing from its wounds. Red, spilling out of the kill shots Robert delivered. It moved forward one last step, then everything happened fast. From behind the monster, something thrashed.

The room was void of sound except for the noise of a sharp blade cutting through a thick piece of meat. Jeremy stood behind the monster with his hands gripped onto the handle of the German-made Dahle professional guillotine paper cutter blade, the same kind of edger Robert used in the office. A brief flash, he remembered noticing its cutting arm had been left on a desk unattached to the platform. The eighteen-inch self-sharpened steel edge had efficiently sliced the creature's head off. Robert watched in slow motion.

Blood splattered forward. The hot wet spray covered Robert from head to toe. He squinted his eyes shut, then wiped the blood away. The blood dripped from the monster, spilled over its severed body onto the floor. Its head fell off, landed with a thud, and bounced on the floor, then rolled, leaving a cardinal path. The body slumped onto the cement. A dark purple thick ooze of hemoglobin poured out from its severed body, then clotted. Dark magic right before their eyes, the creature turned back into Tom Bennett's body, then the corpse decayed fast, years of death poured upon him, withering in fast forward. The creature, Tom Bennett, the monster, was dead.

Robert stood still in disbelief, his entire body saturated with blood. The smell lingered, an iron scent in the air. The heated gore stuck to his face. He couldn't move; he was in shock.

Fear consumed his beliefs. He remembered things his sister had said. All these years Emilie had talked about supernatural things, and he thought she was crazy. Michelle talked about Tom Bennett being evil, and he didn't want to believe her either. *Why? How?* He overwhelmed himself with so many questions and self-doubts, emotions he should have dealt with years ago, all piled high into a stack of feelings he never acknowledged before. *He must be evil, too. He was akin to Tom Bennett. They collaborated, they plotted, and did awful things together.* He stood frozen, hating himself until Michelle snapped him back to life.

"What the hell," Michelle screamed in a shrill voice. "My God, is it finally dead?"

Robert automatically kicked the corpse on the floor with his foot.

"Yes, it appears so. It's dead. What just happened?"

Words came out of his mouth, but he didn't understand how he was able to talk. His mind buzzed with all kinds of crazy. Michelle and Emilie came to his side. The three of them stood there together, three siblings feebly steadying each other, as the scene that just unfolded replayed privately in each of their minds.

Robert looked up and saw Jeremy as he stepped back, away from the dead form, and stood by himself, motionless, with the sharp-edged arm still in his hand. Slowly he raised his head and saw Emilie. Their glances connected, and they shared each other's panic. She went to Jeremy, pulled the cutter from his hand, and let it drop to the floor. It clanged as the hardened steel arm met the hard surface.

"Are you all right, Emilie?" Robert said.

"Yes, Rob, I'm okay. I'll survive now that it's over," she said. "Jeremy, are you all right?"

Stunned, Jeremy remained quiet. Robert sympathized with the guy. He definitely got more than he bargained for with his sister.

"What the hell just happened?" Robert said. "I can't even begin to grasp or accept the scene that just played out in front of us."

Jackson walked up to the withered corpse, his face sad. Robert and Jackson used to be so close when they were in school. *Was Jackson grieving because he lost his father, or relieved?* It dawned on Robert that he hadn't had a real conversation with his friend in years. More regret piled onto Robert, and he imagined he might explode. He raised his hands to his head and squeezed hard. He needed to get out of this place. They all needed to leave, and quick.

"Sorry, Jackson," Michelle said.

Jackson shook his head and walked away; Aunt Victoria stopped him, wrapped her arm around his back, and patted.

Robert looked down at his blood-sodden clothes. He cringed, his body tightened, and he panicked.

"We've got to get out of here now," he called out.

"I'm calling the police," Victoria said.

"No," Robert yelled. "It's not that simple. No matter what story we give them, no one will believe us. We have to leave, now. We can't be here when the police arrive, trust me."

No one moved and Robert grew more disturbed.

"Jeremy, you never killed anything alive in your entire life before, have you?"

Jeremy's face turned red. "Well, that doesn't bloody hell happen every day, now does it?" he said, his heavy English accent audible.

"No, it doesn't. My point exactly. Quick, let's leave now before we're all arrested."

"Rob's right. No one will believe our story. We all need to

leave here," Michelle said.

Suddenly, something warm seeped into his heart, something he hadn't caressed in a long time. It didn't matter anymore. There was no need for secret plans, no more sneaking behind his family's back. Tom Bennett was dead, and Robert's life was born again. He crossed a road and was on his way back home. This feeling seemed like a road that was leading him into recovery. He believed it. *Mother and Father must be smiling, now that we've found each other again,* he thought.

"Let's go." Robert smiled.

Everyone moved toward the exit.

"I'm calling for an ambulance. I think Ramsey is still alive," Victoria said.

"Fine, call from the car, but let's get back to your house before they show up."

They piled into the two cars. Michelle and Aunt Victoria in Robert's car, Emilie and Jeremy in Jackson's. They drove to Victoria's house without mishap.

An hour later, after some of the confusion died down, they called the lawyer's office, a local firm on retainer for the family. Robert spoke on speakerphone and explained his aunt's car needed an urgent tow. He also requested an urgent meet-up as soon as possible.

Two lawyers arrived at Victoria's house by eight that evening. Together the family told a version of the story they all agreed upon, which seemed plausible. They claimed to have stumbled into the area to retrieve Michelle from her car accident. It was hard not to notice the incident, what with gunfire and the racket going on. Of course, any prints of theirs were left when they tried to help. After all, Aunt Victoria made the anonymous 911 call. The family requested that the law firm investigate the situation clandestinely, making sure their names weren't associated with the reported slaughter. They had their statements if the police ever determined they were at the scene. They would be back in Memphis if they were required for anything.

Hours later, Robert remembered a remark one of the attorneys voiced. They didn't know what to make of their story and believed the family was a bit too eccentric for their own good. Similar stray thoughts were just part of the blur he bore that night.

Exhausted, and still in a state of shock, no one could sleep.

He envisioned the evil face of Bennett the monster every time he closed his eyes and feared that the images would invade his dreams. So he kept awake as long as possible. Finally, time won, and he and the others managed some rest for a few hours.

Chapter 35

Emilie

Another cool fall day began with a gentle mist that splashed against the few leaves left hanging on the tree branches. The faint pitter-patter of the droplets hitting the foliage woke Emilie. She rose from the bed, opened the window wider, and took a deep breath, invigorating her body and spirit, recharging her perception of life. The view amazed her. Rain saturated the bark of the prominent topiary that enclosed Aunt Victoria's backyard. The colors of the foliage were vivid, the rain made them look finely polished. The air smelled glorious, fresh, and earthy.

Nature bandaged her, covered her soul with calmness, and encouraged her to heal. Her mind needed to filter the emotional barrage of yesterday encumbered through her clairvoyant nature. She told her family her version of what happened in the warehouse. When she explained how it unfolded through her gift, she had sensed their skepticism in return. Unworldly things frightened everyone, but she could only tell the truth. Their belief in such things remained beyond her control.

Jeremy tossed in the bed. She pulled herself away from the window and went to him, cuddling up close, and wrapping her arm around his strong torso. His body warmed her. He loved her, and she him. Just like his smile, his body shined with goodness. Today he needed some tender care himself.

She understood how horrible he felt. Although Tom Bennett was a monster, the physical violence Jeremy resorted to, chopping off the head, tugged at his conscience. *No one should be comfortable cutting off another living being's head, even spawned evil.* Jeremy was a virtuous man, so he naturally questioned his motives and actions. Careful people are often their worst critic because they try to live the virtues they believe—it's impossible to maintain. Emilie deliberated the idea of virtue and what it meant. The Church taught the virtues of faith, represented by the cross, hope symbolized with an anchor, and charity the flaming heart; the flaming heart—the supernatural virtue that enables us to love God and others more than ourselves. She hoped that her love was enough to get Jeremy through the ordeal that she and her family brought onto him. If they are to be married, they had to find a way to make living with her gift work for both of them.

She reached up, gently combed her fingers through his hair, and thought of yesterday. The gruesome scene played back in her mind. She accepted in her heart they would somehow get through this horrendous experience. Maybe it would even bring her family closer to each other. Exposing the secrets was the way to healing their souls.

Jeremy stirred, stretched his arms out, then looked up at Emilie.

"Good morning, Beautiful."

He took her face in his hands and gently kissed her forehead and lips. She melted inside, knowing they survived the ordeal together.

After Emilie washed and dressed, she left the bedroom to give Jeremy his space. Michelle stood in the hallway, with her back toward her, staring at the floor.

"Good morning."

Michelle jumped as she spun around. Her hand was on her chest.

"My God, you gave me a scare," Michelle said.

"Sorry."

Emilie put her arm around Michelle's shoulder and pulled her in close, kissing the top of her head. "Are you okay?"

Michelle smiled, shaking her head. "Not really. I don't do well being chased and beaten up by a psychopath killer. Guess I'm a wimp."

"Let me see your bruises," Emilie said.

Michelle pulled her arm away. "I'm fine, really. I'll see Doc Hannigan when we get home. I'm alive at least." She smiled.

"And tell him what? The Doc will want to know what happened to you. What will we all say happened?" Emilie said.

Michelle took Emilie's hand and pulled her toward the stairs. They went downstairs to the parlor and sat on the sofa, side by side.

"Okay, Em, this is what we're going to say. Nothing. No one will ask and Doc Hannigan has already seen lots of weird, right? He knows better than to ask too many questions."

Emilie shook her head in agreement.

"Unfortunately, you're right. The real problem we need to deal with isn't a cover story, but our brother. What are we going to do about Robert?"

Michelle closed her eyes a moment.

"Em, remember what you said once before about helping Robert, saving him from himself, because he was, after all, our brother?"

"Oh yes, I remember. And I still believe that too. Nevertheless, he'll need to forgive himself first. If he can't, he'll end up down the same path again and next time there will be no saving him. I know deep down he loves us and Rachael, too. We have to give them a fighting chance to make it work, to carry on their father's legacy. If we both show him some forgiveness, maybe he'll turn back into his real self, and forget all about his lust for power bullshit."

The two sisters sat quietly for a few minutes. The only

sound was humming coming from the kitchen.

"Okay, let's try to forget as much as we can for now. I promise to try to be supportive of Robert," Michelle said.

Emilie grabbed her hand and gave her a firm squeeze.

"We both will. No judgment. For now, we'll try to forget what he did and concentrate on the future." Emilie stood. "Come on, let's see what Victoria is doing in the kitchen."

Chapter 36

Victoria

The big old Victorian house stirred with movement. They all rose from their beds and stumbled down the stairs, piling into the kitchen. They sat around the table, pushing the chairs over to fit more as they filed into place, one by one. Aunt Victoria wore a long house dress with her blonde hair pulled back with a headband, looking maternal. The big coffee pot brewed and the aroma filled the kitchen.

The room was cozy, with deep rich colors on the wall trimmed with fruit borders. Quartz countertops swirled with earthen colors, accenting the maple cabinets stained in warm wood tones, and appliances shined with stainless steel. The radiator banged and clicked as the streaming water passed through the old pipes that rimmed the bottom of the bay window. The air grew comfortable once the heat kicked on and chased away stray drafts. The radiator warmed the nook area, an appendix to the old house. The encircled space harbored the table, a claw-footed family heirloom.

"Okay, no servants here, so give me a heads up. Who wants eggs, toast, cereal? Let me know, folks if you want to be fed."

Victoria clapped her hands together to awaken a response, smiling, and looking around the room at them all.

First, she noticed Michelle, her dear sweet wise-ass. She was close to her heart like her own daughter. Michelle inherited her sister Bethany's bright blue eyes, so filled with life.

Then Emilie, with her long warm brown hair and sweet face, like an angel. Her eyes were like her father's, warm brown. Her fiancé, Jeremy, was handsome, sporting his sparkling hazel eyes, but there was sadness in them today. Watching the two of them interact, it was obvious they were in love.

Jackson—he was infatuated with Michelle, and she had no clue. Victoria wondered what was going to happen to Jackson. Would this ordeal hurt him psychologically? His mother wasn't known as a very warm person, and who could blame her, what with being married to a man—no a monster—like Tom Bennett. Victoria hoped the young man would find a way to stay good.

Last, she noticed Robert. He was her only nephew, and a handsome man, dark curls just long enough, deep romantic eyes, a lean and healthy body. Yes, a prize, and according to Michelle, he was brilliant and witty, too. It was such a shame that he had been brainwashed by Bennett. How deep had Robert invested himself into the secret group? There's still hope for him. What that monster had done to her sister was horrible, and he had stolen Robert's innocence, too. Michelle had told her that Father Eddie had spent time with Robert and Rachael. *Maybe there is hope after all.* Thank God, the beast was dead.

This morning Robert seemed off his mark, his head lowered in what was no doubt, shame. Of course, that meant he still had a chance, he still owned a conscience.

Victoria daydreamed about another breakfast, years ago. It had been a cold morning. She sat close to her sister at this same table, laughing over spilled milk. They hurried and wiped it up together. They had always eaten breakfast together in the morning, starting the day as a family. How she missed Bethany. She prayed her sister's children could find the same feeling of kinship that she had experienced with her sister. It's something to be treasured.

"I'll cook some bacon and eggs, Auntie."

Victoria started. "Yes. Yes, that would be wonderful."

Michelle got up from her chair, went to the cupboard, and

pulled pans out. Then she opened the refrigerator and grabbed eggs and bacon. She moved around behind the stove and seemed to know what she was doing. Victoria watched Emilie, as her eyes followed Michelle. Victoria knew Emilie's empathy was engaged in full capacity, feeling her sibling's unhappiness. She noticed Jeremy as he touched Emilie's shoulder, bringing her thoughts back to her own, and her face became peaceful again. He touched her a lot. Yes, they're a good match, Victoria thought.

"I'll handle the toast," Emilie said.

"My, my, aren't you girls Suzy Homemaker. Aunt Victoria, I hope you don't mind me doing my part by filling my coffee cup," Robert said.

"That's awfully big of you, Rob," Michelle bantered.

"Here, this one is for you, Jeremy. You look like you need it."

Robert handed Jeremy a cup of fresh coffee while reading his face. Jeremy took the cup, his forehead scrunched in pain. Robert's glance lingered, his face questioning.

"Thanks," Jeremy mumbled, then he turned away.

"No problem, old sport. Since we're all in this horrid situation together, we might as well try to get along and be civil. I don't know about you, but I feel like I woke up from a night in hell and lost a huge chunk of my life. For God's sake, did all that really happen? Or did we really go to a horror flick yesterday? I just can't wrap my head around it all," Robert said.

Aunt Victoria saw sincere confusion and wondered some of the same questions. Did any of them understand yesterday's nightmare? What had happened to Michelle and Robert before they arrived? Were the men on the floor even dead?

Victoria stayed busy by helping her nieces set the plates on the table and poured juice. Michelle carried the food and placed the platter in the center of the table. They filled their plates

257

without pretense. The eggs cooked up scrambled, the juice cold, the coffee hot, and the toast burned around the edges. No one joked about Emilie's lack of cooking skills as they mopped up their eggs with the singed bread. The silverware clanged against the china plates as they spread homemade jam on the bread to cover the burnt edges.

Chapter 37

Michelle looked at the faces of the people around the table. Her family was a good-looking bunch, strong features, sharp eyes, and they all proved once again how much spunk they had, capable of dealing with yesterday's tragedy without falling completely apart.

How many tests could they endure in a lifetime? They lost their mother when just kids, and now Father, too. They ended a curse on the family, and now ended the threat of a monster that was bent on killing them all. Michelle was proud of them, even her brother. His tone, his expression this morning— gave her hope that he was worthy of redemption, just like their family priest, Father Eddie, had mentioned once before.

There was so much she wanted to say to her brother, but held herself back, allowing him time. Hell, she needed time herself. Typical, the more Michelle forced herself to stay quiet, the harder it became. Finally, she couldn't take the silence any longer.

"You know, we need to talk this thing through, so we can get past it all, and just in case the police come sniffing around," she said.

"Why do we need to say anything? We'll let our lawyer do that, won't we?" Robert said. "Besides, if Ramsey survives, he won't dare mention our names because if he does, then his involvement in the Black Wolf Society will be compromised. His entire career will be lost."

He wiggled in his chair, looking uncomfortable with the conversation. He dropped his hand to his lap and wiped it on the cloth napkin. *Trying to remove a stain,* Michelle thought.

"Don't worry, Robert, you can talk about everything. Cat's out of the bag already. We know what you planned with Tom

Bennett, and I won't take it personally, or at least I'll try not to. You wanted the company back—I get it. The thing is, dear brother, Bennett wanted to go a bit further. I promise we won't blame you for his added embellishments to the plan. He went way beyond your intentions. I know you didn't really want to kill me," Michelle said.

She was sad that her big brother took part in any plan against her, exposing her secrets for his own gain. Michelle lowered her eyes. *Why?* There were still unanswered questions, and she didn't have a clue how this would end.

"You're too kind to me," Robert said. He avoided eye contact with anyone.

Yes, she distrusted her brother, and she knew that her feelings were warranted. Maybe someday it could all be resolved. She closed her eyes and could still hear the sound of Bennett chasing her. Startled, she opened her eyes, jumping in her seat.

"Michelle, are you alright?" Emilie asked.

"Yes, I'm fine. Still a bit shaky is all. I suppose it will take a while for us to get over this ordeal. I think we need to get back to Memphis."

"Yes, and you need to see the doc right off," Robert said.

She looked toward Jackson. "Are you coming with us?"

"No, sorry. I have to get back to work and then sort things out with my mother. I have no idea what I'm going to tell her. I mean about what happened. I wonder if the police will even figure out it was my father's body. I mean, it was so corroded." He shivered.

"It's okay Jackson. Do what you must, but if you need anyone to talk with, well, you know where we'll be." Michelle gently tapped his arm to reassure him.

"If you ever need to talk, or need anything, we'll all be there for you," Jeremy said. "We understand the bloody hell you went through."

"Thank you, Jeremy. If not for you I'd still be in hell." Jackson nodded and gave a weak smile.

"Of course, we'll all be going through some anguish over this. Jackson, our lawyers are at your disposal, as well. We need to support each other," Emilie said. "Aunt Victoria, will you come back with us?"

Victoria looked back at Emilie, with a loving expression. Michelle knew that look and loved the feeling her aunt had given her on so many occasions. Having Aunt Victoria in Memphis was a great idea. For Michelle, her aunt was the closest thing she had to a parent.

"Of course, I'd love to go to your home in Memphis. Besides, I want to meet Rachael," Victoria said.

She smiled and looked at Robert. He smiled back, though it wasn't genuine, and they all knew it.

"Yes, I need to get back before Rachael gets totally pissed with me. She must be wondering what we're all doing up here. I've no idea what I should tell her," Robert said.

"Start with the truth, Rob," Michelle said.

He harrumphed. "No need to give her ammunition for a divorce."

After everything that happened, Michelle was serious about telling the truth. Secrets only covered up pain and caused trouble. She hoped her brother would consider her words.

"Robert, the truth shall set you free," she said.

Chapter 38

Robert

It was early in the evening by the time the limo pulled up the driveway of the Memphis estate. The air was cool and clean, and Robert heard the rattle of the leaves still on the trees as he got out of the car. A chill in the air sent a shiver through him, though it wasn't as cold as New England, but definitely a cool dip for the Mid-south.

Nina descended from the porch, approached the car with her arms outstretched, and welcomed them home. The cook's frame giggled a bit as she drew close to them. Her embrace touched him with a soft and warm feeling when she wrapped him in a hug, and his mind rested for a moment.

"Lordy, you're all here again! Give me some sugar."

Nina smiled and managed to reach each of them in no time at all. No one could escape her.

"Nina, do you remember Aunt Victoria?" Michelle said as she stepped back.

"Indeed I do." She embraced her as well and guided Victoria toward the porch.

"I have dinner all set, so as soon as you all are ready, just say the word and you shall be nourished," she said.

"You shall be nourished? Nina, you always manage to bring out your corniest. You spend too much time in that church of yours, and now you sound like a walking talking bible toting—"

"You mind your manners," she snapped.

Nina frowned and gave Robert a glaring eye.

"Home sweet home, it's so nice to be back," he said.

"I'll give you corny, your majesty. I suppose you want to eat, so don't fool with the cook."

She left them, shaking her head and laughing to herself as she walked to the back of the house toward the kitchen. Evans carried the bags upstairs, and the family escaped into the parlor. The room glittered, all the lamps lit, and a roaring fire blazed atop the iron grates, adorned with a pair of French Chenets.

Robert walked over to the fireplace, rubbing his hands together to get rid of his chill. He admired the antique andiron; a work of art and still useful after centuries of blazing fires. A few years ago, he had bought the cast iron firedog at an antique show. It was the fifteenth century. Robert stood and admired the design, an arched shape with a sturdy cross on top. The center had a lattice-weave design, topped with a small worn iron head. A head!

He shivered. A memory from the day before flashed as he stared at the fire. He dared to look at the sculpted iron head again. It reminded Robert of the severed head that lopped onto the cement floor in the warehouse. Thoughts about the transformation he witnessed, the image as the corpse turned once again into Tom Bennett, bombarded his mind. The memory made Robert sick, his nerves jumping from his inside. He screamed to get out of his head, every nerve ending seemed sensitive and sore to the touch.

Robert had never been so vulnerable and hurt as he did at that moment, standing there remembering. His face burned as the flames flicked out heat, but Robert didn't move. He only shook his head trying to rid himself of the vision that haunted him.

"Robert, where is Rachael? Should we call her?"

Someone spoke to him but he was too deep in thought to respond. After a few moments, he turned away, his sights fixed across the room. His legs followed and he went straight for the bar and poured himself a strong drink. He devoured the first glass of scotch, then a quick second, then a third. After a moment, feeling more like himself, Robert called out, "Evans, can you tell Rachael we're home?"

Evans entered the room and quietly stood near Robert. He whispered, "I'm sorry, Sir, but Miss Rachael left the day you did, for her father's house."

He disappeared again. Robert's face turned red.

"Rob, call her. She just didn't want to be in this house alone, that's all. Ask her to come back to the house for dinner and meet Aunt Victoria," Emilie said.

He stood there swirling his drink, trying to keep secret fears from playing out across his face. He didn't blame Rachael for going back to her father's place. What kind of husband just ups and leaves without a word?

"Yes, I'll do that."

He finished his third drink. Everyone was quiet and he sensed them watching him as he walked out of the room. Michelle followed him into the foyer.

"Wait, Rob. I want to talk with you," she said.

Robert turned around and acknowledged her big blue eyes searching his face. *She wants to make peace.* After everything he did to her, she still wanted to talk with him. Her bruises had turned from red to a purplish off-color and looked sore. He swallowed back a deep sigh of regret.

He was amazed at her ability to be so tolerant. His little sister ended up being a stronger person than he. Noticing the scrapes on her cheek, he wondered what Tom had done to his little sister before he arrived. The horrid impressions of what she might have experienced made him sick.

"Michelle, what do you need?"

She stopped a few feet from him and tilted her head sideways. She reminded him of a child peeking inside a closet for something hidden.

"I don't need anything. I'm just concerned about you. We all went through so much the past few days. Things must have affected you just as much as they did me."

"Michelle, I'm the one who should be worried about you, and what I put you through. I'm so sorry. I have no idea how to begin making things up to you."

There was a moment of silence.

"Are you worried about Rachael? Her not being here," she said. "As I recall, the last time we were together things seemed like they were going fine between you two. She probably just needed to see her father. I just want to offer you a shoulder, you know, to lean on. If you need mine, I'm here to listen. I want us all to heal, Rob."

Robert jerked. He hadn't expected so much understanding so soon. It was too good to be true. She had always been there for him when they both lived up north while in school. Michelle was always a friend to him, always brutally honest.

He was the one out of line. He swallowed back his angst.

"Thanks, Michelle. You're too kind to me and I don't deserve it. You have every right to be angry with me."

She shook her head and smiled.

"Oh, don't worry. I am angry, but you're still my big brother. Things will work out. Just because you made mistakes doesn't make you a monster. I love you, Robert. But I promise, once the shock evaporates, I'll clobber you—okay? Feel better?"

Robert reached out and hugged his sister. A tear came to his eye.

"I'm so sorry, Michelle; I hope someday I deserve to be forgiven. I have to pay for my mistakes. Even Rachael knows I don't deserve forgiveness. She probably wants nothing to do with me."

Michelle let go and stepped back. She glanced up at him, shaking her head.

"No, you're wrong again. Rachael loves you, Robert — everyone can see that. It's just that sometimes you can be hard to live with, you know. Sometimes you're too demeaning."

He smiled.

"I'm so glad I can count on you to tell me the truth." He smiled, but it turned into a grimace. "When I left the house the other day I was gruff with Rachael. You're right again, Michelle. I'll call her father's place and beg her to come home."

He turned to walk away. Michelle grabbed his sleeve.

"One more thing, Rob."

He turned around and lowered his eyes to the floor like a little boy caught stealing.

"Michelle, how can any of you live with me, knowing what I've done? Actually, you don't even know all of it. I've done some horrible things. You should all hate me."

"Robert, it doesn't matter what you've done — you can do the penance, but you can't change the past. The more important question is what will you do from now and forward?"

He considered her appearance. Her hair was messed up a bit from the long day, but her expression didn't appear tired or judgmental, just his little sister regarding him with her big baby blues.

"What's the one more thing?" he said.

"When you're ready, we need to know the entire truth. I want to know if we're still in danger."

She blinked and stood waiting for an answer of some kind.

Robert's brow cringed. What an odd thing to say — *still in danger. Were they still in danger?* He rubbed his hand through his hair and thought about that possibility.

He didn't know much about the Black Wolf Society, but surely, without Tom Bennett, they were no longer a threat?

Chapter 39

Michelle returned to the parlor and sat on the couch next to Emilie.

"I'm calling Father Eddie," she said.

Emilie put her arm around her sister and squeezed. Michelle experienced a sliver of peace brightening her spirit.

"That's a great idea, especially if Rachael comes back to the house. Eddie's been giving the two of them advice. He can moderate." Emilie nodded at Robert, then pushed her body back into the sofa cushion. She lifted her head and closed her eyes.

"Don't worry, she'll come back," Michelle said. She stared at her sister's face out of concern for the toll this had on Emilie. Her eyes were shut, and her complexion smooth, almost glowing. She didn't seem disturbed at all. Michelle wondered how that could be and wanted to know how her sister was doing. Biting her lip, Michelle searched for the right words.

"Emilie," she started to say.

"Yes?" Emilie said as she opened her eyes and turned to face her sister. Her brow scrunched up with uneasiness.

"Em, you're all right, aren't you? I mean . . . I never saw such a crazy thing as the stuff you did. I can't even begin to articulate all the questions I have. I mean, it was bizarre. I mean, light just streamed out of your hands—" Michelle stopped and fell silent. She pushed herself back into the sofa cushion, too.

Jeremy and Victoria raised their heads and turned toward Michelle at the mention of the word bizarre. They leaned in, neither trying to hide their curiosity.

"I know it's strange, and I can't explain it very well," Emilie said.

"Why bother trying to understand something so other-worldly? I mean, who would have thought this kind of thing even happened." Jeremy shook his head. He was pale and still looked shook up by what happened the day before.

"Well, I knew that man was a monster," Victoria said. "I should have ended things sooner, somehow. But he was more than we dared imagine. Now I at least have some sense of clo-sure after all these years. But I'm still not at peace."

"I'm so sorry, Aunt Victoria." Emilie got up from the sofa and moved to her aunt's side, almost floating. Her small body looked angelic as she leaned to give Victoria a hug. Michelle decided she really wanted to know her sister better.

"Well, I for one want to talk with Father Eddie about all of it. Maybe he can explain a few things to help find not just clo-sure but some kind of peace in our hearts. I'm having a hard time believing that I did what I did," Jeremy said. "Remember the chief said Eddie visited him with your mother. He knows more than he lets on." After a few moments of silence, he said, "I understand I didn't kill a man but protected us from a mon-ster, but still, having killed something alive is eating away at me."

Michelle stood. "First off, he wasn't alive. Bennett said as much when he taunted Ramsey. He said aloud before you were there to hear—that he was already dead. Most important, Jer-emy, is that you saved us. That's what you did. You have no reason to feel bad about taking control of the situation. I've never been so afraid for my life, I thought I was going to die. That monster was going to kill us all," Michelle said.

Weak for a moment, she guessed that they all needed time to get over the trauma, including herself. The need to look over her shoulder still followed her; she was just waiting for some-thing to attack her again. She shivered. *Don't be silly.* Michelle pulled out her phone and dialed the priest.

"I'm calling Father Eddie." She walked away as she spoke to him, then came back in a few moments. "Well, he'll be here soon for dinner. This is going to be some circus."

The grandfather clock struck eight gongs; time for dinner. Everyone moved from the parlor and gathered in the dining room. Rachael had returned home after Robert called, and the two of them strolled into the dining room together. A moment later, Father Eddie arrived to join them as well.

"So glad you came, Father," Michelle said. "I'm pleased to introduce you to my Aunt Victoria."

"It's a pleasure," Eddie said. "Actually we've met, but under duress."

"Of course, you were at my sister's funeral."

Father Eddie nodded and tightened his lips.

"Rachael, glad to see you're home. I wondered where you had gone to," Michelle said. She turned to her sister-in-law and placed her arm around her as they walked toward the table.

"I was at my father's house. After Robert left the other day, this house seemed so empty. Besides, my father isn't feeling well."

"Sorry to hear that," Michelle said.

Robert cleared his throat and groveled. "I'm sorry, Rachael. I was called away to help a friend. I promise that won't happen again, ever."

Father Eddie tapped Robert on the shoulders. "How about we meet tomorrow, you two?"

Rachael nodded. Robert's face turned red. Michelle wondered how much Father Eddie knew about what her brother had been up to. Did Robert tell the priest what happened? Any of it? She imagined he probably didn't, but Jeremy mentioned Eddie went to the reservation before . . . Father Eddie had influence over the family, maybe too much.

"Michelle, how are you? You look like you've seen a ghost," Eddie said.

"No, no ghosts, padre, just a monster."

Aunt Victoria shot Michelle that look.

Michelle scratched her head, wondering why she had even said that. She was punchy. Knowing better than to bring it up at dinner, she refused to talk more about it, especially with Eddie here. Still, his expression seemed suspicious, as if Eddie sensed something was wrong. His deep gaze made her nervous, with those big dark all-knowing eyes. She was compelled to give him her confession, right then and there.

"I meant to say, everything is as good as one can expect right now."

He nodded in agreement. "Okay, whatever that means. I can wait until you're ready to explain."

Father Eddie seemed to accept her answer, for now anyway. Maybe the sage of a man did know what was going on after all.

"Let's hope for the best moving forward. Your brother seems to have had a change of heart. He's . . . different."

Eddie looked across the room at Robert. His head was bowed in deep reflection.

Michelle knew her brother had many issues to resolve. Not only because of what happened yesterday but because of everything that had happened between him and Bennett over the years. Her brother was not only betrayed but he was made a fool of as well. Knowing her brother, that was going to be hard to face. *Welcome to my world.*

"Yes, different. That's one word for it." Michelle wanted to kick herself. "I agree. Things around here are on the mend."

Eddie smiled. Michelle was relieved that she'd been able to give the priest what he wanted to hear. She never knew how to talk with him. Eddie pulled out a chair for Michelle.

"Thank you, sir."

Nina carried platters of food to the table, smiling as she served everyone. Tonight they shared the beef brisket, sides of garlic potatoes, green beans, and cornbread. Michelle noticed Nina sweeping her gaze across them all, then her eyes lifted in praise, her lips mumbling, thanking her Lord. Michelle could never deny Nina her religious beliefs nor her strong opinion that things would always work out. But in her heart, Michelle knew the troubles for her family weren't over yet. There were many buried feelings among them and undertows of anger lingered between siblings.

Michelle had suspicions about the secrets her brother was hiding, and they needed to be fleshed out and soon. Bennett had influenced Robert, they had embezzled from the company and stolen artifacts, maybe even murdered. *No, not murder, not her brother.* He went along with a scheme against her. Worse, he had poisoned Father, yes, though not to the point of killing him . . . *but what else had Robert been involved in?* She remembered when the police had come to the house asking about the murder of Mr. Pierce.

She shook her head, willing all speculations to leave her.

There was also the issue of her sister. *What kind of power did she have?* Michelle hated supernatural stuff, but Emilie's talent seemed to be real. Michelle hoped to find the courage to ask her sister more about it, even though deep down she wished it could be forgotten, and that the last episode had never happened. Unfortunately, it did happen. Her sister was a freak, but a lovable one. She smiled to herself and looked across the table at her sister. Emilie seemed fine right now. Michelle wanted to know her better before it was too late. Before she got married and took off for God knows where.

All three of the de Gourgues siblings had scars, deep scars. Michelle wanted them to heal, but realistically she knew things could never go back to the way they were. They would survive and deal with each other somehow, but part of her resolve was worn, part of her love for her brother faded. The only thing she still leaned on was her sister's strength and friendship.

"Did you enjoy the fall colors?" Rachael asked.

Michelle snapped from her daydream, she had drifted far from the family's dinner conversation.

"Oh yes, the foliage was beautiful this year. Next fall we'll have to visit Aunt Victoria together. We can shop downtown."

She raised her head and saw her brother filling Rachael's plate with more vegetables, never dropping his gaze from her face. His hands shook, Robert wasn't as cool-headed about everything as he pretended, and who could blame him. Rachael planned on staying with Robert, but still, something was off between them. He couldn't have told her about what happened; there wasn't enough time, and Michelle wondered if he ever would. *Did he expect them all to keep it a secret from her?* They obviously had things to deal with other than the Boston incident. *Maybe Em and I can help them smooth things over.* Michelle wanted to be a family again and missed having her big brother around.

They ate dinner without much more conversation. The silverware tapped against the bone china. The tall fan in the corner whirred white noise across the room. Somehow it all seemed familiar and relaxing, in an odd sort of way. Michelle was happy to be in this big house with her family. They had survived a curse, and now a monster, too.

Something still seemed off. An irritating tingle ruffled her skin; she was being watched. From across the table, Victoria stared at her. Michelle acknowledged her, nodding, but wondered what her aunt was thinking. Her face showed deep worry lines between her eyes. After a few moments, Victoria seemed to have awakened from her daydream.

"Rachael, it's so nice to finally meet you. I heard wonderful things about you," Aunt Victoria said.

"Likewise, Miss Victoria."

"Please, just Victoria," she said with a smile slipping in.

"Will you be staying here for a while?" Rachael asked.

"I think so. There's so much catching up to do," Victoria said.

"Good," Rachael said. "My woman's business club will be having lunch tomorrow at the Peabody. Would you like to join me, as my guest?"

"Rachael, Aunt Victoria just arrived. Maybe we should give her a day or so to settle in first before we start gallivanting with her all around town," Robert said.

"Nonsense, Robert," Victoria said. "Yes, Rachael, that would be lovely. I would enjoy joining you for the luncheon. You're so thoughtful to ask."

"Having you there will be a wonderful treat, Victoria. We all read your book and would love to discuss it with you," Rachael replied.

"Victoria, you're an author?" Jeremy asked.

"Yes. I wrote a book about women in business today. It's a collage of business tips for busy women dealing with dreadful men at the workplace." Aunt Victoria laughed, covering her mouth with her napkin.

"Well, I guess you put all us men in our place," Robert retorted with a smile.

Michelle saw Robert's face blush. Suddenly he looked like a vulnerable man instead of her haughty brother. Could there be hope?

Chapter 40

Robert

The dining room quieted. Robert shifted in his chair, uncomfortable having no idea of what they were talking about. He never knew Rachael belonged to such a club, and never knew Victoria wrote a book. He was slipping. Things were going on around him that he wasn't aware of. He chastised himself for permitting himself to become so ill-informed. He should've known these things about his own family. Instead, too busy obsessing over gaining back control of the company; most of his time spent doing Tom's bidding.

Sickened thinking about what a big sap he'd been, duped by the man, he realized he'd been nothing more than a pawn. His self-esteem sank, crushed to an all-time low. Years were wasted idolizing Tom Bennett. The stroking of his ego was a ruse. *He filled me with spite against my father, but Father loved me after all.*

Robert's heart cracked, unable to deal with the rushing feelings. His mind opened to ideas other than hate and vengeance and left him with questions. But he had no answers, worse no idea of where to seek answers. *How can a person deal with the truth about his own horrid behavior and turn their life around?*

His stomach twisted and tightened. He wished he could vomit, then feel better, but it wasn't that kind of pang. His nerves—taut strings, ready to snap.

Robert glanced around the table at his family, watching as they politely dined. Their faces and gestures presented a sense of harmony. None could comprehend his pain, nor did he want them to understand.

"Will you all please excuse me. I need some fresh air," Robert said.

Everyone eyed him with concern. Robert's face burned with embarrassment. He wiped his mouth, dropped his napkin onto the table, pushed back his chair, and hurried from the room.

A bead of sweat covered his brow, his pulse pounded against his temples. The walls closed in on him. Robert loosened his collar, drew in deep breaths, and walked to the front door. He needed fresh air.

Outside on the porch, Robert took in deep gulps of air and slowly exhaled. After a moment, he was calm, but tranquility wouldn't last long. In the pit of his stomach, an odd feeling overcame him. Danger lurked close by, he wasn't alone.

Robert narrowed his eyes. A lone figure stood in the shadows at the far end of the porch. Alarmed, Robert called out.

"Who's there?" A shiver slithered down his back.

A stranger lingered in the darkness, obscured in the far corner of the long front porch. The glow from his cigarette lent a brief glimpse of his outline, a man, tall and thin, wearing a fedora. The stranger exhaled, tossed the butt to the floor, and snuffed it out with the toe of his shoe.

Robert's pulse quickened, beating against his skin. More shivers slithered down his back. He rubbed his clammy hands against his trouser leg.

Was this retribution? Did this stranger intend to harm him? The tension pounded in his head, overwhelming him. How much could one man take, in the span of twenty-four hours? Thoughts of the shady things he had done and gotten away with in the past, flashed in his mind—embezzling money from his father's company. Worse, he had poisoned his father, to make him appear unbalanced and delude others into thinking he was unfit to steer the business—all done to gain control of the company. All his plans, the hoaxing and backstabbing, had failed.

Robert stood still waiting for the next catastrophe. The things that had happened in the past year were too many—he'd never be able to atone for the injustice he subjected his family. Robert accepted that he deserved to be humiliated in public, sent to prison, or whatever punishment his family wished upon him. Still, deep inside, Robert wanted another chance to prove himself. He hoped that there was a path to forgiveness. He wanted to live and prayed this stranger wasn't sent to kill him.

At one time Robert would have done anything to gain more money and power. It was like a sickness inside of him, a deep craving for more. Still, no matter how much he managed to ac-cumulate, it was never enough to fill the emptiness he stom-ached on the inside.

Always associating with others like himself, wealthy men more than willing to take advantage of others, Robert had tried everything, including conspiring with Tom Bennett, his busi-ness mentor. Robert had craved to be a member of an elite group—The Black Wolf Society.

Yesterday changed all that. Everything was different now that Tom Bennett was dead.

Robert swallowed back his fear and prepared for the worst. The man's shadow moved closer. Robert knew in his heart that he deserved whatever was about to happen to him. If this was a member of the Black Wolf Society, sent to silence him, then Robert's time on earth would end in seconds. Do they care it was self-defense? No, they couldn't have known that Tom Ben-nett had already been a dead man, a monster.

A timbre voice with a French accent broke the eerie quiet.

"Mr. de Gourgues, you've been through a lot in recent days. As I see it, you could use some assistance. You don't know us yet, but we can do business together. Take a few days of rest, collect your thoughts, and then, mon ami, I will approach you again. I can help you, and you help me. How you say it, one hand washes the other? Non? We'll be in touch."

The man disappeared, slipping into the cool dark night. A noise startled Robert and he turned to his right. A second person had been standing there in the shadows. The mysterious person slipped away unseen; Robert could only hear the trailing sound of footfalls against the crushed stones that lined the path.

The night was still again. Only the rattling of dried leaves sounded, as the cool autumn wind blew across the almost bare trees.

Robert didn't have enough energy nor heroics to follow the strangers. All he could think of was his family and understood why they were furious with his recent shenanigans. His sisters had been traumatized, physically hurt, and were disappointed in him. Still, after everything he had done, Michelle and Emilie remained concerned about him. He was thankful that his sisters were blind to the worst of his actions, they didn't know how far off the edge of decency he had fallen. Somehow, he had to redeem himself and make it up to them. There was no time to worry about strangers in the dark.

The man hadn't actually threatened him, though he was sure that the shadow-man was a representative for the Black Wolf Society. The thing he had desired most—to be one of them—was now his worst fear. Following the mysterious visitor would have been another rabbit hole that he'd rather not fall into.

He decided at that moment that he didn't care about anything else except how to get his life back on track. No more chasing after money. He vowed to himself that he would find a way to make it up to his sisters and his new wife, Rachael, as well. His only hope was that it wasn't too late.

Acknowledgments

This story is dedicated to my husband Jerry, the most decent man I've ever known. He pretends he doesn't hear me when I walk around the house talking to myself. He understands that I need to discuss the storyline with my characters. He is always willing to listen to my next idea without judgment about my sanity. He is a reluctant Alpha reader, but always there for me. Thank you, Jerry.

Thank you Beta readers. I am especially thankful to MaryLou Paquette, Virginia Duval, Barbara Lipe, and Janice Paquette. You muddled through my very rough drafts and still encouraged me to continue my writing journey. Many thanks to my local critique group for their guidance. Memphislores, you're the best: Barbara, Mike, Suzanne, Bill, Victor, Angelyn, Sri, Tim, and Belinda. You are great writers!

A good story comes from an author's imagination, but a smooth-flowing book can only be accomplished with the help of an editor. Thank you, Michael Garrett. Find out more about the editor at the website: ManuscriptCritique.com

Last, many thanks and best wishes to other Indie Authors who give daily encouragement, advice and support via social media. All of my fellow writers on Facebook, Twitter, and LinkedIn, as well as your fabulous blogs, have been encouraging. You are all awesome!

Please Support Indie Authors and Post book reviews wherever you buy your book copy!

Check out the next book

in the serial Curses & Secrets

SEEKING REDEMPTION

The journey ends with Seeking Redemption.
The de Gourgues family faces a new evil in book three. A stranger visits Robert with an ultimatum that may save himself – his family.
Robert needs to atone and get back his family's trust. He had put them in jeopardy, and they were nearly killed when they had come face to face with the real monster behind Tom Bennett, the man who had once been his friend and mentor. False ideas had been pumped into his mind by his father's enemy, but now that the truth is revealed, Robert realizes the error of his ways.

However, things are not that easy. Robert must also make amends to his new wife, Rachel. He vows to take a new path to build their marriage on trust, but Robert's past is held over his head, and he is coerced to assist the FBI to take down the dark society he once wanted to join. Robert is recruited by Agent Sloan and is running fast and playing games, stuck between good and evil, between the FBI and the Black Wolf Society. Robert's only hope is that he will not lose himself and his family in the process. Is there a way out? Can Robert save Emilie? Can he find his way out of his emotional darkness and discover true happiness?

From The Author

I hope you enjoyed reading the second book of the *Curses & Secrets* serial, **EXPOSING SECRET SINS** where once again, the de Gourgues family came out of a crisis, but more is yet to come . . .

The next in the serial is book three, **SEEKING REDEMPTION**
Please follow along with the family de Gourgues and the siblings' journey through family tragedy and the bizarre.

If you missed the first book, check out:
BREAKING CURSED BONDS

If you could spare a few minutes, please write a review for this book and post at the distributor's site where you bought your copy and/or post at Goodreads, or any other bookreview sites you frequent. Even a few words make a big difference to help future readers discover the story.
I'd be honored to have your review on Amazon—Your feedback
back
Thank you for your time!
Your support is appreciated!

Follow my website for updates:
elisabethzguta.com/
ezindiepublishing.com/

Thank you for reading my story
and leaving your review.